TRIAL OF SHADOWS

ORDER OF THE ELEMENTS: BOOK THREE

EMMA L. ADAMS

PREFACE

The magically gifted have always lived among us.

After centuries of living in hiding, a group of mages banded together and created their own parallel world to the everyday one, a paradise designed as a home for the magically inclined. Mages, vampires, elves, shapeshifters and many others flocked there, and for centuries, they flourished, ruled over by the Council of the Elements.

Then, several decades ago, the spirit mages turned on their fellow Elements and slaughtered them. The resulting war brought an end to the old Council of the Elements and left the magical world in ruins.

Since then, it has remained fractured. Clans of shapeshifters, vampires, and others rule the cities, while the Court of the Dead dominates the areas even the bravest fear to tread. It may be a paradise no longer, but to many of the magically inclined, it's still home.

Welcome to the Parallel.

1

It was always a bad way to start the weekend when the King of the Dead showed up on my doorstep.

With no customers for hours and no missions from the Order of the Elements in the last week, I'd volunteered to watch the front desk for the afternoon in case someone showed up wanting to buy a custom cantrip. Given that the only business Devon and I had had in the last month had been on behalf of the Order, the odds were low, but it gave me something to do that wasn't racking up achievements on Skyrim or designing new D&D characters for more games than I had time to play. Or wondering when the other shoe would drop, and the Order would find out about my illegal use of spirit magic and show up and arrest me.

The threat of the Order's retribution hung over my head like a storm about to break, and when the shop door opened, my hand was halfway to a defensive cantrip when I recognised the soundless footfalls of the Death King. He wore his human face as he usually did when he walked around the streets here on Earth, because a masked faceless monster dressed in black armour would be an alarming sight to the average person. For me, it made a disarming impression to see a pale, handsome face and curly dark hair in place of the obsidian mask of a lich: an immortal death lord with a habit of showing up when I least needed or expected him.

"Oh, it's you," I said, without enthusiasm. "If you're here to ask for a favour, the door's that way."

"How do you know I'm not a customer?" he said.

If this was an attempt to ingratiate himself with me and he thought I'd fall for the ruse, he was sorely mistaken. "What do you want, then? A charm for hair-loss?"

Once, I'd have quaked in my boots at the notion of pissing off the notorious King of the Dead, but times had changed, and I didn't take kindly to people who went back on their promises. Living or dead.

"I would like your assistance," he said. "In an important matter."

"You want to hire me to work for you?" I said. "As I told you the last time, I work for the Order. Not you, and not the Court of the Dead."

"You changed your mind once before," he said, "and you didn't regret the decision."

That was before you ghosted me. The Death King had promised to teach me spirit magic, but every time I'd tried to get into the castle in the last few weeks, I'd found my way barred by liches who said he wasn't taking visitors. Even his Air Element, Ryan—who happened to be part of our D&D group—didn't know what the hell he'd been doing.

"Who are you to say whether I regretted it or not?" I said. "People *died.* I almost died myself. Working with you is about as good a life choice as skydiving without a parachute. Anyway, as I repeatedly told you, I'm not here to solve your people's drama. If one of your liches has got their cloak stuck in a drain or something—"

"It's not the same as before," he interjected. "I'm not asking you to work as a consultant or a retriever of dangerous items. I find myself in need of a security guard."

I stared at him for an instant. "You want me to do *what?*"

"You might recall the incident which cost me my Fire Element."

Did I ever. My own personal fire mage had turned traitor, too. "It rings a bell."

"I intend to hold a contest to pick Davies's replacement," he said. "I will need stringent security around my castle while the contest is taking place, and I thought your unique skills would suit you to the task particularly well."

My mouth parted. That was actually a sensible idea, given how many people seemed to want him dead—or as dead as it was possible for a semi-immortal death lord to be, anyway. But that didn't make me qualified as a bodyguard. I was a novice spirit mage missing the memories of most of my training. He was the King of the Dead. How could I possibly protect *him?*

"You will be well compensated for your time and effort," he went on, "and there is no need for you to be involved in the contest itself. I simply require someone to join my other three Elemental Soldiers in guarding the castle and keeping an eye out for potential transgressors. By opening my doors to mages from the rest of the Parallel, I run the risk of inviting in another threat."

He had a point there. Davies had turned traitor right underneath his nose, after all. "Are you sure this isn't just a ruse to get me to be your Spirit Element in everything but name?"

"Why is that a bad thing?" he said. "Give me one good reason you shouldn't take me up on my offer."

"You're dead."

"Technicalities," he said. "You're qualified for the job, and you're the only mage outside of my three Elemental Soldiers who's proven herself trustworthy."

"We'll discount the fact that I brought a rogue mage into your castle not long ago."

Namely, my ex-boyfriend Brant. Since his betrayal, my quota of fucks to give had eroded to almost nothing, and I'd dearly have liked a reasonable explanation from His Deathly Highness about the last promise he'd broken before I got myself entangled in his business again.

He arched a brow. "Unless you're pursuing a romantic relationship with another questionable character who's likely to be grievously injured in action, that shouldn't be an issue."

Ouch. I'd only gone and rubbed salt in my own wounds with that comment, and the last person I wanted to discuss my dating life with was the King of the Dead. "I'm not. Doesn't mean I'm in need of an extra job, and I wouldn't put it past the Order to kick up a fuss if I take you up on the offer of working for you."

"As I informed you before, the Order—"

"Yes, I know they're wrapped around your little finger." I rolled my eyes at him. "Besides, you can't ignore me for weeks and then come crawling back when you want a favour. I don't appreciate that."

"When have I ever ignored you, pray tell?" he said. "I wasn't aware you felt deprived of my presence. I seem to remember you hated me."

Hate was a strong way of putting it, but we weren't exactly friends. "Try the last few weeks? I'm not here for you to treat like a convenience."

"I don't recall ever using you as such before," he said. "I believe I paid you well for your previous work. Might you enlighten me on what I'm supposed to have done?"

Right... that wasn't him. It was Brant who'd used me. The Death King, for all his numerous faults, hadn't. Yet I'd been working for him when my life had blown up and it was hard for my brain to separate the two. That he'd denied me the magic lessons he'd promised when I was already expecting the Order to put me in cuffs and lock me up in a cell had only poured fuel on the fire of my resentment. "If you're so certain I hate you, why in the world do you want to hire me?"

"You and I might be at cross-purposes, but you're moral to a fault," he said. "You'll do the work and you won't turn against me."

"How do you know that?" I resisted the urge to back away when he walked up to the desk until we were almost nose to nose, and it was hard to remember his face was an illusion and his body wasn't even solid.

"Because I do." He examined an elaborately carved cantrip Devon had left on the desk. "Your friend should consider selling these in Arcadia's market."

"She'd rather cut off her left hand, trust me," I said. "She's working on a mass custom job for the Order. I'm also still technically under the Order's watch, too, so I can't say they'll be thrilled at the idea of me gallivanting off into the Parallel. When is this contest?"

Devon and I had been under house arrest after the furore a few weeks ago, and to be honest, I'd been happy to avoid Arcadia for a bit. I mean, I *had* blown up a house in the vampires' district using the very magic which had cost me two years of memories when I was seventeen years old. Yet I'd been willing to reopen old wounds and run the risk of arrest if it meant getting real lessons in spirit magic from His Deathly Highness himself. Too bad he seemed to have forgotten that promise.

And now he wanted me to do *him* a favour? Yeah, right.

"The first round of the contest starts next Monday and there'll be one round per day until the result is announced on Friday," he said. "For the duration, all the competitors will be housed within my castle, to enable me to keep an eye on them. However, I haven't discounted the possibility that someone will take advantage of the contest to get close to me."

"And steal your soul amulet again," I said. "Unless you're planning to do the same thing as last time and parade it around in front of your enemies on purpose."

"Would I tell you if I was?"

"And you wonder why I don't trust you," I said. "You don't even pretend not to have your own agenda, and I don't need any more enemies than I already have."

"Very well," he said. "I will give you the weekend to consider my offer. The payment I offer will be enough to make up for any Order missions you might receive during the next week."

We both know that number is zero. If he even knew the Order had been ignoring me for weeks, considering he hadn't been around. "I'll consider it, but don't think I've forgotten you promised me lessons in spirit magic."

Not that he'd specified a time frame, and it was obvious that said magic lessons were a lot more important to me than they were to him. He wasn't the one who risked his life every time he exposed his powers. Except for a few brief flashes I'd seen—generally during near-death experiences—I couldn't recall a single minute of my lessons with Dirk Alban. He knew full well how vulnerable it made me, considering he'd been a spirit mage himself back when he'd still been alive. Before he'd given up his old life for immortality.

"I have been occupied," he said. "Both the search for my former Fire Element and my arrangements to hire a successor have taken a considerable amount of my time. However, if it means that much to you, I will endeavour to make time for a lesson or two during the contest."

That's what I got for mentioning the subject, because it seemed that now he'd decided that no bodyguard duty would mean no magic lessons. Why hadn't I guessed he'd wait until he had something to hold over me before he set about keeping his word? That was the sort of thinking that had got me ensnared by Brant's lies. I should know better.

"You seem confident the Order won't question what I have to offer you as a bodyguard, Death King." And their questions would inevitably lead them to the only likely conclusion: I was using spirit magic again. No matter the allure of lessons in controlling my magic, it wasn't worth the risk.

"I'm sure you can think of an explanation." He stepped back from the desk as Devon entered via the back door connecting the shop with our living quarters. Her hair was cut shorter than mine and dyed pink today, while she wore a pair of leggings patterned with unicorns.

"Your phone's ringing," she told me.

"Who is it this time?" The Death King, thankfully, did not have my number. His newfound habit of showing up at my workplace was annoying enough on its own. "Not the Order?"

"Maybe." She nodded to the Death King. "Hey, Grey."

I never should have told her about the nickname Lord Blackbourne had used when he'd spoken to his old friend.

"Devon, is it?" said the Death King, momentary surprise flashing across his face, as though he could hardly believe she'd had the nerve to address him so casually.

"That's me." Devon feared nobody, not even the King of the Dead. If I left her alone in the shop with him, I might come back to find her turned into a lich.

"I will leave you to it, then." He turned and vanished into thin air, taking his shadows along with him.

"Did he just hop through the node?" asked Devon.

"He doesn't need one." Perks of being the King of the Dead. The guy could disobey the usual laws of magic openly and had done so on numerous occasions. "I'll go and answer the phone."

I went into the back room to find my mobile phone lying on the table displaying a missed call from my mother, then hit the return call button.

"Liv!" Mum said. "Devon said you were dealing with a customer."

"Kind of." She'd *met* the Death King, once, when he'd been wearing his human mask, but I'd rather he stayed away from my family for the rest of his eternal life, thanks. "What's up?"

"Just wanted to check in with you," she said. "How're things?"

"Not too bad." Mum and her wife, Elise, didn't know anything about the Parallel, and the bare minimum about the Order, so my main job was to reassure them that I wasn't in imminent danger of losing my life.

In other words, lying. It wasn't fun, but that's what happened when a practitioner was born into a non-magical family. Mum and Elise thought of the Order as like Hogwarts but with less of the glamour and excitement... which was true in a way. No wands or broomsticks at their academy, just reams of exams and lectures on the dangers of magic.

"Good," said Mum. "I'm glad to hear it. I'm glad it's working out for you, despite... everything."

She knew some of my history, but not the extent of the aftermath of the memory spell the Order had used to extract two years of my memories, which was probably for the best. I had quite enough drama in my life without my enemies targeting my family, too.

"I guess." I hesitated. "If you got a job offer from someone that might, erm, compromise your current position, would you take it?"

"It depends who you'd rather work with," she said. "You never liked your job, did you?"

"I guess not." It always seemed to come down to who I

trusted more, the Death King or the Order. And to be honest, I'd always come down on the Death King's side. At least he'd been upfront with me about his manipulative nature.

"Well…" Mum paused for a moment. "Let us know."

She sounded like she'd been halfway to saying something else, but she'd changed her mind. Maybe to offer me advice, not that anyone would be able to make the decision but me. At least he'd given me the chance to think over his offer.

In my experience, it was a bad idea to turn down well-paid work, especially during a phase like this where Devon and I had one big job from the Order and that was it. In our line of work, it was feast or famine, and we'd be wise to save every penny we could for when we hit another rough patch. I wouldn't like to reach the point where I'd end up reduced to selling old trading cards on eBay for rent money again. Or worse… having to take on independent work in the Parallel.

On the other hand, I had zero training in being a bodyguard. Granted, my abilities in spirit magic might be an asset, but I couldn't help thinking that the Death King was acting as though I'd accepted the other position he'd offered me. A chance to be his own personal Spirit Element. *In your dreams, mate.*

I went back into the shop to find Devon speaking on the phone herself. She hung up after I walked back in. "You're not going to believe who that was."

"The Order?"

"You've got it." She scowled. "They're denying they received the last shipment I sent them."

"You mean the shipment they came here to pick up

yesterday?" I frowned. "What did they do, leave it on the bus?"

"Don't ask me, but they're insisting it never reached their base."

I gave an eye-roll. "They must have forgotten to fill out the paperwork. Even Judith isn't unobservant enough to leave a box of cantrips lying around in public."

Like many people at the Order, she disliked me on principle due to my past involvement with spirit magic. She'd been my classmate at the Order's academy, and she was also one of those people who'd thought the academy years had been the best of her life, which made her even more difficult to like. Still, she wouldn't have 'accidentally' lost a whole box of cantrips on purpose. Even Judith wasn't that vindictive... right?

"They're being insistent," she said. "I wouldn't ask you to go, but—"

"But they'll come here next, and we don't need that shit," I said. "I've already turned down the Death King today, so I might as well go and piss off the Order, too."

"What did he want with you, anyway?" she asked.

"He wants me to play security guard at his contest to find the next Fire Element."

She arched a brow. "Wow. He trusts you not to let anyone in who shouldn't be there?"

"After last time? I know." A familiar sense of dread rose within me at the reminder that the Order currently held my ex-boyfriend captive inside their headquarters. I wouldn't lie, I'd been avoiding the place ever since.

But I had to go, for Devon's sake, if not my own. Besides, they were still technically my employers, even if they'd pretended that I didn't exist for the better part of a month.

I headed upstairs, swapped out my glasses for contacts and grabbed my Parallel bag as though I was off on a mission to the Court of the Dead. Which I might be, at this rate. It was that sort of day.

2

The bus to town showed up the instant I reached the bus stop, a rare stroke of luck which was soon dampened by the only available seat being next to the usual woman who insisted in describing her medical problems to me in graphic detail. Some things were nothing if not predictable.

I'd have gone to the Order the easier way—namely, through the node on top of our house—but they were watching the node outside their headquarters closely after a fire mage had tried to burn the place down the other week and it wasn't worth the risk of drawing their ire. I'd been lucky to escape without punishment after that incident, and I'd rather not run the risk of pissing them off even more.

The Order's headquarters was located in an office block which looked deceptively ordinary from the outside, and the two security guards on the doors spent an excessive amount of time scanning my ID—specifically, the black mark which indicated I'd broken one of the Order's major rules—before letting me inside. Nothing new there, but it didn't help my mood in the slightest.

Hardly anyone was around in the lobby, aside from the woman who worked on the reception desk and a few employees milling around, talking and carrying boxes of goods from the Parallel to the delivery bay through the back doors. The Order had continued buying cantrips from the Collective of Spells at Arcadia's market despite the illegal dealings that'd come to light in the wake of the Crow's death, and while they'd also taken a massive custom order from Devon, it'd taken the Death King's intervention to persuade them to keep us on their staff. As if I needed another reminder of the tightrope I walked.

I headed down into the basement where the retrieval unit was located, and found Mrs Carlisle, the department head, sitting behind the computer desk. Her dark hair was pulled back into a bun, her face lined in a severe way that suggested she hadn't smiled in years.

"Olivia," she said. "I don't recall asking you to come into the office."

"I'm here on Devon's behalf," I said. "I'm told the shipment that two of your employees picked up from our shop never made it here, so I wanted to check up on it."

"That isn't my department."

"Isn't it?" I gestured to the boxes stacked around the room. "Didn't you see them bring in a box?"

"I'm afraid I don't spend every second of my life here in this room, Olivia," she said. "You'll have to check with the delivery unit."

Anything to avoid responsibility, huh. "Is there any work going in the Parallel at the moment, then?"

"You'll hear from me when I have any missions available."

Translation: not anytime soon. Recklessness rose inside me, and before I could question my decision, I said, "So I assume it's fine if I take employment from the Death King in the interim? I assume he's visited recently?"

"Yes," she said, her tone frosty. "He has. You are free to take on any work from him you may desire, but if any member of the upper room decides otherwise, I will not be able to prevent them from intervening."

Then we'd better hope I don't attract the wrong attention again. If it took an unstable alliance with the King of the Dead in order to make the Order notice I existed, though, it was better than a punch in the face.

The sound of footsteps echoed downstairs, and a young Order assistant came into view.

"Olivia Cartwright?" said a pimply kid who hardly looked old enough to drive. "You're wanted upstairs."

"Upstairs?" I echoed. "Where?"

"Mr Cobb's old office," said the kid. "Mr Holland would like to speak to you."

Oh, boy. Holland was head interrogator and had been the one who'd given Brant an extended jail sentence a few weeks ago. He'd also been involved in my own trial, come to that, so I'd bet he hadn't invited me into his office to chat about the weather. One of the most annoying parts about my glitchy memory was that I never knew if Order members were friend or foe until I met them face to face.

Bracing myself, I headed upstairs and towards the office which had once belonged to Mr Cobb, before he'd been arrested and locked up in the same jail which now held my ex-boyfriend. I didn't disagree that Brant had deserved his punishment, but the Order knew we'd been involved with one another, and for that reason, I'd feared they might suspect I'd been involved in his criminal activity, too. There was no denying that it would have hurt less if he'd let me in on his dodgy dealings, but if he had, events would have taken a different turn.

One black mark on my record was enough for a lifetime.

I halted outside Mr Cobb's office door, then I knocked on the wooden surface.

"Come in," said a voice.

I entered the room, and a rush of familiarity hit me at the sight of Mr Holland, a tall man with neatly trimmed grey hair, sideburns, and a pair of spectacles balanced on the end of his nose that almost masked his startlingly clear grey eyes.

"Olivia Cartwright," he said, in a soft voice. "I've intended to speak to you for some time."

My gut clenched. Icy fear flowed down my spine. *This is it. They've found out I've started using spirit magic again.*

"And why's that?" Somehow, I managed to keep my voice even. His intent stare caused memories to swim in the forefront of my mind, only to be whisked away an instant later. He'd been involved in my trial, all right, and from his unfriendly tone, he hadn't voted in my favour.

"Your fire mage companion." He gestured towards a seat opposite him. "Won't you sit?"

Damn. So it *was* about Brant after all. I'd been lucky the Order hadn't insisted I attend Brant's trial, but that didn't mean they wouldn't be looking into the connection between the two of us. Because the universe couldn't just give me a break for once.

I sat down, perching on the edge of my seat, and tried to ignore the overwhelming instinct to flee for my life.

"Brant Edwards has been found guilty of conspiring against the Order and misusing our permits several times over," said Mr Holland. "You were involved with him while he was working against us."

Not this crap again. "I didn't know he was conspiring against anyone," I said wearily. "He was working against me, too. I didn't have a clue until I visited his apartment in Arcadia and found it full of illegally acquired cantrips."

"Then you confronted him?"

"No, because he ran away." I skipped over the part where a lich had attacked me in Brant's bolt hole, because that would lead to questions the Death King would not be pleased with me for raising. "I was on the lookout for him when I heard he attacked the Death King and got thrown in jail."

"Which he later escaped," added Mr Holland. "I have this report from the Death King claiming his ex-Fire Element was the one who attacked our headquarters and not Mr Edwards."

"Brant's guilty of a lot of things, but he's not the one who started the fire," I said. "The ex-Fire Element, Davies, came here to break out the three vampires who were held in custody in this very building."

"And where are those vampires now?"

"Dead," I said. "They died in the confrontation with the vampire who called himself the Crow. He was an ex-employee here, I heard."

"That is neither here nor there."

Right. It's only suspicious when I'm the one whose name comes up in connection with the enemy, not the Order in general. Okay, the Order had thought the Crow was long dead, and they'd been right, technically. He'd fled justice by turning into a vampire and hiding in Arcadia, establishing himself among the vampire elite while scheming to turn himself into a living human again. Yet it was another ex-Order employee, the late Dirk Alban, who connected all of us like the tapestry of a spider's web, and I had no way of knowing which other people in this building were as entangled as I was.

"Just passing on what I heard," I said in casual tones. "I've told you everything I know, and my report has been verified by the vampire council and the Death King. Why do you need me to repeat the same information?"

"I'm finding it difficult to believe you ended up at the scene of the vampires' attack by coincidence alone," he said. "Much less that you escaped."

"The vampires held me hostage in their hideout because they were angry with me for bringing them into the Order's custody," I said patiently. "The Death King came to confront the Crow and helped me escape capture."

"How did the Crow die, then?" said Mr Holland. "His remains were barely recognisable."

"Brant tricked him into using one of his own dodgy cantrips to turn into a living being again, which then backfired and took him to pieces." I folded my arms across my chest. "He also set the safe house on fire, which you'd know if you read the reports."

His mouth pressed into a line. I'd given him an iron-clad alibi, not to mention mostly told the truth. "Why would Mr Edwards choose to aid you after betraying you as he did?"

A fist clenched around my heart. "He still cared about me. He felt he had no choice but to ally with the vampires. Now the Crow's dead and Brant is in jail, so it doesn't matter what he thinks."

"I beg to differ," he said, "because the vampires have requested for Mr Edwards to be brought to stand trial in front of their own council."

My heart skipped a beat. "They have?"

"Yes." He scanned me. "I wanted to confirm there'll be no interference on your part."

"If you hadn't told me, I wouldn't have known it was happening." *The vampires are putting him on trial?* I'd barely begun to heal from the damage Brant had inflicted, and yet I didn't want him to face trial by vampire. Not when their punishments were believed to be even harsher than the Order's.

"Then there's nothing more to be said." He rose to his feet. "A tragic waste of a life, but the vampires' word is law."

And just what is that supposed to mean? He might well be trying to get a rise out of me, or to get me to admit to some treacherous thoughts about the Order's attitude to mages. Maybe he wanted to hand *me* over to the vampires, too.

"Only in the Parallel." Instinct screamed at me to get the hell out before I said something that caused him to turn the sentence on me instead. "The Order is the authority in this city, and you arrested him before the vampires did."

"If what you said is true and he was not the arsonist who attacked our headquarters, then the vampires have more reason to convict him than we do." He waved a hand. "You may leave."

Fucker. I hadn't guessed that telling him Brant wasn't the person who'd attacked the Order would cause the upper room to condemn him to a worse fate than an eternity in prison. To add insult to injury, Davies, the ex-Fire Element, had run away and was unaccounted for, so he hadn't suffered in the slightest for his crimes.

Mr Holland, on the other hand, seemed to be looking for a reason to convict me along with Brant, and I wasn't about to give him one, so I left the room and walked out into the lobby. I was halfway to the doors when I remembered the 'missing' package, so I headed for the back exit instead.

Stacks of boxes littered the walled yard at the back of the Order's headquarters, and a skinny Asian guy accosted me at the door. "What are you doing here?"

"I'm looking for someone I can ask about a delivery that you picked up from my house yesterday," I said. "The Order claimed it never showed up here, but we saw two staff pick it up in person."

"Huh." He scanned the boxes around the yard. "Lemme see."

Most boxes were labelled with the COS's logo, containing shipments of handmade cantrips. Others contained magical junk confiscated from practitioners on this side of the nodes, items which weren't allowed here on Earth without the Order's express permission. Judging by the cawing noises coming from the cages stacked in the corner, someone had been breeding vampiric chickens again.

He picked up a box from among the piles around the

yard. I peered over and read Devon's scrawled hand-writing on the side. "Yeah, this is yours. I'll get it logged in."

"Thanks." He might well just be saying that to placate me, but my head was not in the right place for an argument, not now I was aware that Brant would be on his way to his death within a few days. Only the Death King had the clout to fight the vampires, or at least get them to reconsider their sentence.

Oh, Elements. What choice did I have, though? The vampires were as ruthless as the Death King and had no reason to spare Brant's life, and they didn't seem thankful in the slightest that I'd helped save them from the Crow's rampage.

It looked like I'd have a reason to strike a bargain with His Deathly Highness after all.

—————

I returned home to find Devon closing up the shop for the night. Friday evening was our weekly D&D session, and while it was normally my favourite night of the week, worry gnawed at my insides as Brant's plight weighed on my mind.

"What's wrong?" Devon, who wasn't the most obser-vant person, nevertheless always knew when something was bothering me.

"Brant's going on trial in front of the vampire council." I exhaled in a sigh. "You know what the vampires do to most transgressors."

Execution. Usually without any trial at all, which was one point in his favour, but not enough. Brant had been involved in an operation which had threatened to under-mine the vampires' rule over the city of Arcadia, and while he'd also killed the vamp who'd been responsible for pushing him into it, he was one of the few who'd survived long enough to be jailed.

"Oh." Devon looked as though she didn't know what to say. "Is there no revoking it?"

"Not alone." I walked through the shop to the living room and slumped on the sofa. "The Order won't help. They're happy to hand him over to the vampires and be done with it."

"Bastards," she said. "What about the package?"

"They promised to get it logged in," I said. "Not that their promises are worth much. Even less than the Death King's."

I needed to speak the man himself in person, and soon, but I wasn't about to miss D&D night. Besides, there was a member of the Death King's contingent among our group.

I didn't have to wait long. Within the hour, the first arrivals showed up. When I answered the door, the Air Element, Ryan, entered, dressed in ordinary clothes instead of the armoured outfit they usually wore. Two sprites floated behind them, each shaped like a minia-ture humanoid figure. One glowed with orange-red flames, while the other hovered in a cloud of purplish-green.

"Hey, Dex." I waved the sprites into the house. "And Aria."

The air sprite swooped ahead of Dex. She'd attached herself to the fire sprite ever since we'd rescued her from a cage in a vampire's basement and the pair of them had been living in the Elemental Soldiers' section of the Death King's castle for the last few weeks.

The Air Element followed us through the shop into the back room and sat down at the table Devon had set up the dungeon on.

"Hey, Ryan," I said. "Has your master mentioned he visited me today?"

"He did," they said. "He also said you turned him down."

"There's been a change of plans." I glanced at Devon, then back at the Air Element. "If I said I'd accept your boss's offer if he promises to help me save my ex-boyfriend from execution at the hands of the vampires, is he likely to say yes?"

Their eyebrows shot up. "The fire mage is going on trial in front of the vampire council?"

"According to the Order." I picked up a stack of character sheets and began dispensing them around the table. "I know he betrayed us all, but I'd rather he spend years languishing in a cell than face public execution. Those vampires don't play nice."

"Yes, and my master prefers to stay on their good side," said Ryan. "It's vital to maintain the peace in the Parallel. Interfering in one of their trials might upset that balance."

"I thought so," I said. "It's got to be worth trying, right?"

"You might as well ask," they said. "He seems to really want you to help at the contest. It's quite... unconventional."

"Guess I'm a rare commodity," I said dryly. "The Order isn't giving me any work either, but they've stopped fighting me on working with the Death King, for a wonder. That's why I figured I might get away with taking the job."

"Talk to him," they said. "In person, I think he'd prefer."

"I have the weekend to decide, so I'll head up there tomorrow." I took my own character sheet in hand and sat down. "I don't know why he's set on me acting as his security guard. When I worked for the Order, I was usually the person breaking into places, not guarding them."

"I gathered," Ryan said. "That said, I might not understand my master's decision to add you to the team, but we'd be grateful for your help."

That brought me up short. The Order had never, not once, expressed the slightest bit of gratitude towards me. But that didn't mean it wasn't risky for me to agree to guard the Death King's castle from a contingent of potential rogue fire mages. What if someone *did* take advantage of him opening his doors? There were only three Elemental Soldiers working for him, and the contestants might well outnumber his own forces. And that's if someone else didn't sneak into the castle while everyone's attention was on the contest. A hundred possible things might go wrong… but that was the point, wasn't it? That was precisely why the Death King wanted his security to be as tight as possible, and despite the mistakes I'd made, he trusted me to do it.

And to save Brant's life, I'd accept his offer. If it wasn't already too late.

The door rattled with another knock. I walked into the shop and opened it to welcome the rest of our team. Craig walked in, accompanied by Red, while Trix the elf brought up the rear.

"Hey," said Craig. "Carla can't come today. She's on the night shift at the Order. Did you hear about their new shift schedule?"

"Nope." Great. Craig and Carla both worked for the same department in the Order as I did, on the admin side. If they were reshuffling things, it never worked out in my favour. "I'm sure they'll let me know at some point. Like five minutes before my shift."

"You aren't wrong." He joined the others and picked up his wizard gunslinger gnome miniature. While we missed Carla, we still had Trix, who played a dwarf fighter whose speciality was walking headfirst into traps to spare the rest of us. We also had Red, who played an elven cleric who served as our group's healer, while Ryan was our most recent member who played an angry half-orc monk with antisocial tendencies. And there was Dex, of course, who took on the role of various NPCs, occasionally assisted by Aria.

I picked up my dice and got on with guiding my tiefling rogue through the dungeon in pursuit of an evil lich lord. Though the spectre of Brant's upcoming trial hung over me, it didn't stop me from bringing out the slimy troll monster I'd based on his character. Nor did it stop Devon from coming up with an elaborately graphic description of his demise after a lucky roll.

If reality went to hell, I could always count on gaming to make everything right.

3

The node's current of blazing energy came to life inside me, and I stepped across the gap separating the ordinary world from the Parallel, landing in the swampland outside the castle gates.

I'd done my best to put my upcoming meeting with the Death King out of mind for the duration of our D&D game and got an early night before getting up early to pay a visit to His Deathly Highness in person, but now all my worries had come screaming back. I'd opted to use the node in the middle of our house to cross into the Parallel despite my misgivings about the Order finding out I'd done so without a permit. Never mind that any other Order employee in my place would have done the same. Why waste such a convenient mode of transport into the Parallel?

Two liches stood on guard outside the gates, as usual—identical cloaked shadowy forms with masked faces—while the fence extended from each side of the gates and circled the castle from behind. The guards parted without a word, allowing me to enter.

Behind the gates, Cal, the Death King's Earth Element, walked around the expanse of swampland in front of the castle, his hands outstretched. The ground bubbled and rose, reforming into earthen walls which surrounded a wide area in front of the steps leading to the castle doors. Felicity, the Water Element, stood opposite him, using some complicated water magic to move the swampy water around and leave the ground behind the earthen walls dry. I'd never seen mages use magic with such precision before, but they'd got the job working for the Death King for a reason.

The Water Element, a curvy black woman wearing a vibrant blue-lined cape over her armour, gave me a wave. "Hey, Olivia. Or do you prefer Liv?"

"Liv is fine," I said. "Is this where the contest will take place?"

"That's the plan," said Felicity. "Are you here to see the Death King?"

"Yeah, if he isn't too busy." The walls of what I guessed must be the arena for the contenders stood just high enough for me to be able to see over them, while the area covered enough ground for fifty or so people to comfortably stand inside. If he'd had so many applicants for his contest, I grudgingly understood why he'd 'forgotten' about giving me lessons in spirit magic, but it would be nice if he remembered I existed when he *didn't* need a favour from me.

"He's inside the castle with Ryan," she said.

"Thanks." I glanced at the Earth Element, but he kept his attention on the arena. Cal hadn't said more than four words to me before, but Felicity seemed friendly enough, and Ryan and I had gone from adversaries to allies in the last few months. Considering I could count the number of allies I had within the Order on one hand, perhaps this wouldn't be too bad.

I climbed the stone steps and rapped my knuckles on the oak doors. Ryan answered a moment later.

"Liv," they said. "You came."

"I did." I entered the main hall of the castle. Polished wooden floors stretched out before me, bordered by pillars made of human skulls and other assorted bones, a representation of the Death King's commitment to maintaining an aesthetic. My footsteps echoed as I walked up to the dais near the back upon which the Death King stood. This time he didn't have his human face on, and his mask was as inscrutable as ever.

"Olivia," he said. "I thought I'd be seeing you soon."

He didn't have to rub it in. "Because Ryan told you?"

"They didn't need to," he said. "I assumed you'd have brought a list of conditions, but I have to admit, I didn't expect the man who betrayed you to be one of them."

A familiar cold, hard fist clenched around my heart. Maybe throwing myself on the mercy of someone who'd viewed Brant with contempt even before his betrayal was a bad idea, but how else could I possibly save Brant's neck from the vampire council?

"Then you probably know Brant is going on trial in front of Lord Blackbourne any day now," I said. "I imagine you also know the average survival rate for someone who betrays the vampires, too."

"Close to zero," he confirmed. "So you wish for me to

stride into Lord Blackbourne's home to plead on your behalf?"

I'd be willing to do the pleading in person if it got Brant out in one piece, but the Death King had some nerve mocking me when someone's life was at stake, even if it was someone who'd betrayed the both of us.

"I want you to ask them to lower his sentence," I said. "No pleading necessary, unless you want to. Might be entertaining for the rest of us."

If he'd had his human face on, I imagined he'd have raised an eyebrow at me for that comment. "The vampires are unlikely to take my opinion into consideration."

"Yours holds more sway than mine does," I said. "You're an equal authority to them. I'm the troublemaker who blew up one of their houses—and I might add that the Order are getting suspicious about that as well. Their head interrogator gave me a grilling yesterday."

"So you wish for me to plead with the Order, too?" he said. "I already spoke to them about the situation with your friend's business."

You don't need to remind me everything in my life depends on staying on your good side. "Yes, I'm aware you did. I'm not asking you to speak to the Order, I'm just reminding you that I'm not responsible if they decide I'd be better off in a cell than serving as your guard."

"But you are offering to take the job?" he said.

"Yes, with conditions," I said. "The ones Ryan outlined to you."

"You wish for me to save your friend's life from the vampires," he said. "And I will endeavour to do so, provided you keep up your end of the bargain."

"Which is...?"

"You will work as my security guard in the castle from the beginning of the contest until the end," he said. "Regardless of what the Order says, or anyone else. Do this, and I will do my level best to save your friend."

Translation: if I backed out of the job for any reason, Brant was a goner. What else had I expected of the King of the Dead, though, really?

"Fine," I said. "I'll do it."

"Was there anything else you wanted?" he enquired.

A goading note to his voice piled more fuel on my anger. "You didn't mention whether you'd decided to give me lessons in spirit magic or not."

"I told you it was part of our deal," he said. "But it would help if you specified what you wanted to learn."

I had no memory of my lessons from Dirk Alban and what I'd learned in the last couple of months had massive gaps in it. It had taken me far longer than it should have to find out that the Death King had become head of the liches due to his former status as a spirit mage, back when he'd still been alive. As a result, he was the only person, living or dead, who might teach me what I needed to know. I couldn't waste this opportunity.

"I thought I was clear enough," I said. "I want to be able to hide my spirit mage nature. I want to be able to look the Order in the eyes and have them conclude I'm not a threat to them, and I think it would be a lot easier to stop them from kicking up a fuss about me working for you if they didn't think I was a loose cannon."

"I cannot erase their judgement of you," he said. "Nor can I control how they perceive you, no more than I can stop the vampires from enacting a death sentence on someone."

Unfortunately, I suspected he was right. "Then I want to learn more spirit mage tricks. I'm sure you can think of one or two. It's your area of expertise, after all."

"In that case," he said, "I will give you a lesson or two in exchange for your cooperation."

"Deal," I said. "So, when do I start?"

"Now," he said. "Ryan will introduce you to the castle and show you around. We'll start on our first lesson afterwards."

Good. At least if I was working with the Elemental Soldiers and not directly with him, there was less chance of me losing my temper and punching him in the nose. Not that it made me resent him any less now my ex-boyfriend's life and my own safety depended on me doing the Death King's bidding.

Ryan cleared their throat behind me. "If you'd like to come with me..."

I turned away from the dais. "Sure. Lead the way."

One unexpected perk of taking the job: I'd finally get the chance to have a proper look around the castle. So far, I'd only seen the hall of souls and the corridor where the Elemental Soldiers lived. I'd also seen the jail, though that lay outside of the castle in a separate block enhanced with magic that made it almost impossible to escape.

Yet I'd managed to do exactly that, with Dex's help. Maybe the Death King had a point when he thought I was suited to work in security, if just because I'd managed to evade said security myself. More than once.

Ryan took me through a door into a large hall filled with weaponry. Suits of armour hung from the walls, along with an array of swords, shields, and other paraphernalia.

"No wonder you always dress so smartly," I remarked. "This stuff must cost a fortune."

They gave a rare smile. "The Death King does like us to look the part. You can pick anything you like to wear for the duration of the contest. Feel free to choose any weapons, too."

Each Elemental Soldier wore the same gear, including a cloak lined with the colour of their Element and embossed with the Death King's seal—a skull surrounded by the symbols of the other four elements. I didn't particularly care about that part, but the armoured clothing would be more than welcome, given how many pairs of jeans and shoes I'd ruined when traipsing through the swamp.

"How often does he recruit new liches for his army?" I walked down the row, examining each outfit. "I mean, I'm assuming not all of them are trespassers punished for breaking into the castle grounds. There'd be more mutinies if they were."

They hesitated. "My master alone has access to information on the liches who serve him. I can tell you anything you need to know about the rules governing the Elemental Soldiers, but as for matters involving the liches…"

"They're his business alone. Got it." When Ryan's brows rose at the evident bitterness in my voice, I added, "I know he used to be a spirit mage, like me, so I'm a little concerned that there might be an ulterior motive at play here. I mean, he did offer me a job as his Spirit Element, which I turned down."

They frowned. "My master has no intention of turning

you into a lich, as far as I'm aware. Is that really a concern of yours?"

"I think he wants me to work for him whether I'm dead or alive," I admitted. "He also promised to teach me magic and then backtracked. It's kind of a sore point, since Brant told me he could get my memories back and teach me how to use my magic and then turned out to be working with the Crow."

And why was I telling the Air Element this? The two of us had been adversaries not long ago, and yet they were one of the few people who might understand the precarious position I was in.

They shook their head. "My master might not be easy to understand, but he keeps his word. Restoring your memories is beyond even him, but I'm sure if you asked, he would teach you what you want to know."

Then I hoped His Deathly Highness would stop intentionally ticking me off before I got myself fired.

"I'll check back with him on that later," I said. "So… can I really pick whatever I like from this room? Even a full suit of armour."

"Sure," they said. "My master has a wide selection of sizes, so you should find something that fits. And when you're ready, I'll take you to get some cantrips."

Nice. I'd never had proper battle gear before, like the snazzy uniform for the upper Order members who took part in major conflicts in the Parallel. The rest of us had to supply our own gear, which in my case consisted of a semi-waterproof coat and boots which didn't quite keep out the muddy water of the swampland.

I opted to go without the full suit of armour. The heavy

layers would weigh me down, and wouldn't do much against a spirit mage, besides. Instead, I picked out a durable pair of trousers and a belt for my cantrips and changed in the back room. I also chose some waterproof boots and a padded coat which was immune to the elements. It was surprisingly warm, too. I wouldn't freeze to death during the trials… though I was more likely to be in danger of catching on fire. We were trialling new fire mages, after all.

"They're fireproof, don't worry," said Ryan, when I mentioned this after meeting them outside the changing room. "Standard part of the design. That's why none of us were worried about picking fights with Davies."

"Hope you have better luck with the next Fire Element," I said. "How is the Death King finding people to take part in his trials, anyway? Is he putting out an ad in the newspaper?"

"In a way," Ryan said. "He's been travelling around the Parallel for the last few weeks, putting out word among all the local magical communities in Arcadia and beyond. He wants the widest possible choice of mages. He won't pick just anyone."

"Hmm." It seemed he didn't mind everyone knowing he was one Element short, but then again, if he put out word far enough, maybe someone would track down the former Fire Element and hand him straight back to the Death King. "Where are these cantrips, then?"

Ryan led me through to the adjoining room, which was almost as impressive as the armoury. I scanned the shelves of gleaming cantrips, admiring the array of spells on offer. "Whereabouts do you get your cantrips from? Not the market?"

The only place I'd seen so many cantrips was at the

COS's stall at the back of the warehouse in Arcadia, but the Death King was loaded. No way would he settle for mass-produced cantrips rather than fancy homemade ones designed especially for his army.

"No, my master has them custom-ordered," they said, confirming my guess. "I will help you select which ones you need, if you like."

Within twenty minutes, I'd filled my pouch with more cantrips than Devon normally made in a week, and I was more than ready to deal with whichever misfits came here hoping to take on the position of the next Fire Element.

"Ooh, snazzy." Dex flew up to me as I left the room. "Thought I heard your voice. Are you really taking up full-time employment here?"

"No, I'm just playing bodyguard at the contest next week," I said. "You're welcome to join me."

"That was the plan." He touched down on my shoulder. "Can I have my own suit of armour?"

"I doubt there's one designed for sprites, but you should be fine without it," said Ryan. "Maybe a lich cloak…"

"That would look good on you," I said. "Aria would love it, I bet."

He flew overhead and flipped over. "Don't make fun."

"I'm not, but you're spending all your time with her," I pointed out. "Don't think I didn't see you two flirting like crazy during the intermissions in our D&D game."

Dex turned away. "I won't listen to these accusations."

I wouldn't have thought it was possible for a fire sprite to blush, but he managed it. I grinned. "Joking, joking."

I hadn't thought romance was even an option for a fire sprite like him, but he'd proven me wrong. I was happy for him. I mean, Dex had nearly died recently—*had* died, in fact, before I'd used the node's energy to heal him. Spirit magic could do impossible things, like when I'd healed Brant, but it could also cause great damage.

After all, it wasn't for no reason that I'd been discovered by the Order next to Dirk Alban's dead body with blood all over my hands. It hadn't got there by accident, I knew, and yet part of me resisted the implication that I'd been the one who'd put it there.

So many questions, and only one place that might contain the answers. Never mind the contest for the next Fire Element: the real test would come when I faced my spirit magic head-on, and in the process, found out what I'd really done which had led to Dirk Alban's death.

4

Ryan gave me a tour of the rest of the castle until I was reasonably confident in my ability not to get lost in the winding, draughty corridors. Then I returned to the main hall, where I hovered on the balls of my feet, waiting for the Death King's lesson to kick off. He'd better keep his word after I'd taken the trouble to come here on a weekend. Okay, the new armour and weapons were definite perks, but I'd come here to learn magic and I was damned if I'd leave without it.

The door at the back of the hall opened and the Death King glided in, his footsteps making no sound on the polished floor. He looked me up and down—or I assumed he did, considering his eyes were hidden—and said, "The armour suits you."

"Um… thanks?" Was he making fun of me? I was pretty sure I'd never heard him give me an actual compliment before, and it was beyond me to figure out why he'd even want to. "Ready to teach me your tricks, then?"

"What did you want me to teach you, precisely?" he said. "If you simply want to know how to conceal your nature from the Order, you're going to be disappointed. The only way to disguise yourself in any capacity is to become a lich."

"What?" I folded my arms. "You have got to be kidding me. I thought I was more useful to you alive."

"This isn't about how useful you are to me," he said, as though I was barking up the wrong tree for even suggesting it. "This is about the Order. They know of your history of using spirit magic, so you're only likely to be in danger of them suspecting you to be an active spirit mage if you expose your magic in front of them."

"Of if one of the vampires gives the game away." Like, say, when the Order escorted Brant to the vampires in person. Oh, *fuck.*

"If you want to learn how to work your powers of persuasion on the vampires, that's also a futile exercise," he said. "It depends if you feel Lord Blackbourne is likely to tell the Order you used your magic recently."

"You need to work on your 'reassuring' tone." I drew in a breath. "All right, then. Forget hiding my nature. What I did to Dex—bringing him back to life—could I do the same to a living person?"

"No," he said. "Dex is a spirit, essentially formed of energy, and our gift as spirit mages is the ability to manipulate that energy. That's not the same as making a deceased person's heart beat again."

Okay. That made sense. "I accidentally drew his power into me a couple of times, too. It enabled me to use his magic. I take it only spirit mages can do that?"

"You did?" He paused. "Yes. Most spirit mages can't do

more than manipulate the energy of a node, but the strongest among us can draw on the energy of other sources. Like sprites, or…"

"Liches?" I studied him. "Wait. I did the same to you, didn't I? When we fought the Crow."

"You drew on my power because I gave it to you," he said. "Most liches would not take kindly to you using their life force as a conduit."

"Life force?" I echoed. "Damn. You were putting your life force into that barrier. No wonder it nearly killed you."

Which meant that if I wanted to, I could drain the life force from a lich like drawing energy from a node. Not that I wanted to end up on the bad side of the Death King's army, but if I ever ended up on the end of a hostile lich's attack again, that'd be one hell of a useful way to incapacitate them.

"I wouldn't advise you to try the same," he said. "My own resources are unusually high due to my status as a spirit mage turned lich. As long as my soul remains bound to an amulet, nothing can kill me. You, on the other hand…"

"I'm a living human who has no intention of becoming a masked phantom who turns to dust if I ever step away from a node," I finished.

"There are ways around that."

"I thought you weren't planning on turning me into a lich." My hands curled into fists as I felt his stare boring into mine even with the mask concealing his face. "If I can drain anyone of their life force, another spirit mage can do the same to me, can't they?"

"Yes," he said. "With ease."

"Then teach me how to stop them from doing that," I said. "It's not a stretch to think I'll end up facing another spirit mage sooner or later, and I could stand to be better prepared next time."

The Crow might be dead—permanently—but he'd been a spirit mage, and so had Cobb. Dirk Alban's former allies had scattered, but some of them had survived, either by turning into the living dead or by being stripped of their magic. Besides, I never knew if I might find myself on the wrong end of a lich's attack again.

A cold sensation slid over my skin, raising goosebumps on my arms, then a sharp tugging sensation gripped my chest and manifested in a stream of energy, threading from me to him.

Hey! He might have given me some warning before he started sucking out my life force. I took a step back across the floor, but he simply moved with me, the current of energy brightening and the temperature dropping until my hands numbed.

"How do I fight?" I said through chattering teeth. "Can I break the connection?"

"I'm sure you can figure it out."

Not helpful. So much for him giving me a fighting chance. I backed further across the hall, but the thread of energy connecting us didn't break no matter how much distance I put between us. When I tried to grab the thread of energy, my hand passed right through it.

Time for a new approach, then. I reached out for the glowing stream of energy as though drawing it from a node. The pressure lifted a little as the glow transferred to my hand, only to reform in front of my chest again. My body locked to the spot as the pressure on my chest peaked, like a heavy, solid object sat on my ribcage, crushing me slowly. He was literally sucking out my life force without even removing my soul.

"Slow down." I caught the energy current again with my fingertips, but his grip was too damn strong. "How do I break this thing?"

"You don't," he said. "If you end up against someone as powerful as I am, your only option is to finish me off before I drain you for good. If we'd been in a real battle, you'd be dead."

"Excuse me?" I reached for the thread again, alarm seeping through me, but it didn't break. "What if you weren't an all-powerful lich lord? If you were just a regular mage?"

"Then yes, you should be able to break it," he said. "The lesson here is not to get drawn into a fight you can't win."

And with that, the thread connecting us vanished. Sensation surged back into my limbs with an impact that sent me flying backwards. I landed on my rear on the hard floor, struggling to catch my breath.

"Ow," I said. "That was deliberate, wasn't it? You tricked me."

"I think that's enough to be getting on with for now," he said. "If you want, you can go home. Present yourself here at nine o'clock Monday morning for the first round of the contest."

Arsehole. It seemed his new strategy was to get out of teaching me magic by annoying me into quitting.

Challenge accepted, then.

———

After a relatively relaxing weekend, I left the house early on Monday morning to start my new job as the Death King's bodyguard. Or punching bag. His lesson had got through to me, I'd say that much, but it seemed my best bet for fighting someone like him was to rely on my tried-and-tested method of running for my life. Or just ripping out their soul before they got their paws on mine.

I used the node to cross over into the castle grounds and headed to the newly constructed arena just inside the gates. Liches formed a shadowy barrier around the inside of the castle grounds, parting to let me through and then moving back into place again. The three Elemental Soldiers paced around the arena, calling inexplicable orders to one another.

"It's all systems go in here," I remarked to Ryan. "What's the first test for the aspiring Fire Elements?"

"A free-for-all," they said. "Essentially, the first stage is to weed out the weaklings among the contenders. Then we can get on with narrowing down the list to find the best person for the job."

It didn't look as though they'd left any gaps in their security, but the main threat was more likely to come from among the contestants than from outside. If I were out to assassinate the King of the Dead, that was how I'd go about it, anyway. His Deathly Highness himself wasn't anywhere in sight, and I wasn't clear on whether he'd be showing his face during the contest or not. The guy liked to keep things unpredictable.

Dex flew up to me. "Hey, Liv. Ready to rock?"

"Not sure what it is I'm even supposed to be doing," I said. "Where's Aria?"

"Hiding in the break room," he responded. "She wants to stay away from all the noise."

I didn't blame her. The air sprite's imprisonment had left her skittish, and besides, who knew what chaos the contenders would bring with them? "Are you guarding the grounds, then?"

"I've been instructed with watching the hall of souls." He puffed up his chest with pride. "The place is securely locked up, but His Deathly Highness expressly asked me to watch the doors."

"Nice going." Of all the people in the castle likely to steal a soul amulet, the sprite stood at the bottom of the list... mostly because he couldn't actually pick anything up. A good choice, on the Death King's part, if a surprising one. I turned to the other Elemental Soldiers. "What does the Death King want us to do, then?"

"My main job is to put out fires," said Felicity, the Water Element. "Literally, I mean. Cal will be watching the arena. You and Ryan will join the liches in keeping an eye out for anyone trying to break into the castle."

"Sure, I can do that." *I hope.* While the Death King knew about my spirit magic and so did Ryan, I hadn't told anyone else. The liches, though, probably already knew by now, but as long as nobody let anything slip in front of the Order, I was safe.

"The first contestants are on their way," said Ryan, nodding in the direction of the gates. "Once they've been searched for weapons, that is."

I rotated on my heel. A number of mages had gathered just outside the gates, surrounded by shadowy liches. Almost all of the aspiring Fire Elements looked utterly terrified, and I didn't blame them a bit. I knew how disconcerting the cold touch of a lich was when you hadn't experienced it before. As I watched, one contestant sank to the swampy ground in a dead faint.

"That's one way to thin down the competition," I remarked.

Two of the mages picked up their fallen companion and fled the scene, while several others muttered excuses and left. Admittedly, having the liches conduct the weapons search *was* a good way to judge who had what it took to serve the Death King. They wouldn't last long in the job if they were frightened of liches.

The shadowy lich guards herded the remaining mages into the castle grounds and towards the arena. From what Ryan had told me, it sounded like the aim of the first day was to drive off anyone who didn't meet the Death King's criteria. Those who remained would stay in the castle for the duration of the challenges.

The contestants made their way through the gap in the low earthen walls surrounding the arena. They ranged from old to young, with some of them appearing barely out of their teens.

One had the pointed ears and silky hair of an elf. I indicated him to Ryan, who said, "Don't worry, the first challenge will eliminate anyone who isn't a fire mage. I expected at least one person to try skirting the rules."

The actual fire mages seemed to be determined to live up the stereotypes. One burly guy had conjured three flames and was juggling them openly, while several others held leaping fire in their hands to stave off the cold. Fire mages tended to be quick-tempered and prone to rash actions like setting things—and people—ablaze, and I hoped everything in the castle was fireproofed like my uniform was. It was lucky we had a water mage on call, really.

When the arena was full, the liches withdrew, and Felicity strode out to address the participants. "Welcome, all, to the Court of the Dead."

The contestants fell silent, looking around uneasily. Nobody spoke a word.

"You have all come here to compete for the honour of serving the Death King as his chosen Fire Element," said Cal, stepping up to Felicity's side. "There will be five days of challenges, and at the end, only one of you will remain."

"And some of you will be eliminated long before then." Ryan raised their hands, and a current of air smashed into a patch of bushes, unearthing two hidden figures. They both yelped in unison as Ryan levitated them into the air. "As will anyone who breaks the rules. Don't think I didn't see you two masquerading as liches in the crowd back there."

"We just wanted to watch our friends!" squeaked one of the floating teenagers. "We don't mean any harm."

"Tell that to the liches." With a blast of air, Ryan sent both of them flying towards the gates, where the security liches swiftly moved in to remove them. *I guess they used cantrips to disguise themselves.* At least Ryan had thought of that… though the two intruders had some nerve trying to outwit the Death King.

The Death King, who still wasn't here. Maybe he wouldn't show his face until the final round. Who knew? You'd think he'd want to see his potential Fire Elements rather than sitting alone in the castle, but I'd learned not to waste my efforts wondering what his reasoning was. Maybe he had a secret passion for throwing dance parties when nobody else was around. Who knew?

As the contestants returned their attention to the Elemental Soldiers, Felicity began to outline the rules of the contest. I, meanwhile, edged closer to Ryan. "Please tell me you let those two kids inside on purpose."

"Of course," they muttered back. "I had to use someone to set an example, and those kids were harmless."

"Let's hope they're the last." I scanned the arena, my gaze panning across the gathering crowd listening to Felicity. "Does your boss think there are likely to be any troublemakers among the participants?"

"He said it's more likely than not," said Ryan. "Some people wouldn't be able to resist the opportunity."

"Then I hope he's still inside the castle and isn't gallivanting off." Given that the last Fire Element had helped steal from the hall of souls himself, it ought to be a top priority. Twice, in fact, the Death King's soul had gone missing—though admittedly, the second time had been a deliberate ruse on the Death King's part.

"The first contest is a test of endurance," said Cal. "Anyone who is left in the arena after the timer goes off will go through to the next round."

At that point, the entire arena caught on fire. An inferno surged up to the sky, while screaming rang out from within. Two contestants tripped out through the gap in the earthen walls, their clothes singed and their eyes wide. One of them was the elf from earlier, his pointed ears red-tipped and his eyes watering.

I whirled on Ryan. "Was that *deliberate?* Did the Death King seriously order someone to set the arena ablaze to lure out the non-fire mages?"

"It worked, didn't it?" Ryan stepped in to help the liches escort the disqualified contestants out of the Death King's territory. They didn't look to be seriously hurt—the flames must have been for show, mostly—but the Death King seriously pulled no punches. I wouldn't want to be among those competing for the chance to serve him.

Then again, he'd offered me a position anyway. *He's utterly bonkers. They all are. What kind of contest is this?*

The flames began to die down, leaving the remaining contestants shaken but standing. Several of them wore expressions of false bravado which didn't hide their trembling hands. Others cowered behind their friends. The loud trill of a timer rang out, and the Earth Element addressed them again.

"That ought to take care of anyone who doesn't belong here," he said. "Those of you who wish to remain will follow Felicity to the castle to settle in before the next trial."

Muttering broke out among the gathering mages. It seemed a fair few of the participants thought someone in charge had a screw loose. I couldn't say I blamed them an inch.

"Where in the castle will they be staying, anyway?" I whispered to Ryan.

"The east wing, near our own rooms." They did not look thrilled at the prospect. "So we can keep an eye on them."

Good call, given the location of the hall of souls, though it surprised me that they'd be allowed to stay in the castle at all.

"What are we supposed to do now, then?" I asked Ryan.

"According to my master, our job is to transport the contenders' possessions to their dorms, after they've been searched."

"Hey, he never mentioned that in the job description," I said. "I'm not his Fire Element's personal valet."

I was starting to have second thoughts about this whole situation, but I ought to get the chance to complain directly to the man himself if I waited for long enough. He still owed me a lesson or two, after all.

I walked with Ryan into the castle lobby, where Dex hovered in front of the door to the hall of souls. A large number of suitcases and other bags were lined on the polished floor.

Cal entered through the doors behind us. "I'm told you're an expert on dangerous magical artefacts, Liv, so your job is to search all these bags for anything that might pose a threat to our master."

"We have to search all these?" I said disbelievingly. "Also, 'expert' is not the word I'd use." Identifying dangerous items was more my area than bodyguard duty, admittedly, but still.

"Not my problem," said Cal. "Felicity and I will help the guests settle in, and you and Ryan are to search these bags. Boss's orders."

He has got to be kidding me.

An hour of searching suitcases later and I'd unearthed a small heap of cantrips, ranging from healing ones to more aggressive spells. I'd also formed a pile of other dubious items I wasn't sure were magical or not.

"Nobody said I'd be pulling cantrips out of people's underwear when I took this job," I said to Ryan. "Or confiscating Jaffa Cakes and M&Ms."

"It's a character-building exercise." Ryan had gathered the suitcases belonging to the participants who'd already left, which left me to determine who had brought in anything dangerous enough to merit being kicked out. "What've you got?"

"Mostly harmless cantrips." I indicated the pile on the lobby floor. "What's the policy on snacks?"

"Confiscate them all," they said. "Just in case anyone is planning to poison the other contenders. You never know."

"We're seriously going to be on their shit list after this," I remarked. "First we terrify them with liches and magical fires, now we're stealing their chocolate bars."

"They can have them back after the contest finishes," said Ryan. "Those are all regular cantrips... what's that?"

I examined the pointed instrument they'd indicated. "This? It's one of those tools used for carving cantrips, like Devon uses. A few contestants brought reusable cantrips."

"So we have a practitioner among our contenders." Ryan's mouth pressed together. "It's not unheard of for a mage to have that skill, I suppose."

"No, I guess not." Mages were rare even in magical families, so the odds of having a child with multiple talents were very slim. Still, it didn't necessarily mean the contender was up to no good. "Should I take note of whose suitcase I found these in?"

"Go ahead." Ryan passed me a clipboard and pen, and I scribbled down the name. "Now we have to take the suitcases to the dorms."

"This just gets better and better."

Between us, we made several trips from the lobby to the east wing of the castle, by which point the dorms were empty and the contestants had followed Cal and Felicity outside once again. My arms ached from the exertion, and I found myself even less well-disposed towards the Death King for not mentioning physical labour would be a part of my duties.

When we'd dropped off the last batch of suitcases, Ryan and I headed towards the other Elemental Soldiers outside the arena, where Felicity outlined the rules of the next contest. I lingered outside the castle, debating swiping a cantrip to remove the ache from my limbs, when my gaze snagged on the node inside the castle grounds, a hundred metres or so from the arena's boundary.

The current of energy shone bright, but something inside it darkened the glow. *Is someone trying to break in?*

Nobody else appeared to be paying attention, but now I looked closer, I could see a shadowy form within the current of energy. Was it one of the Death King's people? I didn't want to create a fuss for no reason, so I edged around the arena alone, one eye on the node. It was impossible for anyone to come into the Death King's territory via that route. When I'd tried it myself, I'd been ripped out of my body and ended up astral projecting instead. To top it off, I'd then been chased off by the Death King and his lich guards. Whoever it was, they couldn't have come here by accident, surely. One did not accidentally trespass in the Death King's territory.

I halted in front of the node, squinting to see who was inside it. The shadow remained, unmoving. Then a torrent of energy surged at me. I raised my hands in defence, and the current of energy hit me dead-on, sending me skidding backwards. Another beam of power knocked the breath from my lungs and knocked me sprawling onto my back. Winded, stunned, I lifted my head to see a shadow fall over me.

The Death King strode past me, his shadowy hands held up. The torrent of energy ground to a halt, and then reappeared, more solid than before, connecting the Death King to the person in the node. The human-shaped figure inside the node visibly shuddered, and my stomach turned over. The Death King wasn't just taking energy out of the node… he was taking it out of the person inside it.

"Hang on!" I wheezed, pushing to my feet. "Don't you want to find out who it is before you kill them?"

He lowered his hands, and the connection broke. "There's no need. The attacker has gone."

Dammit. They must have used the node to escape unharmed, leaving nothing behind but the gleaming current of white light.

"Who was that?" I said. "Was it a lich?"

"No," said the Death King. "It was a spirit mage."

5

I wobbled on my feet, suppressing a wince. I'd hit the ground hard but hadn't taken too much damage. I was more shaken by the Death King's revelation that another spirit mage had been the one who'd attacked me. Even if they hadn't actually got inside the castle.

I'd expected to meet another one at some point, but not so soon after my lesson from the Death King. *Who the hell was that?*

Several gasps from the contenders drew my attention to the arena again. Dark shapes spilled over the earthen walls, bearing down on the participants. Phantoms.

"Please tell me this is part of the test." I turned to the Death King, only to see him walking away, back towards the castle. "You aren't going to help them?"

"No," said the Death King. "Attacks from phantoms are par for the course here in the Court of the Dead, and they'll have to learn to deal with them sooner or later."

Right, because the Death King gave nobody any excuses, and he wasn't someone to expect mercy from.

The phantoms were easy to fend off with simple fire attacks, but the spirit mage was a different story. I walked in behind him until I caught up at the castle's steps, wondering if anyone inside the arena had glimpsed the intruder. Given their predicament, though, it was unlikely.

"Are you sure the attacker won't come back?" I asked the Death King's retreating back.

"Not if they have any sense, they won't," he responded.

"You're way too calm about this." *He knew.* He must have expected an attack of this nature... which meant he'd known there were other spirit mages out there the whole time. "Also, you might have given the rest of us some warning."

"I thought I did." He swept up the stairs towards the castle doors. "During our lesson."

"That wasn't a warning," I protested, climbing the stairs behind him. "Also, I'm the one who brought up the subject, and I was *not* prepared for a spirit mage to try to kill me before the end of the first day of the trials."

"I beg to differ," he said. "I believe I was the target myself."

"Then why'd they stay inside the node?" I asked. "To draw you out of the castle, or to stop you from recognising their face?"

"Ostensibly." He halted outside the castle doors. "I believe I told you to guard the arena alongside the Elemental Soldiers. If you wish to speak with me, wait until the day's trials are over."

"You can't tell me there's another spirit mage and then expect me to forget all about it!" I found myself addressing the nearest skull instead of him. The Death

King, of course, had passed right through the doors and vanished into the castle. I rolled my eyes at the skull. "That's what I get for taking a job from the guy who turned you into a decoration."

Someone had tried to kill both of us, and he wasn't even stationing extra security around the node. Okay, perhaps he'd considered the threat and had assessed it as not worthy of attention, but he wasn't the one playing security guard. And not all of us were as unbreakable as he was.

Incensed, I marched down the steps and halted beside Ryan. "I can't believe him."

"What's going on?" they asked.

"A *spirit mage* just astral projected into the node and attacked me," I whispered. "And His Deathly Highness seems as unbothered as ever. As though it doesn't matter. What's wrong with him?"

"A spirit mage?" Their eyes widened a fraction. "Are they here now?"

"No, they fled back through the node," I said. "Might have gone anywhere. I didn't even see their face, and they were probably astral projecting anyway, but your boss might have forewarned me of potential spirit mage intruders."

He'd also used his powers to draw the life force from the spirit mage while they'd still been inside the node. That was more advanced than what he'd taught me, but what had I expected? The guy ran on expert mode and trampled all competition into dust.

"First I've heard," Ryan murmured. "Are you sure it was a spirit mage?"

"Your boss said it was, and I doubt he'd lie." Even for him, that would be taking it too far.

I kept one eye on the node as I watched the contestants battle the phantoms, fending them off with flames. Impatience gnawed at me. If it was possible for me to follow the intruder through the node, I'd probably missed my shot already, but it was worth having a look around in case they came back.

I skirted the arena and walked back to the unbroken current of energy in the middle of the swampland. Maybe I'd luck out and find a trace the spirit mage had left behind which might point to their identity. While the current of energy looked the same as ever, that didn't mean an enemy wouldn't materialise from inside it again. There wasn't a way to turn a node off, as far as I was aware…

Movement caught my eye from the direction of the castle, and I glanced up. A shadowy form filled one of the upper windows, a pair of invisible eyes watching me from a distance, and I heard the unspoken message in the Death King's stare. If I walked through the node, I'd lose my chance to save Brant's life.

Muttering curses under my breath, I backed to a suitable distance from the node and heard rustling in the bushes nearby. *Another intruder?* No living creatures existed in the swampland, much less inside the castle's boundaries.

I trod closer to the intruder's hiding place. Energy blasted from my palms, crashing into the bush and unearthing a young woman. She landed in a crouch, her eyes wide. A tangle of dark curls surrounded her pale, pointed face. Her muddy clothes had seen better days, but a defiant tint to her expression told me she wouldn't give in without a fight.

"Who are you?" I demanded.

"Whoa," said the young woman. "I just got here. What's the problem?"

"Someone tried to assassinate the Death King," I informed her. "You don't happen to know anything about that, do you?"

"No, I told you." Her tone was indignant. "I'm here for the contest."

"Is that why you're hiding in a bush?" I said. "Paying a visit to someone in jail, were you?"

"No, I overslept and I was running late." She met my eyes, as though daring me to challenge her. "I'm not breaking any rules."

"We'll see what the Elemental Soldiers have to say to that," I said. "Are you even a fire mage?"

She held up her hands, between which a flame leapt to life. Definitely a fire mage, not a spirit mage... and I'd hit her in the face with spirit magic. So much for keeping it between the Death King and me.

"Broken rules or not, you clearly have a death wish," I commented.

"I wouldn't be applying to work here if I was afraid of death." She rose to her feet and turned towards the arena. "That's where the action is, right?"

"Yes, but you're too late," I said. "You can't just walk into the middle of—"

She ignored me, striding toward the arena. I followed suit, catching up as Ryan cottoned on to what was happening. "Who's that?"

"Intruder," I told them. "Claims she's here for the

contest, but I found her hiding in the bushes way over there."

Had she sneaked through the node? Surely not. The defences kept out even spirit mages.

"Hiding, was she?" said Cal. "Kick her out."

"There's no rule against latecomers being allowed in," Felicity argued. "She *is* a fire mage. And we've already expelled more contenders than we'd expected to at this stage."

I left them to their arguing. At least the intruder was their problem now, not mine. Or rather, the Death King's. Her appearance might be a case of bad timing, but I didn't trust her a bit.

———

By the time the day's events came to an end, I was in a foul mood, to say the least. The contestants seemed to be in a competition as to who could bend the rules the most, but the Elemental Soldiers insisted brawling wasn't a good enough reason to disqualify someone. Nor was setting their opponents' clothing on fire. Despite the rules against carrying excess weapons, the contenders had chosen to hide both knives and cantrips in creative places, and that wasn't even taking into account their tendency to shoot fireballs at one another.

The remaining contenders returned to their dorms at the end of the day, while Ryan and I stood and watched them leave. Even now, the Death King didn't come out to speak to them.

"Is he serious?" I remarked to Ryan. "He's just going to hide in his room all day?"

"My master has a considerable amount of work to do."

"Like plotting how to kill spirit mages he doesn't even tell his own security about?" I said. "How do you stand it? He seems to have zero respect for us."

"He respects us," said Ryan. "A damn sight more than any of the supervisors I've met at the Order."

"Okay, you've got me there," I admitted. "But come on. A *rogue spirit mage* on the property. Shouldn't he at least have warned us?"

"He would have done if they were still there," said Ryan. "Or if anyone had got a glimpse of their face."

"I might have seen them if I'd been allowed to follow." I shook my head. "I know, I know. I dug my own grave when I accepted a job from an evil lich lord. Whatever."

"I wouldn't use the word 'evil,'" said Ryan. "I'm going to ask him what to do about that intruder."

"The one I found in the bushes?" I arched a brow. "I know the rules of the contest are a little lax, but I'm pretty sure she sneaked past the liches to get in."

"Which is why I need to speak to her," they said. "I want to find out how she got past security and if anyone else is likely to try the same. I'll ask my master about the spirit mage while I'm at it. Maybe he'll be more likely to answer me if I ask nicely."

I snorted. "Pretty sure 'nice' isn't in his vocabulary."

He did seem to respect Ryan more than he did me, but I didn't hold out much hope of getting answers. If the Death King had wanted me to know why he'd expected an attack from a spirit mage, he'd have told me right there and then.

I was tired and starving after a long day with little reprieve from the contestants causing trouble, and I was all too ready to foist them off on someone else while I went home to Devon. Without looking back at the castle, I stepped through the node, wondering idly if I could follow the spirit mage that way. The node, however, took me straight home without any detours.

"I bet he did that on purpose," I muttered to nobody in particular. "The dickhead."

"Wow," said Devon, looking up from carving a cantrip on the sofa. "That bad, was it?"

"You might say that." I kicked off my shoes. "My first day at the new job involved picking cantrips out of people's underwear, the Death King setting the arena on fire and terrifying everyone, and a rogue spirit mage trying to get in."

"A rogue *what?*" Devon's eyes bulged. "You found another one?"

"I only have the Death King's word to go by, and he refused to explain anything." I hung up my coat and made straight for the Xbox, more than ready to blow off steam in a game of Skyrim. "It's beyond ridiculous that he expects me not to ask questions after *that* happens."

"Whoa, back up a step," she said. "You saw the spirit mage, right?"

"Nope." I turned on the TV. "They astral projected and hid inside the node until the Death King drove them off. I didn't see or hear them. Neither did he, but he doesn't seem all that bothered."

"Damn." She whistled. "He's confident they won't come back?"

"I think he's hoping *I'll* fend them off, despite the fact that I had no idea they even existed until one of them attacked me." I picked up the controller, fury seeping through me. "He's reached a new low. But if I don't see this one through, Brant's dead."

There was no other option. The Death King had me trapped and he knew it.

Devon shook her head. "So you aren't going to want to hear the news I got from the Order's direction?"

"What, they located your 'missing' package?" I asked. "They're asking me to bring in a rogue again? Or some other mission?"

"Nah, it's more directed at both of us," she said.

"They aren't threatening our business again, are they?" I watched the loading screen. "Come on, just tell me."

"They're hosting a school reunion." She pulled a face. "For those of us who graduated ten years ago. It's a snazzy event at a hotel in town."

"Devon, that is not good news."

"I never said it was *good* news, did I?" she said. "Nobody likes school reunions except for the people who actually enjoyed school."

"So, Judith French," I said, with a theatrical shudder. "They don't seriously expect me to show up, do they? I haven't done anything to make the academy proud."

"Maybe I can tell the future graduates how I created my business making cantrips instead of studying," she said.

"At least it's more honest than the drivel they told us," I said. "I can tell them what it's like playing security duty for the Death King and finding all the creative places people hide cantrips in their laundry. That is, if His Deathly Highness would take a school reunion as an excuse to let me out of his sight."

She snickered. "Don't worry, I know you're busy this week. The reunion is this Friday night, though."

"Great." A school reunion. Just what my week needed. "I think I'll pass. I'd almost rather take on a rogue spirit mage than face the people who fucked me over after the memory-loss crap."

The academy hadn't directly been involved with my punishment after Dirk Alban's death, but they'd punished me in their own way when they'd failed me on every exam I'd taken, despite my malfunctioning memory erasing years of study. Not to mention they were the ones who'd invited Dirk Alban to speak to my class to begin with. I didn't entirely blame them—I was the one who'd taken the bait, after all—but that didn't mean I had any intention of revisiting bad memories any more than I had to.

"Are you going back to the Court of the Dead tomorrow?" she asked.

"Every day this week, yeah," I said. "The liches take over as security at night. Generous of them."

"Hmm," she said. "So… what's the plan?"

"Whoever said there was a plan?"

Devon tilted her head. "You aren't going to do everything the Death King says, are you?"

"If I want Brant to live, I can't go chasing down rogue spirit mages," I said. "Not while I'm on the clock, anyway."

"But outside of it?"

I picked up the Xbox controller. "What can I do? The spirit mage is probably long gone by now, and besides, the Death King is looking for any excuse to let Brant be sentenced to death. He doesn't care about him, and he only made this bargain with me so that I'd take him up on his job offer."

"Then turn it around on him." Devon grabbed the controller and hit the pause button. "Seriously. You're acting like he holds all the cards, but he doesn't. You're a living spirit mage—one of the handful of people who might give him a run for his money. You *removed his soul* once, in case he's forgotten."

"Devon, I think he'd have words to say if I held his soul hostage as a bargaining chip." And as he'd proven already, there was no other way I could best him.

"You don't have to." She gave me a serious look. "That other spirit mage could have done the same. You're the one thing standing between him and them."

"He didn't need me, though," I said. "He took out the spirit mage himself. I didn't do anything except get taken by surprise."

"You'll be prepared next time," she said. "Besides, with the number of attacks there's already been, I can guarantee you'll end up saving his arse again sooner or later."

"That's just it," I said. "The only way I can make sense of him being so blasé about the attacks is to assume he deliberately stuck a neon target on his head so that they'd all come to the castle at the same time. Just like he did with the soul amulet when we faced the Crow."

"So, that gives you a way in," she said. "Get creative. I believe in you."

"Glad one of us does." My anger had begun to melt away, though, to be replaced with a steely resolve.

Screw the Death King. I'd make him thankful for having me around to fend off those who wanted him dead —spirit mages or otherwise.

6

My plan would be a lot easier if I got Ryan and the other Elemental Soldiers on my side, which meant getting up at the crack of dawn to head into the Parallel before the contest started for the day.

I arrived at the castle and found Felicity guarding the doors, clad in armour with her blue-lined coat swirling behind her. I wondered how hard I'd have to plead for the Death King to let me keep the uniform after the contest finished. I had to admit it was nice to have decently durable clothing for once. And boots which didn't leak.

"Hey, Liv," she said. "The boss isn't around, but the others are in the break room."

"That figures." It'd been too much to hope for that His Deathly Highness would show up to assuage my concerns about his attitude to potential attacks from rogue spirit mages. Maybe Ryan had had better luck when they'd addressed their concerns to their master yesterday, but I didn't hold out much hope.

I entered the castle via the back door and joined the other Elemental Soldiers in the break room, which lay down the corridor from their living quarters. Half the space contained a large sofa big enough to seat at least four people, along with a TV mounted to the wall, while the kitchen at the back was stocked with snacks brought in from the other side—Ryan had explained yesterday that they had a rota on who did the week's shopping, since the liches didn't need to eat or drink. Ryan and Cal occupied the sofa, while Dex and Aria flew around the ceiling in a game of chase.

"Nice place, this, isn't it?" said the fire sprite, spotting me. "I always assumed His Deathly Highness made his people sleep in the dungeons."

"The dungeons are involved in today's tasks," said Ryan. "Or so Felicity says, anyway. She won't tell me why."

"Perhaps the Death King is planning on locking the contenders in there all night as an endurance test." For all I knew, the whole contest was entirely for his own amusement. It wouldn't surprise me at this point.

"You should speak of him with more respect," Cal said. "The next Fire Element needs to be ready for anything. And we need to weed out any scumbags who are plotting against our leader."

"There shouldn't be any left, surely." Felicity entered the room. "The non-fire mages are all out."

"And did he tell you about the spirit mage?" I asked the others. "Because as far as I'm concerned, that shows a glaring lack of any respect for his employees."

"I told the others," Ryan added. "I also spoke to my master. He claims that scaring off the intruder ought to have deterred any other spirit mages from trying the same thing."

I'd believe that if I hadn't found another intruder hiding in a bush five minutes later.

"Did the spirit mage really attack you during the trials?" asked Felicity. "I didn't see."

"The Death King scared them off," I said, addressing Cal as well. "He also claimed he was likely the target and used that as his reasoning for not warning us first. But if he knows who the spirit mage was and whether they might come back, he wouldn't say. Did he tell any of you?"

"No," said Ryan. "Honestly, he just doesn't want us distracted from our jobs. Our goal is to keep all enemies out of the castle and from interfering in the trials, and we aren't trained to deal with spirit mages."

Except for me. If you counted half a lesson as proper training anyway. "I understand that, but it doesn't exactly set a good precedent for the new Fire Element. I mean, I'd be concerned if my employer wasn't telling me the potential risks before I took the job."

"Protecting him *is* our job, though." Cal rose languidly to his feet and walked out of the room. "I'm going to check the arena. Felicity, are you done?"

"Sure." She turned on her heel. "Ryan, don't fall too far behind. The boss wants us outside in ten minutes."

"Got it." Ryan climbed off the sofa. "The Death King has too many enemies to count, and not all of them are worthy of the same level of attention. Right now, his focus is on keeping potential intruders out of the position as Fire Element. The rest, he can deal with later."

"I know." Frustration burned beneath the surface. "But

I can't do my job if I'm walking around blindfolded. I'm not supposed to be the one on trial here."

Or maybe I was, and this was a test to see if I was worthy of taking on the position of the Death King's Spirit Element. A position I wanted less and less with each passing day. I wouldn't back out now, though. For Brant's sake, if nothing else.

"If you've already told him that, there's nothing more I can do," Ryan said. "Sorry, Liv. If it's any consolation, things will go back to normal around here after this week is up."

"I'll try to hold off on punching him in the nose before then." I gave a grim smile. "You'd think my ex-boyfriend's life hanging on the line would be enough of an incentive, but he's seriously testing my patience."

The Death King might not like me, but he wouldn't reprimand the other three Elemental Soldiers for asking questions. If they started pressuring him over the issue of the spirit mage, too, then he'd have to cave eventually and tell them the truth. Right?

The two of us left the break room at the same time as a contender walked past, from the direction of the main part of the castle. I recognised her as the young woman from yesterday... the one I'd found spying on the contest after the spirit mage's attack.

"He actually let you stay?" I said to her.

"Oh, it's you." She turned to me. "Turns out I performed well enough in the rest of the tasks yesterday to be worthy of a place in the trials."

What the hell was the Death King playing at this time? I looked at Ryan, who glanced over their shoulder at both of us. "I'll go and catch up to the others. Don't forget you have to be outside in ten minutes… that includes you, Bria."

Evidently, they didn't want to discuss their private meeting with the Death King in front of any of the contenders, but they'd given me an opening.

"That's your name?" I asked the woman. "Bria?"

"Yeah, why?" Her defensive tone wasn't unexpected. I wasn't normally this much of a grump, but several brushes with death coupled with the Death King's attitude problem were starting to grate on me. That, and the fact that she'd sneaked into the trials under the liches' noses and had still been allowed to stay.

"Some mages use aliases." I watched Ryan walk out of sight. Wait, had they left me with her on purpose? Maybe. There was no rule saying I wasn't allowed to speak to the contestants—or ask them pointed questions. She *had* already seen me use spirit magic and hadn't commented on it. Was it a usual sight to her, or had she been more concerned with not getting kicked out?

"C'mon," I said to her. "You have to join the others. What're you doing alone in here, anyway?"

She'd been coming from the direction of the main part of the castle… which was supposed to be out of bounds to the contenders, as far as I was aware. *Hmm.*

"Forgot my coat." She indicated the plain dark uniform which all the contestants had been given at the end of the previous day. "Then I got lost. This place should come with a map."

"The Death King doesn't normally have visitors," I said. "As you may have gathered."

"What's it like?" she asked. "Working for him?"

"A trial." I opted for an honest approach in the hope

that it might make her open up a little about how she'd sneaked in without being noticed. "Don't tell him I said that."

She grinned. "I can see why it would be. I haven't seen the man himself yet. What's he like?"

My mouth parted. She might be innocently curious, but her questions were those a spy might ask, and I still didn't trust her motives in being here. On the other hand, she'd given me an opening.

"Dangerous," I said carefully. "I mean, he's an immortal lich lord who's been in power longer than I've been alive, and then some."

"Huh." She frowned. "Not what I heard. I thought he only got the job a decade or so back."

"Really?" I tried to hide my genuine surprise. "How'd you know?"

"I thought everyone did." She shrugged. "I guess if you don't live here in the Parallel, you might have missed it."

Or rather, my missing memories had evidently eaten that particular piece of information, too. "Yeah. I don't live in the Parallel. This is a temporary job."

For her, though… it might explain her lack of reaction to my use of spirit magic. Rare or not, it wasn't a crime on this side of the nodes.

"Fair enough," she said. "I imagine he pays well. That's one of the reasons I want the position as Fire Element."

"Pay isn't everything," I said. "There are risks, too. But I guess you knew that."

"Meaning, the risk of getting killed by a phantom?" she said. "Oh, that's old school. We get them everywhere back home."

"Do you get liches, too?" I said.

"Nah, they're all conscripted into the Death King's army, aren't they?" she said. "They can't turn on us."

"Actually…" I doubted the wisdom of telling her the Death King's secrets, but if she was working against us, she already knew, and if not, she'd need to know what she was up against if she wanted the job of the new Fire Element, once way or another. "Actually, there have been a few incidents recently. Thought you should know in case you end up getting the job without anyone telling you."

"Thanks for the reminder, then," she said, turning to the door Ryan had gone through. "Is that the way out?"

"Yeah, we should head outside before we're late."

We walked out of the exit and towards the arena. While part of me doubted she'd sneaked in using legal means, her comment about the Death King had knocked me off-balance. How much more had the gaps in my memory swallowed up? Brant used to be my go-to person for reliable info on the power structures in the Parallel, but he'd left out some pretty major things. Like his own criminal enterprises. And now, it seemed, how long the Death King had been in charge.

As I neared the arena, a shadow fell across my back as though conjured up by my thoughts. I slowed my pace, letting Bria walk ahead. Then I turned to the steps, and the masked figure looking down at me.

"Decided to welcome your potential Fire Elements in person?" I queried.

"You were talking to that contender," he said. "Why?"

So he had been paying attention, then. "She asked what I knew about you. Since you're so elusive and mysterious."

"And what did you tell her?" he said.

I tilted my head. "Why? Worried I'm bad-mouthing you behind your back?"

"Simple curiosity," he said. "Well?"

"I said you were a deadly immortal lich lord who's been in power forever," I said. "She corrected me on my dates a little. Seems I was misinformed on how long you've been in the position of Death King."

Which meant there were people in the Parallel right now who'd known him before he'd become Death King. No wonder the vampires had known his old nickname. They were ancient enough that it would have still made sense if he'd been a century old, admittedly, but perhaps I could make use of that information later down the line.

"Your point?" he said.

I shrugged. "Just found it interesting. I'd also like to know why you let her stay in the contest after she showed up late and tried to hide in the bushes. Not exactly soldier-worthy behaviour."

"I have a policy of giving everyone at least one extra chance," he said. "Including yourself."

"If you ignore the time you locked me up for days before letting me explain myself." Second chances? He'd locked me in a cell, the dickhead. "Why are you suddenly giving everyone the benefit of the doubt? Because if you're intending to lure your enemies in so you can force them to expose their treachery, you might have held the contest somewhere which didn't literally contain the lives of yourself and every single person in your Court."

"I didn't know you were so concerned for my well-being."

My hands clenched. "I'm concerned that you're

making it bloody impossible for me to do my job, Death King. If you're going to keep secrets from me, invite people with dubious motives onto your property and allow latecomers to sneak in, don't blame me if I accidentally kill the wrong person."

"I'm honoured that you're so dedicated to the cause," he said, "but I doubt you have reason to worry. Anyone who's foolish enough to get on your bad side deserves their fate."

"Do you include yourself in that number?" I said, before I could question if it was wise to anger him at a time like this. "Because you've spent longer on my bad side than otherwise."

"Really." His tone dripped with scepticism. "If you're reconsidering your offer to work for me, then I would remind you to think of the others who would be impacted by your decision."

As if I could ever forget. "Nobody said anything about quitting, but if I end up with your soul in my hands again, I'm seriously considering whether it's worth the bother of putting it back where it belongs."

He didn't drop a snide comment or threat, as I might have expected. He simply vanished through the doors into the castle, at the same time as silence swept across the arena, signalling the start of the second round.

I blew out a breath. "Note to self: next time get a job working for anyone but the most ungrateful wanker in the Parallel or otherwise."

I didn't particularly care if he heard me. Turning away, I went to join the other Elemental Soldiers at the arena's side as the second day of the trials kicked off.

7

"The goals of today's trials," Ryan told the participants, "are to test your ability to improvise and use quick thinking to solve problems. Everyone who isn't in the contest, I'd advise you to get out of range."

That meant me, then. I backed up to the castle steps, along with Felicity and Cal, as Ryan raised their hands.

A whirlwind shot towards the arena, knocking the contenders over like skittles. I braced my feet on the steps as the air current rippled over our heads.

"I see why we're supposed to keep our distance," I remarked to Felicity.

Ryan's magically conjured whirlwinds lifted a number of baskets across the grounds, levitating them above the arena. *What's going on this time?*

"Your task is to catch as many discs as possible," said Ryan. "And don't drop any. Everyone takes one basket. *One* basket, Sledge." They addressed a heavyset guy with a mullet and a scowl who'd started a few fights already.

There followed a flurry of activity as everyone scrambled to grab a basket before the air current knocked them over again.

Once everyone had a basket in hand, the wind picked up again, sending a handful of blank cantrips surging above the participants' heads. To no surprise, the first participants to catch any cantrips in their baskets were those who could jump the highest. Or climb on the others. One short, skinny girl climbed a taller contender like a tree, grabbing for the discs. Ryan raised their hands and the air current reversed, knocking her off the challenger's back.

"You're having fun with this, aren't you?" I called down the steps.

"It's rare that I get to make full use of my gifts." They shot me a grin and returned their attention to the contest.

By the trial's end, three participants were still on their feet. One was Sledge, who looked like he was part boulder; the second was a smaller girl who'd survived by hiding behind the bigger, sturdier contenders—and the third was Bria. She caught my eye and grinned—whether mockingly or triumphant, I honestly couldn't tell. After our chat earlier, I still didn't know where we stood, but I hadn't seen her openly break the rules. She must be quick on her feet, that's all.

"That's enough," said Ryan, lowering their hands. The wind died down and the remaining discs bounced into the mud. "Who has the most discs?"

Sledge dropped his basket, revealing it overflowing with gleaming gold discs. "Did I win?"

"Nope." Bria casually stepped aside, revealing a basket piled high behind her back. "I did."

The smaller girl looked a little annoyed, but she revealed her own stash of cantrips without a fuss. One by one, the other contenders began to rise to their feet and show their spoils. Ryan helped count them, while the rest of us watched for any signs of trouble. Like Sledge trying to steal other contenders' discs, for instance. If it were up to me, I'd already have disqualified him, but that wasn't my decision to make.

"The next trial will take place in the dungeon," said Felicity. "Come with me."

She descended the stairs and led the contenders around the back of the castle, while Ryan, Cal and I went through the main doors into the lobby. Inside, Dex had taken up his usual position in front of the hall of souls.

The fire sprite gave me a wave as I walked past. "Not much action in here, is there?"

"Don't speak too soon." I followed Ryan and Cal through a side door which led to a balcony overlooking a wide room.

The dungeon itself contained nothing of note, only a pair of oak doors which opened with a reverberating creak. The candidates filed into the room behind Felicity and assembled on the ground below our balcony, which was covered in what appeared to be sand. When the doors closed behind them, Felicity climbed a stone staircase to join the three of us on the balcony.

"Stay up here." Felicity told us. "Word of advice... you're definitely going to want to keep your distance from this one."

I shot Ryan a puzzled look, but Cal stepped in first. A grating noise came from below, and a large slab of stone slid across the sandy floor, blocking off the stairs Felicity had climbed. Another covered the door the contenders had entered through, trapping everyone in the dungeon… including us.

"Your test is to find a way out of here," Felicity said to the fire mages below. "Don't bother trying the stairs over here. They're barred. And so is the way you came in."

Then Felicity raised her hands, and water began to fill the room, sweeping across the sandy floor. The fire mages' faces twisted with alarm and shock, but there was nowhere for them to run. In no time at all, the water rose to block the doorways, while the mages found themselves submerged to their ankles, then their knees.

I turned to Felicity, whose face was pinched in concentration, then back to the others. "What's she doing? I thought the trials were supposed to test their skill at fire magic, not put it out."

"The fire magic is on hold for a while," said Cal, looking entirely too pleased with himself. "They won't be much use if they can't fight back when their magic is disabled, can they?"

By now, most of the contenders were treading water. "Is the test for them to *swim* out of here?"

"That's the plan, yes," said Cal. "I'm the one who hid the keys."

"Please say the Death King has safeguards in place to prevent anyone from drowning," I said.

"Hey, we all get a chance to cut loose," said Cal. "Ryan already got theirs, and now Felicity gets to try hers out."

I doubted she'd let people die in the middle of a challenge, but it was clear the Death King himself had no intention of intervening in this one. If anyone was unlucky enough to drown, he could always turn them into a lich and conscript them into his army. Or turn their bones into decorations. Arsehole.

The water stopped at neck-height for most of the participants, but the shorter people had to tread water or stand on the higher parts of the ground in order to keep their heads above the surface. I scanned the room, wondering where in the world the way out must be... then spotted a glimmering section of stone diagonally across from us.

One of the contenders had found it, too. She pushed against the wall, then shook her head. My eyesight wasn't good enough to see what was wrong, but Ryan leaned in and whispered, "There's a keyhole. They need to find the key to get out."

"And it's hidden in this room."

The key must be below their feet, then, concealed in the sand. There was nowhere else it might be.

Several of the contenders had already figured it out, diving below the water to search the sandy floor. A furore rose when the big guy, Sledge, grabbed a smaller candidate and shoved her under the water, limbs flailing.

"Stop whining and grab the damn key," he said.

"Hey, that's cheating, isn't it?" I readied myself to intervene.

"Yes, it is." Ryan leaned over the edge and sent a current of air at Sledge, knocking him back into the water. "Three strikes and you're out. No drowning the other participants."

"Spoilsport," Sledge spluttered, resurfacing.

"Real team player, that one," I muttered, scanning for other familiar faces. The shorter girl who'd endured the last round dove under the water to search for the key, and Bria did likewise.

Then the crowd surged to one end of the sandy floor. Had one of them got the key? Judging by the way the crowd piled up near the door, I'd say so. Ryan shouted again, and their magic pushed the crowd apart, allowing the contender to reach out and unlock the door.

A doorway in the wall sprang open and the contender jumped through it to safety, but when the others tried to follow, they found the way blocked. The door had closed, and nobody else could get out.

"There's more than one key." Now I got it. "They have to find one each. Without drowning one another in the process."

That seemed a tall order. Whenever one of the participants found a key, others would try to snatch it from their grip. Within ten minutes, five or so of them had left the arena, but the rest of them had to keep diving underwater to retrieve the keys from where they were buried.

"There aren't enough," I said to Cal. "Are they? You deliberately did that to disqualify half of them."

"Guilty," he said. "In my defence, it was the Death King's idea. All of this."

"Of course it was." Sledge was still in there. So was Bria. Neither had been lucky enough to find a key, nor keep hold of it for long enough to unlock the door.

Another participant escaped through the door and Sledge tried to drag him back out. As the two grappled, Ryan's magic sent Sledge flying into the water again. He disappeared with an angry shout. The water levels appeared higher than they had before, covering half the exit. *That's new.*

"Felicity's not doing that, is she?" I looked at the Water Element.

"No, she isn't." Ryan shot her a concerned look. "Someone else is using magic. Everyone—get back from the edge."

I took a step back, and the water gave another surge, dragging the contestants downward. Felicity swore under her breath. "I can't stop it. The person doing this must be a mage. We have to get them out—"

In a rush, the water surged up to the ceiling and over the balcony. Icy water drenched me, a powerful current dragging me into its wake. I kicked out, my feet seeking the stone floor, but the balcony wasn't beneath me any longer. My hands touched the ceiling, and panic shot through my nerves. There *was* no surface. The water filled the entire hall. The only way out was to swim through one of the doors which had been sealed for the contest— or find a key.

Luckily, I had one ace up my sleeve in the form of a water-breathing spell. I fumbled in my pouch for the right cantrip, my already-poor eyesight hindering me further. Then I turned on the cantrip and a bubble appeared around my head, bringing a relieving surge of oxygen. I dove below the surface, spotting Ryan treading water beside the oak doors the contenders had entered through. Air shot from their hands and the doors burst open, sending a current of water and mages surging out into the main castle.

Oh, hell. Now the whole castle was in danger of flooding. The nearest contenders took their chance to swim through the now-open doors, while others kicked and climbed over one another in an effort to escape the water.

Felicity remained behind, directing the stragglers towards the doors, while Cal had disappeared. Maybe he'd made a run for it. I turned on the spot and caught sight of the earth mage floating unconscious nearby. *Or maybe not.*

I grabbed his arm—he might not have been particularly nice to me, but I didn't want him to *die*—and swam towards the open doors. The water level was no lower on the other side, and by now, it filled the corridor almost to the ceiling. Gritting my teeth, I pulled Cal through the doors and towards the others swimming for freedom up the stairs into the main castle. I pushed Cal up the stairs ahead of me, relieved to find the water levels above only came up to my ankles.

In the upper corridor, Ryan was performing CPR on one of the contenders. They caught my eye as I dropped Cal off, and as the contender stirred, Ryan moved to Cal's side. I glanced behind me, still seeing more contenders escaping the hall. Most of them had already fled, but some of them might have been left behind. Including, perhaps, the person responsible for the flood.

I swam down the staircase back into the dungeon, pausing to allow a couple of stragglers to swim past me to safety. My feet touched down on the sandy floor, unearthing a key. Might there be a cantrip hidden under here, too? It was that or a water mage had got in... which was unlikely, given how thoroughly everyone had been searched.

I shoved the sand with my foot, glancing up as Felicity helped another contender escape. Movement stirred below, a faint glitter in the water. Magic?

I swam towards it with strong kicks, but the water current changed direction with a surge that sent me flying back. I hit the wall, and the bubble vanished from around my head. Water filled my mouth.

I rotated towards the door again, my lungs screaming for air. Water overflowed my mouth, and my vision blurred.

The image of Dirk Alban's face flashed before my vision.

"What have you done?" his voice said. *"Olivia Cartwright, you have doomed us all."*

I opened my mouth to respond, but no words came out. My sight turned grainy, like a corrupted video recording, and the voices blurred into one, the faces merging before my eyes before darkness clouded my vision.

———

I choked on a breath, then coughed up a torrent of water. Cold hard stone cushioned my back, while my eyes opened to see the Air Element leaning over me.

"Good, you're alive," Ryan said.

"Thanks." I coughed up some more water. "Who did that?"

"I don't know," they said. "Thanks for getting Cal out. I couldn't help everyone at once. The water moved too fast."

A few more contestants lay scattered around the corridor, soaking wet and shivering. I wobbled to my feet and walked up to the staircase leading into the dungeon, where the water had almost cleared. I held onto the wall for balance as I descended the stone steps until I came to the balcony. Felicity stood alone, her face set in an expression of concentration. In the dungeon, the water levels were lower, but puddles covered the floor along with sand and unearthed keys. Nobody had been left behind. *Did I really see someone use magic, or did I imagine it?*

If that had been a person I'd seen, they'd tried to kill me. I retreated upstairs into the corridor, where the contestants huddled together in bedraggled groups. None appeared obviously guilty, though it was hard to tell from outside appearances. Further down the hall, the door into the castle's lobby lay partly open. I walked through, finding the hall slightly damp but not flooded, and it didn't look like the doors to the hall of souls had been opened. The mental image of fishing soul amulets out of random places for the next week was not an appealing one.

"What the *hell* is going on?" Dex wanted to know. "Did His Deathly Highness try to drown his contenders? Has he forgotten one of his security guards is a fire sprite?"

"It wasn't him," I said. "I thought I'd find him in here. Is the hall of souls okay?"

"No thanks to whichever fool flooded the place." He flounced over to the doors. "Storms and quakes. This job will be the death of me."

"I'm starting to agree." I turned around as Felicity walked in, dripping-wet.

"I swear I didn't do that," she said, as Dex puffed out smoke at her. "Either another water mage got in, or someone used a spell to make the water rise."

"Like a cantrip?" I said. "Are all the contestants in one piece?"

"More or less," said Felicity. "Ryan and I got most of

them out. The trial itself ended inconclusively, but what can we do?"

"Never mind the trial." Someone had flooded the castle with the intention of sabotaging the trials without a care for who might have died in the process. "Where's the boss?"

"Pretty sure he can't drown," said Felicity. "He'll be in his hall of souls, I don't doubt."

"He isn't," said Dex. "Nobody has been in there, not even me."

"Do you think the person who did this was intending to distract everyone so they could steal his soul amulet again?" I asked.

Her expression shadowed. "Maybe. Truth be told, I don't know if a contender did it or not. If it wasn't a water mage, a cantrip would have turned to dust after its use, which would have vanished in the water."

She had a point. From above, none of us would have seen someone set off a cantrip underwater... but the other contenders might have.

"You're right," I said, "but I reckon if they did, someone must have spotted them. It's hard to do something like that surreptitiously. And there was a lot of bad behaviour going on in there."

"Like that bully Sledge," said Felicity. "I'm going to dry out the castle. Can you ask Ryan to find me when I'm done?"

"Sure." I turned back to the bolted doors behind Dex. "The water won't have got into the hall of souls, would it?"

"No," she said. "It's protected by magic the rest of the castle isn't. None of us expected the place to end up flooded from the inside, but anti-elemental shields only cover the jail and the hall of souls."

"I'd pity the person who had to rearrange every soul amulet if they didn't," I commented. "Who knows, maybe the Death King is hiding somewhere in there after all."

"It's locked," said Dex.

I had an unlocking cantrip, but I had an inkling that wouldn't work. So be it, then. I turned away and went to find Ryan.

"Everyone accounted for?" I asked the Air Element, who sat at the foot of the stairs, squeezing water out of their cloak.

"Sure," they said. "I'd get everyone assembled outside, but I'm pretty sure they'll catch their death of cold if I do. We need to find some cantrips to dry them out."

"Bring them into the hall," I said. "The contenders, I mean. We can grab the cantrips while we're at it."

"Oh?" Ryan climbed to their feet. "What's the plan, then?"

"Play detective." And if necessary, convince His Deathly Highness to step in and do some of his own damn work for himself. "I've got this, don't worry."

"Okay, over to you." They headed down the corridor. "Everyone, get into the main hall. Cal, can you get some heating cantrips to dry them off?"

The Earth Element grumbled a complaint, but I was already walking back into the hall ahead of the contenders. When the hall was full, I climbed onto the dais, wishing I had a dramatic flourish like the Death King to draw everyone's eyes.

"Hey!" I called out, my voice echoing from the high ceiling. "Everyone, pipe down. I need to talk to you."

Most of the noise died down.

"One of the people in this room is responsible for this recent act of sabotage," I told them. "If anyone would like to make a confession, now is the time to do it."

Nobody spoke. Well, it was worth a shot.

"Your choice, then," I said. "All of you are going to be questioned by myself or one of the Death King's Elemental Soldiers. If any of you saw *anything* that might point to who flooded the hall, then you can tell us that information in confidence and it won't be held against you."

"Wait, who are you?" said a girl with long dark hair plastered to her face with water. She was the young woman who'd survived the first round by hiding behind Sledge. "You're not an Elemental Soldier."

"I'm head of security," I said. "And I think you're up first. None of you is to leave this hall until everyone has been questioned."

If the Death King decided to show up in the interim, then it was not my problem. He should be doing this himself, but it seemed he had zero intention of showing up. Dex mimed clapping in the background, though, which I appreciated.

I stepped off the dais and addressed Ryan. "It'll be quicker if we split the questioning between us."

"Sure," they said, to my relief—I hadn't been a hundred percent sure on their cooperation. With Felicity occupied with cleaning up the flood and Cal fetching the warmth cantrips to dry everyone off, the two of us would have to handle this ourselves—which was fine with me, because I trusted Ryan more than I did the other Elemental

Soldiers. "We'll use the adjoining rooms over there. The Death King won't mind."

They beckoned to a contender to follow them into one of the rooms, and I took my own contestant into the neighbouring room. Bookshelves and armchairs filled the space within, which would have been downright cosy in normal circumstances. The girl's distrustful gaze didn't break, and up close, I could see a pattern of scars on her face which hadn't been obvious from a distance. I also recognised her as one of the candidates who'd hidden a dozen knives on her person on the first day, which Ryan had confiscated. It seemed she was no stranger to attracting trouble, but then again, that was probably normal for someone who'd grown up in the Parallel.

I sat down in one of the chairs and indicated to her to do the same. "No need to look so nervous. If you have nothing to hide, this won't be a problem for you. What's your name?"

"Harper," she said, her hands twisting together. "I didn't mean to offend you. I just wondered if you were allowed to call the shots here. I mean, you're not one of his Elemental Soldiers."

She wasn't wrong. "I'm not offended. I'm going to ask everyone the same questions. That okay?"

She nodded. "Sure."

"Do you know who flooded the castle?" I asked.

She shook her head. "No. I don't."

"Did you see anything unusual while you were in the dungeon?" I asked. "Like someone using a spell, or any magic other than fire magic?"

Her eyes were on her knees. "I didn't see anyone else

use magic, no. Our magic got cut off when the water came in."

I'd assumed so… but that didn't mean another type of magic hadn't been used instead. Like a cantrip. Harper continued to fiddle with her hands. She wasn't fidgeting like Devon did, to occupy her hands. She had the distinct air of someone with something to hide.

"And did you see any behaviour from the other contestants which implied involvement in the attack?" I asked. "Or any other unsportsmanlike actions? Say, someone attacking the other contenders?"

"Sledge," she said. "His friend Bark, too. Don't tell him I said that."

"I think we all saw," I said. "And what made you choose to try out for this position?"

"It pays well."

At least she'd been honest. "Okay, that's enough. You can go."

I repeated the same questions to the others. After going through enough contenders that I couldn't put it off any longer, I called on Bria, who came in with her hair newly dried from Cal's cantrip, wearing a confident expression that suggested she had no fears of being caught out.

Once I'd got through the usual questions, I asked a new one. "Do you think any of the other contestants have ties to anyone who might have reason to target the Court of the Dead or its members?"

"I don't know," she said. "I assume whoever did it doesn't know liches can't drown, in that case."

Hmm. "Perhaps. Or maybe they were trying to cover up another crime."

Someone had been up to no good in the castle, and while nobody had targeted the hall of souls, her confidence rubbed me up the wrong way.

"A conspiracy theory." Her eyes gleamed. "I like it. Is your job always this exciting?"

Innocent or not, I could do worse than humour her so that she'd let her guard down. "I'm just here as head of security for the week, so I can't speak to how it usually is. You might find it dull."

"Steady work is hard to find," she said. "Guess you probably know that, being a spirit mage. Work is hard to come by when people think you'll set their place of business on fire. I imagine the threat of ripping someone's soul out is a similar deterrent."

My heart gave a jolt at the words, while cold sweat slicked my skin even though it should come as no surprise that she knew. I'd openly used spirit magic in front of her, after all, and she didn't know I worked for the Order or that I didn't permanently live here in the Parallel. "You might say that. Do you know many other spirit mages, then?

"Not personally," she said. "Ever heard of the Spirit Agents?"

"No..." The name didn't ring a bell. "Who are they?"

"They're, like, vigilantes."

"They are?" I said, disarmed. "Whereabouts are they based?"

She blinked. "Well, if I knew, I wouldn't broadcast it."

Was she aware that another spirit mage had almost killed the Death King recently? If she wasn't from here... maybe not. I found it hard to believe she'd heard nothing at all about the recent upheaval in the region she wanted to work in, though. "Just wondering if I need to watch my back for anything other than the usual suspects. You're not from Arcadia?"

"Nah, Elysium."

"You came a long way." Elysium overlapped with London, and while it wasn't impossible to cut the distance by using the nodes, she wasn't a spirit mage. If she'd never been here before, she must have walked here on foot.

"I did." She rose to her feet. "Should I send the next person in?"

I moved in front of her before I could quite consider what I was doing. "If I wanted to learn more about the Spirit Agents, who would I ask? I'm here working as the Death King's security, and I need to know if there is any possibility these people might be a threat to the contest."

"Nah, they're not here in Arcadia," she said. "I haven't heard any mention of them since I arrived here. I reckon the vampires keep them away."

"So you don't know anyone I can talk to about rogue spirit mages who might target the contest?" I asked. "I don't know how much you know about recent events…"

"Nothing, probably. I've been off the grid."

"A spirit mage attacked the contest yesterday but escaped through the node," I said. "It's why I reacted as I did when I found you."

"Oh." Her eyes rounded. "That explains a lot. I don't know about any spirit mages who might have reason to target the contest. It wasn't one of them who flooded the place, I wouldn't think."

She might be lying, but I'd need to spend more time around her to find out if her story had holes in it. Either way, it couldn't have been a spirit mage who'd flooded the castle. Even if a cantrip had been the cause, a spirit mage could have done a lot worse if they'd wanted to target the Death King.

I nodded. "All right. That does help. I'm asking these questions because this is going to be a major issue for the person who wins the trials and becomes the next Fire Element, and they're going to have to work with all of us to keep the Court of the Dead safe from outside attackers. Anything you can tell me, I'd be grateful."

She frowned. "The Spirit Agents aren't local, but if you want to know more about the local mage groups, I'd start out with the Houses of the Elements. There'll be a branch in Arcadia, no doubt."

Houses of the Elements? I'd never heard of them before, either, but you could bet I'd be probing my contacts. The information was golden, and best of all, Bria had no reason to hold it over my head like the Death King. Even if she was hiding something, she was worth keeping around.

In the meantime, it was time to do a little sleuthing outside the castle.

8

The questioning continued, until Ryan and I had covered all the other contenders between us. One by one, they returned to the hall. Ryan took charge of questioning Sledge, which was lucky, because I wouldn't have been able to resist booting him out for cheating.

As for the others, nobody gave away anything incriminating which pointed me in the direction of the person who'd flooded the castle. And the Death King still didn't come back. Either he was hiding somewhere and eavesdropping, or he wasn't in the castle at all.

After Ryan and I had dismissed the contenders—all of whom had dried off by now—we met up with the other Elemental Soldiers in the hall.

"Any luck?" I asked. "How was Sledge?"

"I gave him a disciplinary warning," said Ryan. "He's still in the contest, but only because he has one strike left and the boss has to personally be involved in an expulsion that isn't for anything too serious."

"He's taking his sweet time showing up," I remarked. "You'd think he'd want to check up on everyone. Unless the flood washed him away."

Which I doubted. The guy was way too well-prepared not to have at least expected an attack similar to this one.

"Which others do you have your eye on?" they asked. "Did anyone act suspicious in any way which didn't lead to outright guilt?"

"Harper," I said. "She was acting shifty."

"What about Bria?"

"I'm reserving judgement on her." If the Death King wanted to keep his enemies close, then perhaps I could make use of the same strategy.

"The trials are on hold for the rest of the day to give everyone the chance to recover," said Felicity. "Considering half the contenders nearly drowned, it's probably the best move for now."

"Good to know." It seemed His Deathly Highness wasn't going to come back and actually check on the damage to the castle... or check if his soul was safe. Weird, but who was I to complain? Now I was free for the rest of the day, I could do worse than check Bria's claims held any truth in them.

———

Dex flew up to me when I left the castle, having also been dismissed. "Someone tried to off you again, didn't they?"

"I really don't think I was the target," I said. "If they were aiming for the Death King, though, he doesn't need to breathe underwater. And I'm pretty sure he isn't even here."

"He picked a fine time to go for a walk, didn't he?"

"Finally, someone who agrees with me." I walked out across the swampland and called out to the zombie horse known as Neddie. "Fancy coming with me on an adventure?"

Dex would likely be reluctant to leave Aria behind, but the idea of staying in a soggy castle with a bunch of shivering fire mages wasn't exactly my idea of a good time either. Sure enough, he said, "Okay, but I'm not riding on that horse."

Dex hovered alongside me as I rode through the swampland. I could have taken a shortcut through the node instead, but I wanted the time to think on my decision. With the rest of the day free, I was determined not to squander my chances to make use of the information Bria had given me.

Neddie and I parted ways at the edge of the swampland, and Dex and I made our way past the warehouses into the main part of Arcadia. Trix the elf lived in a rough area, but he seemed by some elven fortune to avoid trouble, for the most part. I knocked on his door, and he opened it with his right hand, the left one rubbing his eyes while he yawned. Even half asleep, his hair was silkier than any human's, his pointed face handsome and eye-catching.

"Hey, Trix," I said.

"Oh, hey, Liv." His expression brightened. "Sorry, I was napping... what are you here for, a mission from the Order?"

"Not quite." I summarised my job working for the Death King, along with today's incident. "I nearly died at least twice on the job and the boss is out of town."

"That's not good," he said. "Can I help in any way?"

"Have you ever heard of the Spirit Agents?" I asked.

"No, but I can find out," he said. "Are they who's threatening the Death King?"

"I don't know, but a spirit mage attacked me, and there aren't that many of us. It makes more sense if there's a collective, whether they're based in the city or not."

"There's a spirit mage *here?*" said Dex. "Another one?"

"I don't know if there is, because they could literally have come from anywhere, on Earth or in the Parallel," I said. "I'm not allowed to go and hunt down rogues while I'm working, so my options for finding them are limited."

"So you want me to keep an eye out for spirit mages?" said Trix.

"Don't put yourself in danger unnecessarily," I added. "But if you hear any mention of the Spirit Agents, I'd be grateful if you could let me know. Also, the House of the Elements."

"Oh, I know about them," he said. "They're magical collectives based in Elysium."

"Wait, they are?" I said, disarmed. "Are any of them likely to want to attack the Death King?"

"I don't know them personally, but there's one house for each Element," he said. "Except spirit, of course."

This was news to me. "I can ask the other Elemental Soldiers, then. Maybe these Houses are trying to do what the vampires did and kick the Death King off his throne."

"I doubt it," said Trix. "I heard they have a binding agreement with the vampires not to march on their territory. I don't see them breaking it and coming here."

Hmm. It figured that the vampires would know these mages... and for all I knew, they were well aware about the spirit mage who'd attacked as well. Unfortunately, they were unlikely to volunteer that information to me. Not without the Death King.

And the next time I'd see them would be during Brant's trial.

An idea slithered into my mind. The vampires *did* owe me for saving their lives… and if I went to them in person, then perhaps I could get through to Lord Blackbourne and his fellow council members before they made up their minds to condemn Brant to death. It was worth trying.

I headed for the vampires' council house, guilt gnawing at me. I might have put Trix in danger again by asking him to get involved, but I had no other allies in the city outside of the Death King's castle. Even Dex was in His Deathly Highness's employment now.

"Ever heard of these Elemental Houses?" I asked Dex.

"Sounds familiar," he commented. "They run Elysium like the vampire council runs Arcadia, except in four houses divided by magic type. Makes sense."

"That I can believe." The mages held a series of hierarchies and rivalries which made little sense to me as an outsider, to tie in with their general distrust of non-mages. There'd be people among the contenders who'd been spurned by their allies for daring to try out for a job working for the King of the Dead. "I wonder if it was one of them who disturbed the trial and flooded the place. If so, though, it probably wasn't a fire mage."

One long walk later brought me to the vampires' council house, which stood near the old Citadel of the Elements. Most cities held one, and all of them were empty vessels where ghostly phantoms roamed. Nobody had dared tear them down, even after the spirit mages had died out. Their haunted halls carried as many unsavoury rumours as the Court of the Dead did.

I found the same kid standing by the door to the council house as last time, pale as milk with needle-sharp bite marks on his neck.

"Hey there," I said. "I'm Olivia Cartwright. I met with Lord Blackbourne a few weeks ago, and I assisted in the fight against the Crow and the other vampire traitors."

"Olivia," he said, slurring the words a little. "I'm afraid my master won't arise until sundown."

"That's okay," I said. "I'd like you to ask if he's willing to speak to me at a time of his convenience. It's about— my friend. The fire mage. He's due to come here for a trial in front of the vampire council, and I'd like the opportunity to talk to one of the vampires before then."

"Council. Fire mage. Got it." He leaned on the door, and I caught it before it closed.

"Only tell your boss," I said. "Nobody else. This is secret council business, do you understand?"

He nodded mutely. Then he closed the door, while I hoped I hadn't made a huge error in trying to speak to the vampires at all. If the impossible happened and Lord Blackbourne let me plead on Brant's behalf, I wouldn't need to rely on the Death King at all. I wouldn't have to keep risking my neck while he hid out of sight.

Now I had several hours to kill until sundown and nothing more to do at the Death King's castle. It seemed foolish to waste that time, but short of ambushing strangers at the market and asking if they knew of the Spirit Agents or the Houses of the Elements, I was out of ideas on how to find them. The Parallel was full of secret groups and societies and people who'd rip your tongue out for telling tales to the wrong person. Yet another reason I hadn't set up a permanent base here.

"Are you out of your mind?" Dex hissed in my ear, ever the pessimist. "You can't beg the vampires to spare fire-boy's life. They'll laugh you into the grave."

"I saved them from the Crow," I pointed out. "If not for me, they'd have been hit by one of his spells and decayed into ashes. Besides, the Death King was going to campaign on my behalf by the week's end anyway. I just got there first, on the off-chance that I accidentally get myself fired before then."

He snorted. "His Deathly Highness has got under your skin again? Ooh, I recognise that face."

I followed his line of sight and spotted a ragged WANTED poster affixed to the wall, adorned with Davies's grinning face. He might have disguised himself, of course, but I had my doubts he'd stayed in the city at all. He knew how the Death King punished traitors.

"Bet he's pissed at being replaced," Dex said.

"That's one way of putting it." I let my gaze pan across the town square and halted at the sight of a figure slipping out of sight, past the vampires' council house. It was Bria. "What's she doing?"

"Going into the citadel, apparently."

I drew to a halt. "What the hell?"

Nobody went into the citadel. Even the vampires didn't. I glanced towards the council house, but nobody appeared or reacted to the unnatural sight across the square from me.

"Liv!" Dex howled and clung to my shoulder as I trod out into the square after Bria. My heart thumped louder the closer I drew to the citadel. The door remained sealed, but Bria had disappeared from sight.

"She went through a side door," Dex muttered in my ear. "I am *not* going inside."

"Keep watch, then." I trod around the corner of the citadel's towering form and towards the dark shape of a door set in the shadows.

My hand closed on the handle, and a shock went through my bones. The world flipped over, and images flashed before my eyes.

"You... ruined... everything...

Dirk Alban's voice faded, to be replaced by Dex's frantic yelps. "Liv! Liv! Don't just stand there."

I reeled on my feet. "Ow. Did you hear that?"

"No!" He grabbed at me until his grip burned my skin. I wasn't all that keen to get another shock, so I backed away from the tower.

"How in hell did she get in there without being shocked?" I shook my throbbing hand.

"Maybe she has a special password to get in." He gave a whimper and hid behind my shoulder. "That place is pure evil."

"It's also an old spirit mage haven." Not that anyone *living* existed inside of it. I reached for the front door instead, but a warning buzz in my ears halted me before I gave myself another shock. "What's the betting that the Death King has his own personal key?"

"Of course he does." He gave a weak chuckle. "Tell you what, if the vamps agree to spare fire-boy, you can ask for a trip into the citadel of doom as a reward for your services to His Deathly Highness instead."

"Thanks for that one, Dex." I wasn't in the mood to

joke around. You'd think a place once built by the spirit mages would have let me in and not a simple fire mage.

Unless she was something else entirely.

I left the door behind after ten minutes of trying to get it open, with my head pounding and my temper fraying worse than ever after a number of shocks which rattled my teeth in my skull. Then I headed for the warehouse where the main market was held, but the crowd outside only served to make my headache worse. Besides, there was nothing to find in there. The Collective of Spells was Order-approved, and now the Crow and his allies were dead, there wasn't anyone making illegal spells on the side to reverse life and death. At least, I bloody well hoped not. The only remaining enemy who wasn't behind bars was Davies.

I headed around the back of the warehouse and towards the tunnels, and Dex groaned audibly. "Liv, please tell me you aren't going down into the tunnel. There are revenants down there."

"I'm not going into the tunnels. I'm going to try out an experiment."

I made for the nearest node and stepped into its path, picturing Bria's face in my head. Nothing happened.

"What was that in aid of?" Dex wanted to know.

"I wanted to see if I can travel somewhere I've never been before," I said. "If, say, I wanted to follow a specific person."

"Not if you can't picture it, I wouldn't think," he said.

"I did it once," I said. "When I followed that water mage and brought you to Earth."

"As if I could ever forget it," he said.

I thought back. At the time, I'd been hot on his heels.

Bria, I hadn't seen go through the node at all. She'd gone into the citadel instead, and even a node couldn't get me through a locked door. The only other option I could think of was astral projection, but the citadel was spirit mage-proofed. People like me had built the place, after all.

But that didn't mean I was giving up. If the Death King refused to teach me spirit magic, I'd learn it on my own terms.

———

That night, I slid out of my body and floated through my bedroom ceiling, hovering above the house. The night sky hid me from the world below, though few people would have eyesight good enough to spot a floating transparent woman hidden in the darkness.

If the spirit mages had enjoyed this as much as me, no wonder they'd created the Parallel to avoid exposing the magical world in front of normal people. I floated through the node and emerged in the streets of Arcadia. Then, I drifted until the Citadel of the Elements stood before me, looking even more forbidding in the darkness. With nobody around to bar my path this time, I ought to be able to give it another try.

A shadowy figure appeared, stopping me in my tracks. Of all the luck. It seemed flying around the city centre back home wasn't the Death King's only nightly hobby. "What are you doing out here?"

"I could ask you the same question." The Death King studied me. "Practising spirit magic, are you?"

"What else?" I eyed the tower. "What's in there?"

His gaze drifted to the citadel. "Any reason?"

"Oh, we're playing this game again?" I said. "I saw one of your contestants walking in there earlier. Couldn't follow. The door gave me a shock when I tried."

"I see," he said. "Which contestant?"

"Bria." At least he hadn't accused me of lying outright. "Why would anyone go into that tower?"

"Why would anyone go to the Court of the Dead?" he said. "Perhaps she intended to get in some practise at killing phantoms."

"Then how'd she get past the door?" I looked more closely at the tower, which emanated a faint glow which was more noticeable at night than it was during the day. "She can't be a spirit mage *and* a fire mage, right?"

"No."

Someone was in a talkative mood tonight. I floated up to the door and extended my hand as though reaching into a node—

A shock went through my nerves, sending me flying back a good five feet. The Death King watched me land in an inelegant sprawl without moving to help me.

"You might have warned me not to do that," I said.

He glanced behind him. "Someone's coming."

I ducked out of sight, towards the node I'd come in by. Whatever was out on the street at night was either a vampire or something nastier, and even in my transparent state, I wasn't in the mood to be harassed by a revenant.

I didn't really expect him to follow me, but when I floated out of the node and into the middle of the city, I found the Death King on the other side. For some reason, we'd come out in the same placee.

"Were you planning on meeting with the Order?" I

asked. "Or do you have a secret contingent of spirit mages who you meet on Earth when everyone else is sleeping?"

"No, I don't," he said. "What were you doing yesterday? After your unplanned interrogation of all my potential Fire Elements?"

"Unplanned? You left us to deal with the flooded castle alone." I should have figured he'd wanted to question me about my unorthodox way of sniffing out intruders. "One of your potential Fire Elements tried to drown me, so I think the interrogation was justified."

"Tried to drown you?" His tone contained enough surprise for me to know that he hadn't realised I'd nearly died during the flood. "Who?"

"I didn't see who," I said. "Hence the interrogation. Have you ever heard of the Houses of the Elements?"

"Any reason?"

"They came up in connection with the fire mages," I said. "During the questioning."

"Yes, I expect they would," he said. "The House of Fire is the largest of the four Houses, so I assumed at least a few of my contenders would be from there. Davies himself was."

My mouth fell open. "You knew? Do you also know who flooded your castle?"

"No, because I wasn't there," he said. "From the reports, it's more likely to be a contender than not."

"I figured, but it would have been nice to hear a little reassurance from the person who's supposed to be running the show," I said.

"I did warn you the job would be dangerous."

"You didn't mention you were going to leave the castle altogether," I said. "I'd have thought you'd be spying on the contenders, not traipsing around the city while everyone else is asleep."

"Spying on the contenders?" he said. "I've already learnt everything I need to know about who might have been involved with the sabotage, so there's nothing more to do but wait and see if they give themselves away tomorrow."

"Sneaking into the Citadel of the Elements seems pretty suspicious to me," I said. "Don't blame me if you get back to find she's swiped your soul amulet, too."

"Nobody but me can get into the hall of souls at the moment," he said. "You removed all cantrips and weapons from the contenders when they arrived, did you not?"

"I did, but it doesn't mean a thing if she picked up more while she was in town." Though it wasn't the first time he'd taken a major gamble with his own safety. "The last two times you let your security lapse, I ended up having to save you from certain death."

He didn't respond for a moment. *Got you there, didn't I?*

"We'll have to agree to disagree on our methods, then," he said. "I'd advise you not to linger here for much longer. The Order might not take kindly to your presence."

"You're the one who brought me here," I pointed out. "And you promised me magic lessons. More than one."

"Have you practised what I taught you last time?"

"No, because I haven't had a surfeit of opportunities to practise draining someone's life force," I said. "How do you do that thing where you freeze someone so they can't move?"

"Lich trick." He extended a hand, and ice-cold chills stiffened my limbs. "How did you escape when Hawker did the same to you?"

Hawker? Oh, he meant the lich who'd betrayed him. I'd never got his name.

"Dex," I said, through chattering teeth. "He loaned me some of his power. There's no other way."

"Maybe after an hour or two, you'll find a way out."

"Don't you even think about it." Alarm blared through my nerves as he turned his back on me. "Death King, I'm serious."

"So am I." He didn't turn back. "You should know, my powers don't work as well on this side of the nodes."

"Shouldn't you fall to pieces here?" I fought the invisible chains binding my limbs, but they wouldn't budge. "I thought most liches couldn't survive."

"I'm safe when I'm astral projecting."

"Yet you still have all your magic." My fingers and toes had gone completely numb. Why had I goaded him again? Some use I'd be if the Order caught me transparent and frozen in the middle of town.

"Not compared to the amount of power I wield in the Parallel," he said. "That remains unmatched."

"So modest," I said. "Okay, forget the freezing trick. How do you teleport yourself between realms without needing a node to be nearby?"

"As a spirit mage, you have access to a larger store of power than most," he said. "You can draw the node's strength into yourself and hold onto it, and if you take enough of that strength, then you should be able to use its power to escape any situation."

I momentarily forgot the frozen sensation binding my limbs. "I could teleport? From anywhere?"

"If you absorb enough power from a node beforehand, without using it all up," he said.

Well, damn. "You use that node by your castle as a recharge point, don't you? Wait, is that why you're always astral projecting around the city at night? You're recharging your batteries."

He inclined his head. "It's also how I kept that barrier going when we were up against the Crow."

I'd figured that much out already. He'd fed his own life force into the shield until it had formed an unbreakable barrier no magic could get through. "You also gave *me* your life force."

"That," he said, "is a rare type of magic that is only possible for two spirit mages. One can take in the energy of another and direct it elsewhere the same way you might use a node. The risk is that if you take on too much, the other mage dies."

"A last resort, then," I commented. "What if the person is like you, and is already dead?"

"Even then, I'm capable of burning out," he said. "As long as my soul remains in its anchor, I will not permanently die, however."

But you will if someone takes your soul again. I heard the unspoken words and dread clutched at my chest. He'd intentionally given the soul amulet to the Crow so that he wouldn't take anyone else's, which meant if I'd drawn too much life force out of him, all the Crow would have needed to do was destroy the amulet and then the Death King's desperate move would have ended his life.

At the same time, I could see why spirit mages were so fractious. Someone like us could determine the outcome of a war even if we hadn't caused it. The original spirit mages must have thought their victory was assured, but in the end, they'd only managed to seal their own doom.

I scanned the dark buildings before me. "Can I travel anywhere on this side? Even the other side of the world?"

"I wouldn't advise it," he said. "The distance increases the risk of death."

"But not for you," I said. "Seeing as, you know, you're already dead."

"I had no idea," he said dryly. "I'd advise you to head home before someone sees you."

"But—" Dammit, my limbs were still frozen. "You can't leave me out here."

"I think it's a useful exercise."

And with that, he vanished. I yelled curses after him until I spotted a drunk below looking blearily up at the sky as though wondering where the shouting was coming from.

Just great.

9

I t took me a good twenty minutes to unthaw enough to make it to a node and transport myself home, and I fell into dreams with relief which swiftly turned to horror.

Blood covered the walls, covered my hands, and the floor of a metal-walled room. Dirk Alban's voice spoke from nearby. *"You ruined everything, Olivia."*

Light bloomed around my bloody hands, revealing the transparent shape of a humanoid figure. A soul, held in my palms.

In the seconds between sleeping and waking, the figure came into focus. The soul in my hands tilted its head back, and the Death King's human gaze met mine.

I jerked awake, gasping for breath. Shuddering, I fell back onto my pillow, my breath coming out in sharp gasps. Not cool, subconscious. Not cool at all.

I pressed my knuckles to my mouth, willing my heart rate to slow down. I should have known openly pursuing spirit magic would bring back the worst memories I could dredge up from the abyss the Order had left in their place. That, though, had just been a bad dream, no doubt born from my encounter with the Death King last night.

Once I'd dragged myself out of bed, showered and dressed in my new armoured uniform, I went downstairs to find Devon working on a cantrip.

"You look even worse today," Devon told me. "Are you sure this job is a good idea?"

"No," I muttered. "In fairness, it's my own fault. Every time I learn more about spirit magic, I send my subconscious into overdrive."

"Bad dreams, then?"

"Yep," I said. "And now I have to go back to my worst nightmare. Oh, and find out if Lord Blackbourne agrees to talk to me about Brant or not."

Despite my best efforts yesterday, I couldn't help feeling I'd made no progress on finding the interloper. Or that I should at least have found a way to get into that damned citadel.

"You're treading a thin line," she said. "What will you do if the vampires say yes?"

"Ask if they'll help Brant out as a favour for saving their lives from the Crow," I said. "And use that as an excuse to give them a questioning about which spirit mage might be after the Death King. It's worth a shot. The worst they can do is say no."

"The worst they can do is rip your throat out," she corrected. "Don't get me wrong, I think the Death King is being a dick, too, but the *vampires?*"

"They're who I'll have to ask to save Brant's life no matter what," I said. "Besides, they have contacts. And if I establish an agreement with them?"

Then I'll have leverage to hold over the Death King. I won't have to rely on him to help me.

She shook her head. "I know the people in the Parallel are nasty pieces of work, but you don't have to turn into one of them to win this."

"I'm beginning to think I have no choice." I fiddled with a piece of loose skin on my finger. "The Order wanted to paint me as a villain all along, and for all I know, that's exactly what I was. My last memory is of Dirk Alban lying dead at my feet with his blood all over the walls. If I was the one who put it there, I'm hardly an angel."

"*That* guy was a piece of shit, too," she said. "I didn't know him, but just from what he did to you, he deserved everything he got."

I looked away. "I can only go by what I've heard. Anyway, have you ever heard of the Spirit Agents?"

"Doesn't sound familiar, no," she said. "Why?"

"One of the contestants mentioned them as a possible connection with whoever's trying to sabotage the trials," I said. "She also told me the saboteur might be involved with the Houses of the Elements, but it turns out the Death King knows who they are and doesn't think of them as a threat. Also, Davies used to belong to the House of Fire."

"The same Davies who betrayed the Death King and tried to kill him."

"Uh-huh," I said. "I'm glad I'm not the only one who thought of that."

"Definitely worth looking into," she said. "Tell you what, I can poke around and see what I find out."

"Talk to Trix," I said. "He's asking around the Parallel

to find out if anyone from one of the Houses is in the contest. Just… be careful."

"Speak for yourself."

This would have to do. I couldn't be in more than one place at once, so I'd have to hope my friends wouldn't face any backlash for asking the wrong questions.

Once again, I headed into the Parallel via the node, landing in the swampland. Neddie greeted me with an enthusiastic *neigh.* At least someone was happy to see me. Aside from Dex and Aria, who followed me into the break room where the Elemental Soldiers had gathered.

"Hey," I said to Ryan. "Nothing happened during the night, did it?"

"No, why?"

Your boss wasn't around. Then again, he'd been gone for most of yesterday, too, and nobody had noticed.

"No reason," I said. "I expected your boss to have words to say about the flood. Or at least come and talk to the contenders in person. But I guess he's busy."

Wandering around Arcadia, apparently. Unless he really had been meeting with the Order when he was supposed to be judging the trials.

"Well, half of them will get eliminated today," said Felicity. "No more water trials, either, so there'll be no more opportunities for anyone to flood the place."

"Instead they'll probably set things on fire," I said. "And you can't confiscate *that* from them."

"Unfortunately," said Ryan, "I think you might be right."

Sure enough, by the end of the morning, my hands were singed all over and I'd used up most of my anti-burn cantrips. Bria won her first fight easily, but with the matches running back to back, I had no chance to ambush her and find out what in hell she'd been doing at the citadel yesterday. She'd be within her rights to tell me it was none of my damn business, but who'd voluntarily go to one of the spirit mages' old strongholds? I still didn't know what His Deathly Highness had been doing there yesterday, come to that.

A yelp drew my attention to where Sledge stood over the body of another contender, pummelling the shit out of him.

"Hey!" I shouted from the side. "Stop. You already won."

Sledge punched the already-unconscious guy in the head. "He didn't surrender."

"He's passed out." I marched over and caught his wrist in my hand. "That's enough. You're disqualified."

"No." He squirmed free and aimed a punch at me. I ducked and swept his legs out from underneath him, and then drew on the power of the node. Energy shot from my hands and blasted him onto his back.

He looked up at me, cross-eyed. "You can't kick me out."

"We can," Ryan said, walking over. "You just blew your last chance. Get out."

"What about my stuff?" he said indignantly.

"It will be taken care of," Ryan said.

I translated that as 'we'll send your suitcase via zombie horse'. Neddie would be thrilled.

Sledge struggled to his feet as two liches glided over to escort him out. Once again, His Deathly Highness had neglected to make an appearance, but that was the least of our problems. I followed after the liches to make sure

Sledge didn't try to sneak back in, and spotted movement on the other side of the gate.

Having hidden in those bushes myself, I knew a human-shaped shadow hiding under the guise of a cantrip when I saw one. I marched on the intruder and yanked out a squirming teenage boy by the scruff of his neck.

His cantrip toppled to the ground, and he yelped. "Let me go!"

"What are you doing hiding out here?"

"Waiting for my sister." He flinched when I put him down. "Don't hurt me. I only wanted to know how she did in the trials."

I arched a brow. "You felt the need to use a cantrip to turn invisible and hide in the bushes rather than waiting outside?"

"I didn't want the phantoms to find me." He shivered. "This place is horrible. Is Harper still in the contest?"

"Last I heard." I glanced over my shoulder at the gates, where the liches were still wrestling a stubborn Sledge from the arena. "You're her brother. Are you a fire mage, too?"

He shook his head.

"What kind of mage are you?"

"I—" He faltered. "Water."

He was a water mage? *Was he the one who flooded the place?* He couldn't have reached the castle from the other side of the gates, but if he'd somehow sneaked in... it was definitely possible.

"I'll see what your sister has to say." I walked back through the gates, steering him in front of me, and beckoned to Ryan. "He was hiding in the bushes. His sister's in the contest."

Harper, who was in the middle of a duel, faltered, and a punch caught her in the face and knocked her onto her back.

"Percy!" She bounded to her feet. "What have you done to my brother?"

"Caught him spying on the castle," I said. "We have to bring him in for questioning. You, too. Death King's orders."

Not that the man himself had given any orders, but he'd want me to talk to both of them. Harper followed after me, looking pale and scared, and accompanied her brother into the same room I'd used for questioning the day before.

I turned to both of them. "Harper, I'm sure you understand why I need to question you, given yesterday's incident. Your brother's a water mage, after all."

"You think *he* flooded the castle?" she said. "No. He couldn't have. He wasn't here."

"That so?" I turned to her brother. "How long have you been spying outside the castle? Were you here yesterday?"

"I—yes, but I didn't come inside the gates," he stammered. "And I didn't use my magic."

Hmm. "Harper, what about you? You were still in the trial when the room flooded, weren't you?"

"Yes, but I didn't do it," she said. "I already told you yesterday."

"Percy, leave the castle at once," I said. "Harper, you can stay, but if you remember anything else, tell me or any of the Elemental Soldiers. And if you let your brother into the castle grounds, for whatever reason, I'll have to disqualify you."

I sent the two of them back outside and followed, skirting the arena as I spotted Sledge standing in front of the liches at the gate. Flames shot from his hands, narrowly avoiding setting the liches ablaze.

"This is bullshit!" he bellowed. "You can't kick me out."

"Get a hint." I marched up to him, stopping at a safe distance from the flames. "You're getting kicked out, matey."

"Fuck off," he spat. "You don't get to tell me what to do. You're not a mage."

Screw it. I reached out with my spirit magic as though I was drawing on a node, snagged the energy inside him and gave a firm tug like a rope. He gasped, staggering backwards, all the fight draining out of him. "You're a spirit mage."

"Really, I had no idea." *I actually pulled it off.* I'd exposed my magic in the process, but there was no way this dude worked for the Order. Besides, look how many people already knew. "Get out of the Court of the Dead."

He lunged at me, and I raised my hand, focusing on the white-hot energy I'd pulled out of him. A current of flames shot from my hands and blasted him off his feet.

"What the—?" He tried to rise to his feet, but a second blast of white-red flames knocked him flat. *Hey, I could get used to this.*

Ryan ran up behind me. "Liv? Did he try to sneak back in?"

"He tried." Triumph flooded me, tempered by the sense that I'd crossed some invisible line. I hadn't cared who'd seen my display when I'd taken him down. "Can you levitate him away from the castle? I don't want him to wake up and start taking shots at the liches again."

"With pleasure." Ryan lifted Sledge off the ground and levitated him through the gap in the gates. "How'd you knock him out, anyway?"

The truth constricted my lungs. Perhaps hiding my power had been a fool's errand from the start. Besides, I couldn't deny it felt damn good to have brought the thuggish bully crashing down using his own power against him.

"Spirit magic." I followed them out of the gates past the liches on duty. "Your boss taught me a couple of tricks."

"Huh." They frowned. "I didn't know he gave you any lessons."

"It's easier for me to fight an opponent who doesn't use the same magic against me." No need to mention how the Death King had decided to leave me frozen in the middle of town last night.

Sledge came to alertness with a bellow of anger, flailing in mid-air. "Put me down!"

"You tried to kill me, arsehole," I said. "You're going home."

"Or if you'd rather sit in the Death King's jail for a while instead, be my guest," said Ryan. "What will it be, then?"

Sledge flailed and kicked, then jumped out of Ryan's reach and straight into the node's path. At once, the current of energy swallowed him up.

Ryan swore. "We can't follow him."

"Like hell we can't." I took a step towards the node, and the sound of someone clearing their throat made me spin around on the spot. Trix stood there, for all the world as though he'd been watching the whole time.

"Need help?" he said. "Who was that?"

"Sledge here cheated in the contest, so we kicked him out."

"Fair enough."

"Can you follow him?" asked Ryan, eyeing Trix. "I mean—it's fine if you can't, but if he's planning anything dodgy, it's better to catch him at it now."

"I will do." Trix stepped through the node and vanished without another word.

"I'd be more inclined to keep an eye on Harper," I said. "Her brother is a water mage, though she claims he wasn't in the castle yesterday. Perhaps some of the others have mage relations who have different powers, though. Not unheard of, is it?"

"No… you're right," said Ryan. "My master did perform a background check on everyone, but he didn't share the results."

"He didn't?" I said incredulously. "Are you serious?"

"He has his reasons."

"Well, they're shit." I'd about had it with the Death King's blasted obtuseness. "And so is the rule that we have to keep the contenders in the running unless they literally set the castle ablaze."

"Most of the troublemakers have gone by now," they said. "As for the mage kid, I'll find out who he is. And his sister. But we have to finish the trials first."

"Fine," I said. "I hope Trix has better luck with Sledge and doesn't get caught."

"Will he be okay?" asked Ryan.

"Sure," I said. "He's resilient and good at spying on people. Sledge won't be able to land a hit on him."

"I'm more concerned about him bringing reinforcements." Ryan turned back to the castle.

"Good point."

Time to head back to the trials… and hope that Sledge had been acting alone.

10

I hardly had any focus left to watch the contest for the rest of the morning. I was starting to think I should have risked the Death King's wrath and chased after Sledge after all. At least Harper's brother didn't make another reappearance, while Bria maintained her winning streak without breaking the rules in any obvious way. With the numbers thinned down, it was easier to watch out for any foul play, but aside from a few fires, nothing leapt out at me.

I didn't have time to talk to the others until our assigned break in the afternoon, at which point I dropped in on Devon to grab some lunch and found Trix waiting on the other side.

"Hey, Liv," he said in cheerful tones. "I was just talking to Devon about Sledge."

"What about him?" I went to the kitchen to put a sandwich together. "Did you manage to follow him? Where'd he end up?"

"He wandered around a bit, then he went to the market."

Hmm. "Did he meet any more fire mages?"

"I don't know. I lost him in the market."

That figured. "Maybe I should have asked you to follow Harper's brother instead."

"Who?"

"One of the contenders has a brother who's a water mage," I explained. "She claimed he wasn't in the castle when it flooded, but it seems suspicious to say the least."

"Is she still in the contest?" asked Devon.

"For now." I carried my sandwich back to the living room and took a bite. "This afternoon, half the remaining participants will be eliminated. Plus Sledge, but he deserved it. Are you sure he wasn't going to sneak back into the castle, Trix?"

"I didn't see him going that way," he responded. "Also, I found out more about the Houses of the Elements."

"You might have led with that." I put the sandwich down. "So, what did you find out?"

"The four Houses have a rivalry going on, but you expect that of the mages," said Devon. "Trix, tell her what else you know."

"The House of Fire is the biggest house and the most dangerous," he said. "Apparently, the vampires don't like them for some reason. Not sure why. The vampire I asked started yelling at me to mind my own business after that."

"Trix, I didn't tell you to question the *vampires*." I shook my head. "Please tell me you aren't on their hit list, too. Don't you remember when you ended up tied up in the basement?"

"Which time?" he asked, all wide-eyed innocence.

I rolled my eyes. "Never mind. So the House of Fire… do you know whereabouts they're based? I heard Elysium…"

"That's the bad news," said Devon. "Turns out they have an arrangement with the local authorities in Elysium which allows them to make the laws for all mages in the city. They're open about the fact that they'd prefer to be in charge of the mages across the rest of the Parallel, too. Reportedly, they aren't a fan of the Death King either."

I swore. "Seriously? You mean they could have taken in Davies without telling anyone?"

"You've got it," she said. "Also, they have safe houses and designated meeting points in every city. He might not even be in Elysium. He might've stayed in Arcadia, if he didn't mind risking being spotted by someone who knew his face."

"Dammit," I said. "I guess we could ask around to see if any of the contenders know where the Houses' local meetup spot is."

I still didn't know what to make of Bria's visit to the Citadel, but I was reasonably certain even Davies wouldn't pick that place as a hideout. Besides, the Houses' main bases were in Elysium. Not Arcadia. Arcadia belonged to the vampires… who really ought to have noticed if someone was making trouble in the citadel, considering how close it was to their base.

"What about Bria?" asked Devon. "She's the one you suspected, right?"

"Yeah." I chewed the rest of my sandwich before asking, "Can you think of a good reason your average person might want to go into the Citadel of the Elements?"

Devon's brow wrinkled. "To fight phantoms?"

"That's what I thought, too." I turned to Trix. "Did anyone you questioned mention the Citadels?"

"No, but everyone knows the Citadels used to host the Houses of the Elements before the spirit mages fell," said Trix.

"I didn't know," Devon supplied.

"Nor me, but you know, defective memory." I tapped my head. "So the Houses of the Elements used to be connected to the Order?"

The Order of the Elements had severed all connection with the original council after they'd died—not hard, because there'd been so few survivors—but they must know of the Houses, surely. Question was, did the Houses still have any of the influence they'd once had when the Council of the Elements had ruled over the entire Parallel?

"Looks that way," said Devon. "Did you follow Bria into the tower?"

"The door wouldn't let me in," I said. "It was magic-proofed. Like the hall of souls. I tried the back door, too."

"Maybe it's where he spends his nights."

"Ha." I shook my head. "I don't trust Bria, but I think I have to gain her confidence if I want her to spill any more secrets. She's the one who first mentioned the Houses of the Elements when I asked if she knew who might be trying to sabotage the contest. She brought up the Spirit Agents, too."

"Maybe she's trying to gain *your* trust in order to get information," said Devon.

"I thought of that, but it's not like I haven't questioned the other participants, too."

The doorbell rang. *Not the Order again.* I dropped off my plate in the kitchen, and, bracing myself, followed Devon into the shop.

Devon peered through the letterbox. "It's your friend."

She opened the door and to my utter surprise, Ryan walked in. "Hey, Liv."

"You didn't mention you'd be dropping in." I stepped aside to let them in. "I'm glad you're not from the Order."

"Are they still giving you trouble?"

"Not right this minute." I closed the door firmly behind them. "Also, does your boss know you're here?"

"No, he doesn't."

"Now I've got you disobeying the King of the Dead?" I grinned. "I'm a bad influence."

They smiled. "Nah, I just think you're right about this situation being fishy. So I did some poking around."

Trix eyed them with interest. "What did you find?"

Ryan held up a wad of paper. "The other Elemental Soldiers and I did some sleuthing, gathering what we knew on the contenders and their backgrounds."

"I knew you wouldn't let me down." I led the way into the living room. "So… what's the verdict on Sledge?"

"A lowlife with no connections," said Ryan. "Bad temper, though. And Bria… weirdly enough, we have no records of her. She's not the only late contender who didn't put in an application, but she must have taken care to hide all traces of herself."

Hmm. "What about Harper?"

"Her name came up in connection with the House of Fire," said Ryan. "Seems she left, though. Maybe because of her brother. He's definitely a water mage, but that doesn't mean he caused the disruption yesterday."

"Maybe we should find out if any of the others have water mage relatives," I said. "How is she connected to the House of Fire, exactly?"

"She shows up on a list of members," said Ryan. "A *long* list. Davies is there, which is to be expected."

"Yeah, about that," I said. "I have some bad news on our odds of finding the traitor."

I filled them in on what I'd just learned from Devon and Trix, about the Houses' myriad of safe houses and their arrangement with Elysium's authorities. The Death King, I was reasonably confident, already knew. That would explain why he didn't have his liches patrolling the Parallel, searching every house for his runaway mage.

"Nobody can hide forever in the Parallel," said Ryan. "If Davies really is hiding in the House of Fire, I'll find him and make him pay for what he did."

I didn't argue. Ryan had earned that right, considering Davies had damn near killed them. "Spirit mages wouldn't work with the others, would they?"

Granted, Bria had insisted the Spirit Agents couldn't be involved in disrupting the contest, but the fact remained that a spirit mage *had* attacked me the other day.

"I dunno," said Devon. "But look at Brant. Was *he* involved with the House of Fire?"

My mouth parted. "You know… there's a strong possibility there. He and Davies knew each other from somewhere, and Brant didn't make a habit of hanging around the Death King's castle."

"Can you speak to Brant?" asked Ryan.

"Not before the Order sends him into the Parallel," I

said. "And even then, I'd be depending on the goodwill of the vampires."

Speaking of whom, they had yet to give me an answer on whether they agreed to my request for a meeting or not. Had I made a mistake in asking them? If I hastened Brant's fate and he ended up dead, everything would be for nothing. Yet how many chances would I have to talk to him again, whether he survived or not? If the vampires spared him, he'd still be stuck behind bars for the rest of his life.

"The vampires owe you a favour," said Trix. "You saved their lives."

"So does the Death King, and you wouldn't know it," I pointed out. "Besides, the vampires have the upper hand in this scenario. Brant was heavily involved in the conspiracy against them, and I know for a fact some of them were royally pissed off with us for not leaving them anyone alive to torture."

Brant's fate weighed on me more than I wanted it to. I didn't blame myself for where he ended up, and yet I couldn't help feeling as though I held his life in my hands again, whether I acknowledged it or not. Yet the fact remained that he might be the only person who could tell me where Davies was, and which of the contestants might be scheming against the Death King.

"Have you spoken to the vampires?" asked Ryan.

"I tried to get a meeting with them," I admitted. "Still haven't heard back."

"You did?" They frowned. "You didn't tell the Death King."

"And I'd prefer it if you didn't tell him either."

"Can we trust you?" asked Trix.

"Me?" said Ryan. "Of course. I'm not thrilled at going behind my master's back, but I understand why you feel you have no choice in the matter. The vampires, though… don't count on them to have your back. Especially where the fire mage is concerned."

"They might say differently if I explain that Brant can help them track down Davies," I said. "He did more damage than Brant did, in the end. If Brant can point us towards him…"

"Even if you find the House of Fire's hideout, it doesn't mean you'll be able to get inside it," Ryan said.

"I'll build all the stealth cantrips you might need, then," Devon said. "I've been making extra on the side."

A stealth mission sounded much more appealing than going back to judge the Death King's contest. "If you ask me, Sledge is more likely to come back and make trouble than Davies. Are you sure you didn't see where he went, Trix?"

"No, but maybe he'll show up later on."

"Not a good thing, Trix." I pushed to my feet. "All right. Time to head back in. If I have time this afternoon, can I look at that list, Ryan? I bet I'll find Brant's name on it."

"Go ahead," they said.

When we returned to the castle, however, it was to find Dex hovering anxiously above the node. "Someone's here to see you."

"To see me?" I looked past him at the gate, and my heart plunged. The liches at the gates crowded around someone who stood in the middle of the path as though they had every intention of walking inside. A *vampire*. The smartly dressed man couldn't be anything else, though I didn't recognise his face.

"He said you asked to see him," said Dex. "Told you it was a bad idea to request to speak to Lord Pointy Teeth."

"No need to rub it in."

An emissary from the vampires had come to the castle, because of course they couldn't just wait until I was alone. How long had the dude been standing outside? Long enough to rile up the liches, evidently. Everyone could see him. Including—if he was here—the Death King. Fuck me sideways.

I approached the vampire, shivering as I passed through the crowd of liches. The smartly dressed man wore dusty clothes which looked as though he'd been wearing them for a few decades, and his glossy pointed teeth gleamed in his wide smile.

"I'm Liv," I said. "Who are you?"

"My master wishes to respond to your request in person." He bowed to the liches. "Send my regards to your King."

Dammit. The Death King would be pissed if I ran off now, but one did not disobey the vampires without facing the consequences. I caught Ryan's eye, and they nodded, giving me permission.

Hoping I hadn't just doomed both myself and Brant at once, I walked alongside the vampire. "I thought you slept during the day."

"We do," he said. "However, as acting liaison between humans and vampires, I am sent on ambassadorial missions such as this one whenever appropriate."

To my surprise, he headed towards the node I'd come in through. Didn't want to get his polished shoes dirty by traipsing through the swamp, I'd guess.

"I didn't know vampires used the nodes so much," I

commented. "I wouldn't have thought you'd need to, with how fast you move."

"It proves useful when we meet with humans such as yourselves."

He stepped through the node. I followed... and came out in the middle of the crowded city centre.

This wasn't Arcadia, or even the Parallel. *He's bringing me to the Order.*

I halted mid-step, the node gleaming behind me. "Is your master in there? With the Order?"

He didn't answer. He took off at a fast pace, and I had to run to catch up with him. How could the vampire lord be *here*? Since when did he meet with the Order, in broad daylight, no less? Something was seriously screwy.

My heart beat loudly in my ears. Either I was in deep shit for using spirit magic—again—or for my job working for the Death King. Or even for stepping out of line and having the audacity to request a meeting with the vampire council.

The vampire led me into the Order's headquarters, startling the guards outside so much that they forgot to scrutinise my Order ID. I walked after him, conscious of the stares I attracted throughout the lobby, and entered the corridor at the back. The vampire stopped outside Mr Cobb's old office and gestured to me to go ahead.

When I entered the office, I forgot all about the vampires. Brant sat in one of the chairs, his hands and feet cuffed, and his head bowed.

11

My shocked gaze went to Mr Holland, who sat at the desk wearing a blandly calm expression. "What is this?"

The Order couldn't know about my scheme to seek out the vampire council and ask them to spare Brant, right? But then, why had the vampire been the one to bring me here?

"Liv." Brant's voice cracked and his eyes brimmed with horror when he lifted his head to look at me. Despite his evident fear, he didn't look hurt. The Order weren't given to inhumane treatment—they obeyed the laws here on this side, after all—but that didn't mean they hadn't done their level best to torment him psychologically until he'd lost all sense of self, the way they'd done to me.

Pain splintered my chest from the inside. I knew how brutal the Order was, and yet I'd let them dictate the terms of his punishment. If they'd taken his memories or magic, punishment at the hands of the vampires might have been be a better fate after all.

"Olivia Cartwright," said the head interrogator. "This man is set to face trial at the hands of the vampire council. As the two of you were acquainted, you are to be sent alongside him as the second emissary at the request of Lord Blackbourne."

Disbelief speared me. *Emissary?* I knew some people in the Order worked hand in hand with the vampires to bring in supplies from this realm into the Parallel, but there was a world of difference between that and transporting a prisoner on foot. I would have thought I'd be seen as too biased to be trusted. Either the vampire had more influence over the Order than I'd thought, or something else was going on.

"Lord Blackbourne asked me to bring Brant to him?" I said.

"Yes, he did," he said. "I trust you're willing to do your part?"

There must be a catch somewhere. "Yes, but I'm not an ambassador, and this isn't typical of my role as a retriever, either."

"I thought it in poor taste to deny the request of the leader of Arcadia's vampires."

Were they trying to set me up in some way? I tensed when a shadow fell over the window, but when I tilted my head in that direction, it wasn't a vampire I saw. The Death King walked past the room, halted for a brief instant, then disappeared from sight.

A fresh wave of shock washed over me. The Death King was *here.* In the Order's base. He must have seen me, yet he hadn't intervened. Why would he? Brant was more his enemy than mine, and he'd gladly see him suffer at the vampires' hands.

At least I wouldn't have to explain my absence from the castle the next time I saw him. Not that that was much of a silver lining right now.

"What is *he* doing here?" I asked.

"The Death King is one of our allies," he said, "and it's our policy to maintain good relations with him and with the vampires for the sake of maintaining peace among the magically inclined."

"And the Houses of the Elements?" The words slipped out before I could reel them in.

Brant's gaze snagged on me, and his eyes widened in a way that suggested he wanted to communicate something with his eyes which he couldn't voice aloud. Not that I had the faintest clue what it was.

"The Houses, too," said Mr Holland. "Come in."

The door opened and the vampire from earlier entered the room. "Is the prisoner ready?"

"Yes, he is." Mr Holland rose to his feet. "Olivia will be accompanying you, as planned."

Not by me, it wasn't. I held my tongue. The vamps might be plotting against me, but they'd just handed me a chance to talk to Brant *and* Lord Blackbourne. If I played my cards right, that is.

"If that is all," said the vampire, "we will take him with us."

He glided to the chair and undid the cuffs on Brant's ankles, then dragged him to his feet with the ease given by vampire strength. A second vampire took Brant's other arm, and between them, they carried the bound fire mage out of the room.

I hesitated, turning back to Mr Holland. "Whose idea was this? The vampires'?"

"Who else?" he said. "You'd better catch up to them before they leave you behind."

Not like I had much of a choice. I went to the door and walked out into the corridor, following the vampires' path through the lobby and towards the doors. Brant made no sound and moved unresistingly, as though all the fight had been kicked out of him all at once. I couldn't say a word to him yet, not with the vampires there. *He must know about the Houses of the Elements.* Had he really belonged to the House of Fire? The head interrogator hadn't reacted in such a way that suggested I was in trouble for knowing, so the Houses must be common knowledge, but what about their link to the contestants in the Death King's trials? To Davies and his betrayal?

"Hey." I caught up to the vampires as they stalked towards the node. "Slow down, won't you?"

The vampires halted beside the node until I caught up. Then light engulfed us, and we emerged out of the node and onto one of the roads leading to the vampires' council house.

The Citadel of the Elements towered above the rooftops, tall, forbidding, and empty. Yet it was the vampires' council house which contained the holding cells where they put anyone who was foolish enough to make an enemy of them. The two vampires halted for a moment to scan the street, and Brant shuffled back, his eyes bulging. I caught up behind him, sensing he wanted to speak to me.

"The Houses—they can't be trusted," he whispered to me. "If they've targeted you, don't seek them out. Don't—"

He broke off with a shout, and I spun around, as did

the two vampires. Someone had thrown a knife at us, which clattered to a halt at my feet.

Another sharp instrument whipped past my back, narrowly avoiding Brant's shoulder. We were under attack. Whoever it was, they were aiming from above, from somewhere among the rooftops. One of the vampires fell into a heap, a knife buried in his chest.

The second vampire let out a howl of fury and scaled the nearest house with elegant grace. I made to follow him, and Brant bumped against me from behind. "Take my cuffs off. Please."

"Brant, I can't—" I broke off as the second vampire flew down from the roof, several knives sticking out of his chest, and landed with a thud in the alley. "What the hell?"

A shadow fell overhead. With a curse, I began to climb the drainpipe to the roof. If I'd brought Dex with me, I might have been able to track down the attacker, but they'd moved too damned fast for me to catch up with. As I halted on the windowsill, movement prompted me to look down as Brant's cuffed form sprinted out of the alleyway.

Crap, Brant was running away. Had *he* planned this?

"Stop!" I let go of the drainpipe and landed in the alleyway. "Brant, for the Elements' sakes—"

The cold hands of a lich wrapped around my throat, choking off my breath.

"Hello, Olivia," a voice hissed. A voice belonging to someone who shouldn't be alive any longer. Someone I thought the vampires had killed.

This time, I knew his name. Hawker. *He was alive all along.* The lich traitor had survived—and set up an ambush. He couldn't have thrown the knives, though, so he must have living allies on his side.

"You're dead," I choked out. "You died…"

Coldness shredded my throat, and dread seized me. If the lich started draining my life force, I was dead for good.

Too bad for him that he'd made the mistake of attacking me right next to a node. I drew on the node's strength and blasted energy at him from behind. The lich's grip broke, but cold still froze me to the bone, deeper than an arctic frost. Could a human outdo a death lord, even a spirit mage like me?

I fought the chill, grabbing for the node's energy. Power blasted from my hands, but he didn't so much as stagger. He was stronger than the others. As a former spirit mage, he had the same power as the Death King did.

Gritting my teeth, I pivoted out of reach of his grasping hands, drawing the node's energy into my palms once more. "How the hell did you survive? I saw you die."

"Are you sure that's who you saw?"

Well… no. All the liches looked the same, and while I'd seen a dead body in the vampires' district which I'd taken for a lich, it'd been in such an advanced stage of decomposition that I wouldn't have known who it'd originally been.

But then, who was it? "There was more than one betrayer."

"Far more than one, Olivia." The lich's chill grip brushed over me again.

I lunged forward and grabbed the thread of energy inside him. White-hot power seared my hand and I staggered back, the connection breaking as suddenly as it had begun.

"He's been teaching you a few tricks, has he?" said Hawker. "He's wasting his time."

I caught my balance. "I'll be the judge of that."

The node's power filled my hands. My teeth rattled with it, and a rush of satisfaction pierced me from within when the lich backed out of range.

Hawker pivoted, eerily quiet, and my attack hit empty air. His voice drifted from nearby. "Good luck dealing with the vampires, Olivia."

I wheeled on the spot, but the lich had vanished. The body of the vampire emissary lay nearby, and the second lay further down the path.

"Shit," I whispered.

He'd left me alone, paralysed with cold and humming with the node's energy, and if the vampires caught me here, I was dead.

12

I stood frozen to the spot for an instant, pulling energy from the node into me, but it didn't heal the ice-cold dent Hawker's touch had left behind. I edged around the vampire's body as I retreated to the node—and towards the dark figure stepping out of it.

About damn time you showed up.

The Death King approached at a soundless glide. "What is going on here?"

I pointed to the body of the fallen emissary. "Assassins attacked us. They killed the vampires. There was a lich, too, but he disappeared. Hawker survived. He didn't die at the Crow's house after all."

"I was afraid of this." His expression was shadowed. Human. He was still wearing his disguise. He'd come here straight from the Order, after all. "The Order tried to persuade me to stay. One would almost think they knew this was going to happen."

My mouth fell open. "Shit."

Someone had set us up. They'd wanted me to take the

blame for Brant's inevitable escape, and they'd kept the Death King away deliberately so he couldn't cover for me again. Even now, he'd showed up too late. Brant had gone, and the vampires lay dead in the alley.

Darkness spooled around the node, and the Death King's expression flattened. "They must have sensed my return."

Liches. As I watched, at least five of them emerged from the node like a tide made of shadow. I called on the node's strength, but the last lich's attack still trembled through my bones. I couldn't beat all of them at once, not if they were all former spirit mages like the Death King. And even if I did, there was no finishing them off without access to their soul amulets.

Light burned my palms, and I fired the node's power into one of the liches. The lich staggered, and I had a brief moment of shock to appreciate the Death King giving me some of his power again before that same magic burst out of my hands and into our adversaries. Cold, invigorating energy surged in my veins in tandem with the node's strength, equally fathomless. *You're in for it now.*

Two liches fell down under our double assault, dissolving into inky puddles of darkness. A third blasted magic at me again and I raised my hands, blocking the attack with the Death King's strength. The two of us broke apart as the remaining liches turned on their former master, and he engaged both of them at once.

The third lich and I fought, hand to hand, or rather, spirit to spirit, fuelled by the same node as we struggled to outdo one another. I was vaguely aware of the Death King standing at my side, trading blows with his own opponents, but I kept my attention on my own adversary. My fist sank into the lich's shadowy form, and I grabbed a handful of life force and *pulled.*

Energy surged into me, into my spirit, and the lich exploded into nothingness. It was only then that I noticed I'd astral projected out of my body. If anyone saw the Death King and I now, they wouldn't have known which of us was living and which was dead.

That was the power of spirit magic.

The Death King's opponent turned to shadows, and the two of us circled the one remaining enemy. The lich retreated with a snarl, and the Death King's power burst from my hands once again, turning the lich into shadowy dust.

"They'll be back." I breathed out, my hands trembling from the rush of handling so much power. "Where are their soul amulets? In the hall of souls?"

"No," he said. "They aren't mine."

"Huh?" I said. "Yeah, I'm lost. That lich I saw earlier... Hawker... he died. I was sure the vampires killed him using that spell which reversed life and death."

"For a time, I believed the same," he said. "However, he's not the only lich to have turned on me. I've lost a number of my liches since the recent attempted coup."

Shock punched me in the chest, and I stared at him for a moment. I'd assumed the lack of liches in the castle had been because they were staying out of the way of the fire mages' contest. "Why? Who else would they follow other than you?"

"Anyone who can offer them what they need," he said. "My recent decisions have proven somewhat divisive. I took power in a time of instability, and while I have held my Court together for this long, it's clear some have other plans."

The notion of him losing his power seemed impossible, and yet I had no other way to explain where the swarm of liches had come from. Nobody else could create them, right?

I drew in a breath. "Not to make it all about me, but if we stay out here, Lord Blackbourne will think I'm the one who killed the ambassadors. How am I supposed to defend myself from his accusations with Brant and the assassins gone?"

"You aren't." If I didn't know better, I'd say he sounded worried. "That was the intention, I don't doubt."

"Why were you meeting with the Order, then?" I said. "What was so important that you had to be at their base instead of at your own trials?"

He shook his head. "Trust me when I say my meetings with the Order are of the utmost importance, but whoever is responsible for engineering this attack is no ally of mine."

"The vampires are going to have my head for this," I murmured. "And Brant…"

He'd run. Like he always did. Yet what choice did he have? He was a dead man otherwise, no matter who caught him. Except, perhaps, for the House of Fire.

"Forget the fire mage," he said, a bite of impatience in his voice. "The vampires need to be told the truth, as soon as possible."

"It would help if we knew who threw the knives." I jerked my head at the fallen vampires. "We can't just leave them here, either."

"Whoever they are, they didn't use magic for a reason." He picked up a discarded knife. "I will show this to the vampires as proof and return their dead to them. I want you to return to my castle and tell the other Elemental Soldiers."

"I think Brant ran away to the House of Fire," I told him. "If you know whereabouts the nearest base is, now's a really good time for you to tell me."

"I don't," he said, "but I highly doubt the House ordered this attack."

"What gives you that idea?" I said. "Do you know everything about the Houses of the Elements?"

"I know a considerable amount," he said, "because the Court of the Dead is all that remains of my own House."

My heart missed a beat. "You mean... there *was* a House of Spirit?"

"Yes," he said. "Every spirit mage who belonged to the House of Spirit was afflicted by the same curse following the war."

A thousand questions exploded into my mind, but he cut me off before I could get half a syllable out.

"I will talk to the vampires," he said. "If you're here when they arrive, you're likely to be punished."

"You can't just leave me hanging like that," I said. "Not after dropping *that* bombshell on me."

"Go back to the castle, Olivia," he said. "Don't ask my soldiers for details, either. They don't know."

"Because you never tell them anything, either." The words fell from my mouth. "And maybe one day, they'll have had enough, too. Good luck dealing with the vampires."

I left him in the alley and walked through the node, driven by anger which swiftly turned to guilt. Infuriating though he might be, he'd helped me fight the liches, and was about to argue with the vampires on my behalf. Yet his word might not be enough if the vampires decided I was the one who'd killed their emissaries. Or the Order, come to that.

"Liv?" Ryan caught up to me on the other side of the node. "The vampires—what did they want?"

"They wanted me to escort Brant to their holding cells," I said. "The Order's idea, allegedly. Then a group of assassins attacked us on the way and killed the vampires' messengers."

"Shit." Ryan's eyes widened. "Where's the fire mage?"

"He ran, of course, as soon as he had the chance to," I said. "The Death King showed up after the attack. He was at the Order, for reasons he won't tell me, and he insisted I came back here to tell you and the others he's gone to explain the situation to Lord Blackbourne."

"Then we need to tell the other Elemental Soldiers." Ryan ran back through the gates to the castle, and I followed. "Are you okay? You didn't get hurt?"

"No, the assassins weren't aiming for me," I said. "A group of liches tried to kill me, though. Almost succeeded, too… if not for your boss."

Ryan stopped inside the gates. "The traitor survived?"

"More than one traitor," I said. "We never caught the assassins either, but they ran away through Arcadia. They were climbing on the roofs."

"Human?" Ryan's mouth pressed together. "I can take them down."

"I don't think that's wise," I said. "Your boss isn't in the best mood."

Ryan snapped their fingers and Aria swooped over.

"Can you tell Felicity and Cal that I'm going into the city to fight someone who was sent to kill my master? Also, tell them not to let any of the vampires in if they come here."

"Or the Order," I added, as the air sprite left, resigning myself to going along with Ryan's spur-of-the-moment plan. If nothing else, the Death King couldn't pin this one on me.

Ryan headed back through the gates and out into the swampland. "Lead the way, Liv."

"I can't take us back to the crime scene if I don't want the vampires to catch us." I ran towards the node, regardless. "We'll have to go elsewhere in the city and hope Lord Blackbourne isn't prowling around."

"He won't be out this early. It isn't dark yet." Ryan strode over to the node. "Besides, he's meeting with my master."

"Yes, and I think we should have told the other Elemental Soldiers that." Then again, if this didn't take too long, we'd be back before the Death King knew it. I didn't think much of our odds of finding the assassins even if they were still on the rooftops, but who knew, maybe Ryan's air magic could knock them down. "The attack happened on the west side of town, near the city square."

Ryan and I stepped through the node and emerged into the city. We hurried down a side street, a current of wind propelling us along courtesy of Ryan's air magic. I bloody well hoped the vampires weren't anywhere nearby, because it was a little difficult to hide.

As for Brant, I saw zero signs of him. He'd probably hopped through the nearest node as soon as he could and fled for his life.

Ryan eyed the rooftops and conjured a gust of wind strong enough to rattle the nearby windows and force me to brace myself against the alley wall. "That ought to flush them out."

Why did I agree to this again? "I think you just knocked someone's roof tiles off."

Ryan shrugged and kept walking, their foot catching on something on the ground. I caught up as they lifted a knife into the air. "Is this one of their weapons?"

"Looks like it."

Ryan conjured up another breeze, this one even stronger. A muffled thump sounded from the neighbouring road, and we ran around the corner to find ourselves faced with two masked figures, both looking somewhat windswept. Both wore generic dark clothing and carried carved knives in their hands.

Ryan raised their hands and blasted both assassins off their feet. One hit the wall, the other landed in a heap at my feet. I flicked on a paralysing cantrip and both of them froze. Ryan grabbed one of their knives and pressed it to the nearest assassin's throat.

"Hold on!" I warned Ryan. "If we kill them, we won't be able to prove to the vampires that they were the ones who murdered their emissaries, not me."

Ryan scowled. "What are we supposed to do with them, then?"

"Lock them in the Death King's jail," I said. "I'm sure he won't object."

Ryan lifted one of the assassins into the air. "Fine."

I dragged the other assassin behind me as I followed them back towards the node. "I don't know about you, but I'd like to know who sent these guys. Someone hired them, and it sure as hell wasn't the vampires *or* the Death King."

Were the traitorous liches acting alone, or had they rallied around whoever was disrupting the trials? The only way to know for sure was to talk to them myself… or get the Death King to spill his secrets.

When we landed in the swampland, the assassin squirmed out of my grip and tried to make a run for it.

"Who might you be?" Dex appeared in a flash of light, and the assassin tripped over his own feet in an effort to avoid the sudden burst of flames.

"Assassins." Ryan levitated both of them into the air with an irritable gesture. "They're coming with us."

Between us, we dragged the assassins into the jail and shoved them into cells side by side. The doors slammed, and my skin prickled at the memory of my own captivity. It wasn't the first time I'd been locked up, nor even the worst, but I'd forgotten most of my stint in prison before my trial at the Order.

At this rate, I'd be lucky to escape a similar fate at the vampires' hands, since someone in the Order's ranks had tried to set me up to take the fall for the vampires' emissaries' deaths.

The Death King likely wouldn't be pleased with me for bringing the assassins here, but I wasn't about to squander my chance to get information on who was giving them orders.

I approached the cells. One of the assassins lay in a heap on the bench. The other had begun to twitch as the paralysing spell wore off. He lifted his head, his mask askew. "You won't get away with this. The vampires will tear out your innards."

"I don't think so." I stepped closer. "Why did you attack us? Who sent you?"

He flipped me off. "None of your fucking business."

"Wrong answer." Ryan's hands rose, and a blast of air slammed the assassin into the wall. His mask fell off entirely, revealing an unfamiliar face. Human. Not a mage, otherwise he'd have revealed his magic by now.

"Who sent you?" I repeated. "Not the Order?"

He laughed, a trickle of blood streaming down his face. "The Order is as good as dead."

I stepped up to the cage doors. "Says who? Was it the House of Fire?"

He gave another laugh, more blood bubbling in the corner of his mouth. "Sure, why not."

"This isn't funny," Ryan snapped. "Tell us the truth. Who sent you?"

He continued to laugh, high and reedy, blood streaming from his mouth. His body hit the floor as he slumped into a heap, his laugh turning to a rattling cough. Foam spilled from his mouth.

"Shit," I said. "I think he poisoned himself."

I wheeled around to the other cell, whose occupant lay unmoving on his back, his eyes half-open and sightless.

Ryan swore. "They had a backup plan ready in case they were caught."

"Dammit." I slammed my foot into the cell door. "What the hell was that supposed to mean? The Order being as good as dead?"

"You think I know?" Ryan stepped up to one of the cells and unlocked the door before entering and crouching over the assassin's body. A moment later, they emerged holding a piece of paper.

"He was carrying this note," they said. "Better than nothing."

"Maybe it'll tell us where Brant is hiding," I said. "The location of the House of Fire."

Ryan shot me a sceptical look. "I doubt it. It'll be a local meeting point… but there's a chance some of their people might still be there."

"Worth a shot." I walked out of the jail, leaving the dead assassins behind, and squinted in the fading light. We had an hour or two before sundown. Then the vampires would come out to play for real.

Dex hovered nearby, a wary expression on his face. He was about as much of a fan of the jail as I was. "Any luck?"

"The assassins killed themselves before admitting anything," I said. "But Ryan found a note with an address on it. Want to come with us and check it out?"

"Ooh, are we storming a castle?" said Dex.

"Not quite a castle, but it depends how dramatic the House of Fire is," I said. "Let's just hope this address isn't a giant trap."

"Bring it." Ryan closed the jail door and beckoned two liches to take over from them. "Can one of you tell my master those two are the assassins the vampires are looking for?"

"He's going to be majorly pissed off that they died before he could rip out their souls," I remarked.

Ryan shrugged. "The liches will keep an eye on our deceased visitors on the off-chance that one of them wakes up."

"I think they've missed their chance to be liches, to be honest." I skirted the arena at Ryan's side, and we made our way through the gates to the node once again.

We landed in an alleyway and we began to follow the winding road, referring to the address on the paper Ryan carried.

"I know this place," said Ryan. "I've been here before. It's a known haunt for mages."

We made our way down the street on swift feet. The sinking sun brushed the rooftops and shadows filled the alleyways, but Ryan's armoured clothing and aura of purpose kept the beggars and thieves at a distance, and we found the address without being accosted.

We came to a halt outside an unremarkable brick house painted in faded grey and white and bearing a crooked sign proclaiming it the Withered Oak. Greasy windows revealed a dingy pub filled with the type of mages who wore travelling cloaks wherever they went as though they'd walked straight out of an LARP session. I didn't see Brant among them, but he was surprisingly good at blending into crowds for a fire mage.

Dex flew up to the door, his hands sparking. "Want me to chase fire-boy out?"

"Not sure your flames will do much to a group of fire mages, Dex," I said. "Besides, we need to find out who employed those assassins."

"Worth a shot." He zipped over to my shoulder. "Someone's coming."

The door wrenched open and two people appeared. One was a young black man with curly hair. The other was an older white guy, wearing a scowl on his pock-marked face.

"Who are you?" said the older guy.

"I'm here on behalf of the King of the Dead," said Ryan,

"and we found your address in the hands of a pair of assassins who tried to kill us."

"Don't look at me," said his companion. "This is a safe house for mages."

"And assassins?" I peered past him into the hall, where a faded carpet led up a set of crooked stairs. "I don't think they were mages, but they may have been in league with the House of Fire."

The merest shift in his expression drew my suspicion. "The House of Fire, you say?"

"Know them?" I said. "Have you seen a man called Brant Edwards?"

"Who?" said the older man.

"He might be using an alias," I added. "What did he used to call himself… Flare?"

"*Flare?*" said the younger dude. "Haven't seen him in months. Thought he was arrested or dead."

So they have heard of him. "He's on the run. If this is a safe house, he might be on his way here."

"I know you, though," said the older guy. "You're Liv Cartwright, aren't you?"

Brant had told them. I was going to kill him.

"I'm not here to talk about me," I said evenly. "I'm here to ask about where Brant is hiding, if not here."

"How am I supposed to know?" said the younger dude. "Flare disappeared months ago without so much as a word."

Yeah, well. He ended up losing his soul to a vampire, so that turned out well.

"And the assassins?" Ryan put in. "Mind if we look around? If not, my master will have to pay you a visit in person."

The two of them blanched. At least they had a healthy fear of the King of the Dead.

"Fine," said the older guy, "but don't harass my guests and don't touch anything."

They stepped aside to allow us to enter. A door on the left of the stairs led into the pub. I didn't recognise any faces, and from the unfriendly stares we got from those nearest to the door, the Death King was not popular here.

"The fire mage isn't in here," Ryan murmured.

"Guess not." But what about the assassins? If they'd planned to meet up here following their mission, anybody here might be their ally, but we wouldn't win ourselves any friends if we walked around accusing everyone in the room of plotting against the Court of the Dead. We were already taking a major risk being out in public right after the vampires' murders and Brant's escape.

"Satisfied?" The older man escorted us to the door. "You're making our guests nervous."

"Good," said Ryan. "Someone here was meeting with two assassins. If it turns out you're covering for them, the King of the Dead will shut this place down."

The mage winced. "There's no need for that. This is a safe place."

"For some people, maybe." I eyed him. "Ever met him?"

"No." He shuddered. "Creep. No offence."

He sounded genuine enough for me to wonder if the assassins had carried this address in order to cover their traces. Brant hadn't mentioned this place, but of course he hadn't. He'd wanted me to see the best of him.

Now I knew more about what I'd done while working with Dirk Alban, it seemed an absurd idea. I'd been neck-deep in this long before I'd even met Brant.

And yet as long as my memories remained gone, I'd be at a disadvantage. I'd been haunted by Dirk Alban's ghost for too long, yet for all that, I'd never really faced my history. Never dared to guess the worst of what I'd done in those missing years.

Maybe I'd belonged among the Death King's people after all.

13

After we'd searched the whole safe house and came up empty, there was nothing more for us to do but head home. With the Death King gone and the contest's events temporarily on hold, I was only making myself a target by staying in the Parallel, and if I drew the vamps' attention, I'd end up in worse trouble.

Besides, if Brant hadn't gone into hiding in the Parallel, maybe he'd come back home. To Earth. Part of me expected to find him waiting on the other side of the node, but instead, Devon's crushing embrace caught me as soon as I reached the house.

"Whoa." I caught my balance against the sofa. "You heard?"

"The Order called me," she said. "They said you were supposed to be on an ambassadorial mission but there was some kind of attack and they lost contact. When they figured out that I didn't know what they were talking about, they clammed up. What happened?"

"One of the vampires must have contacted the Order,"

I said. "They pressured me into escorting Brant to the vampires for his trial, but the vamp ambassadors were assassinated on the way. Now Lord Blackbourne and his fellow vamps are probably going to blame me for it if the Death King can't convince them otherwise, the assassins committed suicide rather than telling me who they worked for, and on top of that, I'm still on the hook to judge this bloody contest, if I don't get arrested first."

"Shit, Liv," she said. "Who assassinated the vampires?"

"Not mages, I don't think, but they're working with the same liches who betrayed the Death King before," I said. "We thought they all died along with the Crow, but we were wrong. If His Deathly Highness hadn't shown up, I'd be dead."

"Good timing." She frowned. "Did he know?"

"I don't think so, but he was already at the Order, for reasons he won't tell me," I said. "Holland set me up. Him and others at the Order are in league with the enemy."

"He was working with the vampires?" she said. "No, he can't have been, if he had the ambassadors killed."

"To frame me," I added. "Someone in the Order wanted to ensure I took the heat for Brant's escape, too. He took off the instant I turned my back."

"What does the Order have to gain from *him* escaping?" she said. "He broke their laws. And no offence, Liv, but he's not much use to them dead *or* alive."

"Yeah, I know." I rubbed my forehead. "I think they wanted to pawn him off on the vampires, since Lord Blackbourne wanted him to stand trial in the Parallel anyway. But someone decided it'd be a good time to get rid of both of us at once."

"You said you caught the assassins?" she said. "How?"

"Ryan and I tracked them down," I said. "They committed suicide in the Death King's jail before we could confirm who sent them. The address they were carrying on them turned out to be a dead end."

"Holy crap," she said. "Does the Death King know that?"

"Ryan will tell him, which is not going to go well," I said. "But he's the one who left me hanging, and he didn't tell Ryan not to go after the assassins. Nor did he tell me his liches are leaving in droves. The only useful piece of information he's given me is that his own Court used to be the House of Spirit—which would have been nice to know earlier."

Her eyes rounded. "Of course."

"You guessed?"

"If there's houses for the other four elements, it stands to reason that there would have been a collective of spirit mages, too," she said. "I'm more surprised he told you."

"Don't get too excited. He dropped that bombshell on me and then disappeared without saying another word."

"Sounds about right." Her eyes glittered with amusement, for some reason. "Another traitor in the Order? The school reunion is going to be interesting."

I groaned. "Don't remind me. You're not planning on going, are you?"

"Maybe." An inexplicable grin appeared on her face. "Did you see the photo online?"

"Devon, I couldn't possibly be *less* interested," I said. "And I thought you weren't interested, either. What does it even matter, anyway?"

"I don't want to go to the bloody reunion, I want you to look at the photo."

My head hurt at the very notion of another trip down memory lane after the day I'd already had. "What photo? I don't want to see my godawful school pictures."

"Someone uploaded a picture of our class on social media, and I think you want to see it."

When Devon focused, she *focused*. She wouldn't let this drop until I did as she asked.

"All right," I relented. "But don't forget that time you were convinced I'd look amazing with hot pink hair. You know how that turned out."

I picked up my phone and found I had indeed been tagged in a few photos by overly keen people who seemed under the impression our days at the academy had been the best of our lives. I scrolled down and found the picture Devon had referenced, which depicted our entire year group standing in the auditorium at the academy. I spotted my teenage self in the middle row, looking decidedly plain. Terrible hair, check. Terrible school uniform, check. Terrible classmates… hang on a moment.

My gaze snagged on a guy on the right, near the back, his face slightly turned away from the camera. I cast my mind around in search of his name, then saw someone had tried to tag him as 'Greyson Beaumont' but he had no social media account. Even in our terrible maroon uniform, a jolt of recognition hit me at the sight of him. His hair was shorter than it was now, but his face was almost the same.

"Devon," I said slowly. "Is that who I think it is?"

"Finally she gets it," she said. "I *knew* the guy looked familiar when he first walked into our shop. And get this… Greyson vanished from all contact not long after graduation. I don't think he was ever on social networking sites. I asked a few of the others from our year and nobody knows where he ended up. Everyone else left a trail, even the ones who moved abroad. Not him."

I cast my mind around. Had we been in any of the same classes? All my memories of the last two or three years of school were fuzzy and filled with gaps. Did he remember me? He must do. It wasn't like I'd changed all that much, nor had he suffered any memory loss the way I had. So why in hell hadn't he brought up the fact that we'd been classmates?

"Before graduation." I checked the date on the photo. He must have disappeared weeks, months at most after the picture was taken. Nobody else seemed to have put two and two together, but who would have thought their classmate from the Order's academy would become the King of the Dead? "Why didn't he tell me?"

"He didn't want you to know how low he sank?"

"I wouldn't call becoming one of the most powerful people in the Parallel 'sinking low'." I'd thought he'd never met me before. And in a way, he hadn't. Not as the Death King, anyway.

As Greyson Beaumont, though? *Grey.* The vampires had known. The liches must know, too. But me... I'd known his name all along, and yet I hadn't recalled a damn thing.

"Good news, then," she said. "You have some ammunition to use against him if he tries to manipulate you again."

"Not really," I said. "I'm depending on him to stop the vamps punishing me for the double assassination. Especially when I tried to interrogate the assassins and they ended up dead."

"Yeah, that's bad luck," she said. "And Brant… I wonder where he is now?"

"Hiding, if he has any sense," I said. "With Davies in the House of Fire, maybe. The mages I spoke to denied having any knowledge of where he ran off to, but who else would have taken him in?"

For all I knew, the Death King might have tracked him down, handed him over to the vampires, and cleared my name all at once. Yeah, and maybe I'd make it to this week's gaming night without being arrested. Some things were less likely than rolling a critical on a D20.

"Oh, yeah, I finished these." Devon held up a handful of cantrips. "These are for all your stealth needs. Invisibility, sense enhancing, hiding your own traces, and a few paralysis ones. All set to disintegrate on contact. Not the reusable ones. You don't want to leave any traces."

"Good." I took them. "Thanks, Devon. I have a feeling I'll need them when I hunt down whoever's working against us."

The bitter truth was, I couldn't take them on alone. Every time I'd fought a spirit mage alive or dead, I'd needed to rely on the Death King's help. Yet even though I'd ultimately trusted him with my life, and vice versa, he hadn't told me who he really was. Unlike me, his past didn't lie buried beneath the haze of a memory spell, which gave him no excuses. Perhaps he didn't trust me with that information. Or he thought I'd hold it against him.

Back in those days, he'd been a spirit mage, too. Yet as

far as I knew, he hadn't been foolish enough to get caught like I had.

Greyson Beaumont, huh. Maybe I could make use of that little snippet of information.

———

I hadn't intended to astral project in my sleep, but I found myself drifting through the ceiling and up into the sky the instant my eyes closed. The city spread out beneath me, and when I stepped through the node, I found myself in front of the Citadel of the Elements beside the shadowy form of the Death King.

"Why here?" I asked. "Why do I always end up here?"

It wasn't like I'd been looking for the guy, but maybe Devon's words had been weighing on me more than I'd thought.

"Because it's always easier to astral project on a path you've already travelled," he said. "You and Ryan went out alone earlier to pursue the assassins, didn't you?"

Ack. Admittedly, the dead assassins in the jail would have been difficult to explain away, so Ryan would have had no choice but to tell their master how they'd got there. "I wanted to find out where their employers were hiding. I didn't expect them to die."

"I would guess they were instructed to take their own lives in the event of their capture," he said. "The same would have happened if I'd found them myself. Besides, we know who hired them."

"And... Lord Blackbourne?" I asked. "Did you tell him who killed the emissaries?"

"I did," he said. "I gave him the evidence, and he might

have taken my word for it if not for the fire mage's escape."

Shit. "According to the mages, he's not at their safe house, which was the address we found with the assassins."

"Yes, Ryan told me that, too." Exasperation laced his tone. "Not only are you incapable of obeying direct instruction, you seem hell-bent on getting my Elemental Soldiers to break the rules, too."

I bristled. "Sorry I didn't ask permission, but you stormed off and I wanted to find out where Brant was hiding. The mages at the hideout insisted they don't know, but where else might he be? Unless he's hiding in your spare room or something."

"I'd advise you to forget about him," said the Death King. "He's not looking out for your best interests."

"I figured that out when he sided with the dickheads who tried to have me killed, funnily enough." My hands clenched. "With him on the run, you know the vampires will keep blaming me, don't you?"

"The same would be true if they'd taken him in," he said. "The connection between the two of you paints you as guilty in their eyes."

"Fuck that." I scowled. "Besides, if we hadn't found those assassins, they might well have killed someone else or hunted us down at your castle. It doesn't take a genius to say someone in the Order hired them, or they know who did. Someone with links to the liches who betrayed you."

His gaze travelled past me, towards the shape of the citadel etched against the night sky. Beyond it, nodes shone like pillars of light piercing the heavens. While travelling to the Order might be simple, I'd be visible to anyone even if I infiltrated the place via astral projection. Here, the cloud cover and darkness prevented me from being spotted. Unlike the Death King, I didn't wear a dark cloak and a mask over my face, though right now his face was visible enough that I couldn't believe I'd forgotten him.

That damn school photo was going to haunt me until I asked him what the hell had happened after graduation. It seemed absurd to think that I'd been preparing to retake exams while he'd been taking over the Court of the Dead. Yet I'd seen the evidence for myself.

When he didn't respond, I added, "Do you think the Order might be involved with whoever is trying to intervene in your trials, too? Is that why you were visiting them?"

"No," he said. "It is no great secret that the Order dislikes the power I wield, as do many others, but I doubt the person intent on infiltrating my Court is the one who freed the fire mage and tried to frame you for murder."

"No, the universe just decided I needed another enemy to deal with," I said. "I wonder why the betrayer didn't stand and fight."

"Because he fears me, even now." His words carried an undercurrent I couldn't quite place. "I am the one who holds his soul in my hands, after all."

And I could create a lich in the same way, if I had a soul amulet to hand. A dangerous power… and even more so in the hands of someone like the Crow or his followers. I had zero doubt that many, like Dirk Alban, would have abused that power. But then, what did that make me?

"Do you all give up your names when you turn?" I found myself asking. "Or is that just you… Greyson?"

He stilled for a moment, then his head tilted in my direction. "You figured it out."

I tensed inexplicably, as though part of me expected him to strike me down for using his real name. "You should pay more attention to social media if you want to hide your identity. Why didn't you tell me?"

"It isn't hidden to anyone who wants to know," he said. "I doubted you'd remember me as well as I remembered you. Besides, it's irrelevant."

So he did remember me? "Coming to the school reunion?"

"No," he said. "Are you?"

"Over my dead body… not that that's an invitation," I hastened to add. "I wasn't being serious. You couldn't pay me to set foot in that hellhole again."

It was bad enough that half the Order would no doubt be gossiping about me being involved in the mysterious deaths of two vampire ambassadors. I didn't need to stand there and listen.

"I thought not," he said. "There was little in our education that was remotely relevant to my career."

"You mean, being King of the Dead." A grin swept my mouth. "I'm having trouble imagining you in a classroom."

"I was rarely there," he said. "It's hard to discipline someone who's going to be dead in a few years, so the academy never bothered to chase me up."

"They *knew?*" But if the Order had known he belonged to the former House of Spirit, then they'd known exactly what was coming for him. "Haven't the liches been around forever, though? How long has this curse been going on?"

"The liches have existed for as long as the spirit mages have, yes," he said. "But before the war, it was very different."

"The war," I said. "But—does that mean you're...?"

Damn. The liches had once been the very spirit mages who'd slaughtered the council and started the war. Except they hadn't died out after all.

They'd been transformed.

"The survivors of the Council of the Elements enacted a punishment on the House of Spirit for their actions in the war," he said, his voice soft. "The curse they unleashed crept into the bloodlines of every member of the House of Spirit, and all of them were faced with the same choice: to turn lich, or to die. The same curse still lives on in every member of my House and is set to strike the instant they reach a viable level of spirit magic. For most of us, that's around the age of eighteen."

The illusion had always been his real face. He'd always been someone I knew, from the world before my memories had split down the middle and left me stranded on the wrong side.

"So, the spirit mages never died?" I could hardly believe the Council had *let* them live... forever, even. "Some of them survived?"

"Not every spirit mage fought in the war," he said, his tone distant. "Some disagreed with the whole notion. Others were cast out for the same reason. Regardless, the punishment hit every member of the House, guilty or not, and ultimately brought an end to the war. If their intention was to prevent the spirit mages from ever rising to power again, they succeeded."

"Damn," I whispered. "They cursed the spirit mages' children, too? Bit harsh."

"They judged us all culpable for our parents' wrongdoing," he said. "You know how the Order operates."

The Order did it. It was *them.* "But... you still have power over the other liches. Right?"

"Provided I behave," he said, with no hint of irony in his tone. "The Order and the vampires made a deal with the heads of the Houses of the Elements to ensure none of them ever rises to their former glory."

"Then... the Order *wants* me to join you, as a spirit mage." My voice dropped to a whisper. "That's why they gave up trying to stop me from working with you. They figured out you're probably teaching me magic and they decided the only solution is for me to stay in the Parallel."

And either turn lich or die, in the end. If I died, it didn't matter. If I survived long enough to turn lich, I would no longer be a threat to them. Either way, they'd won.

He inclined his head. "You weren't supposed to exist. What Alban did... teaching independent practitioners magic... it was intended to create new spirit mages in the only possible way."

"By picking ordinary people and unlocking their potential." Bitterness laced my voice. "Knowing what the Order would do if we were caught."

Which at least proved that ordinary mages *could* turn into spirit mages, given the right training, but that made the punishment inflicted on the House of Spirit seem all the harsher. To close that loophole, the Order had banned the use of spirit magic, and they'd condemned the liches to a living death in order to stay on top.

"Why do you think I ensure I maintain my authority over the liches?" the Death King said. "It's entirely intentional that I keep a reputation as a callous ruler who punishes anyone who crosses him. The Order wouldn't accept anything less from the person elected to keep the other liches—and spirit mages—in line."

"Aren't you stronger than the Order?" I said.

"Here, yes," he said. "In their realm, though? I certainly can't single-handedly take on the entirety of the Order's worldwide presence at once."

I couldn't wrap my head around the idea of him being anything other than the undead overlord of his territory. But that was the point. He'd cultivated his reputation on purpose. He needed the Order to see him a certain way. So he wouldn't end up like me. Or worse, Cobb.

"Were you born on Earth, then?" I asked. "If your parents were liches, how is that possible? I mean..." *Immortal death lords can't fuck,* I almost said, before remembering who I was talking to.

"I wasn't aware you were an expert."

"You're *dead.*" I'd walked headfirst into that one, and I had nobody to blame but myself. "Also, I doubt I'd be thinking about getting laid if I was cursed to a living death."

"Are you sure?" he said. "Given enough practise, most of us are capable of using our illusion skills to recreate almost any human experience."

"I do not need to know about your sex life, Death King."

"You were the one who asked the questions," he said.

Yes. I had. And I had more than a few other queries which were more important than the improbability of a lich getting laid. "Why would the other liches turn against you, if you're the only thing keeping them alive?"

"There have always been defectors," he said. "Now they've heard of the spells the Crow had in development, they believe that if they find a way to replicate them and return to life, it will set them free and bring an end to the curse. They're wrong, of course."

"You mean the cantrip that turned them into living beings only for them to die again?" I said. "They think there's really a way to use a similar spell break the curse?"

"There isn't." He snapped out the words, and I flinched. "I would know."

"I guess you would." An ache filled my chest as he turned away, leaving me wondering at what point I'd become comfortable enough to talk to him, and to feel pain at everything he and his people had suffered. And now I knew the hold the Order had over him ran as deep as their grip on my own life.

The Death King vanished, and I blinked awake, closer to answers but more lost than ever before.

14

nother day, another challenge. Two more rounds of the contest to go, assuming the castle didn't catch on fire first, that is. Today's round involved magical combat, yet the constant bursts of flame weren't the reason my concentration levels were non-existent. The vampires' looming threat didn't help, nor did the Death King's absence and the shadow of the revelations he'd piled on me last night. Instead of watching the contest, I found myself watching the shadowy forms of liches glide around the swampland, wondering who they'd been before they'd been bound to a living death.

The House of Spirit had never died. Not permanently. Question was, how many of them had already left the Court of the Dead, now the enemy had promised them the one thing the Death King had never been able to give them? The other liches would never be completely under Hawker's control as long as the Death King survived, which probably meant his end goal must be to steal the soul amulet again.

The Death King… or his real name, Greyson. Had we ever spoken at school? I couldn't recall anything, and yet I was missing so many memories from those years that we might have been in the same D&D group and I wouldn't know it. And as for what he'd told me about the Order and their hold over his Court and his family…

Someone screamed, startling me out of my reverie. Harper flew back across the arena floor, dodging torrents of flame, and hit the ground hard. Her hands rose, flames fluttering from her fingers, then they died out.

"What's going on?" I strode up to the earthen wall bordering the arena.

Harper scrambled upright, puffs of smoke emanating from her hands. "My magic isn't working."

"It isn't?" I looked around the arena at the other pairs of fighters, but I didn't see any obvious obstacle which would stop her from using her powers. No water on the floor or raindrops or mist.

Her hands ignited, but the fire went out an instant later. Her opponent advanced on her, his own hands blazing, only for the flames to die out before he could launch his attack. He looked at his hands in confusion.

The other contenders were having the same difficulty. Flames sputtered and died, as though something unseen was suppressing the contenders' magic. I walked around the arena to join the other Elemental Soldiers. "What's going on?"

"Is there another water mage around?" said Cal.

"Not that I can see." Felicity peered over the arena's edge. "I'll keep an eye on them. Can the rest of you search the grounds? If it's a spell, the caster can't be far away."

"I'll root them out." Ryan's magic blasted several bushes to pieces, but no water mages materialised.

If Harper was affected, too, it should mean her brother *wasn't* responsible—unless she wanted to lose, but that made little sense. I walked around the arena's edge and spotted Bria standing over her fallen opponent. *She* didn't seem to be having any trouble conjuring fire, but that didn't necessarily make her guilty.

Come to think of it, I never had followed up with her about the House of Fire. I'd been more concerned with the vampires, the assassins and Brant's escape, but who knew, maybe it was all linked. Someone in here wanted the Death King off his throne, and she'd told me to go to the House of Fire herself. It was a tenuous link, I'd admit, but not one I could overlook.

Might the other Houses still bear a grudge against the Court of the Dead for the spirit mages' actions in the war? Had they faced punishment, too, or was the House of Spirit alone saddled with the consequences? During my conversation with the Death King last night, I'd forgotten to ask how if the other Houses had faced a similar punishment from the Order after the war, if not as severe as the Court of the Dead. Overnight, I'd thought of a million other questions I wanted to ask, but they'd have to wait until he came back.

I caught Bria's eye as she knocked her opponent flat on his back. "Hey."

She lifted her head. "Why are you looking at me funny?"

"A bunch of people are losing their magic." I gestured around the arena.

"Don't blame me," she said. "Maybe they spent too long in the shower."

"Ha." Her tone didn't hide any visible guilt, but I'd been looking for an excuse to talk to her either way. "Either it's someone in here, or another outsider."

"Did you kick Sledge out for good?" She sauntered over to the fence and leaned over to speak to me. "Maybe he's the culprit. I mean, he's bound to be pissed off at losing his place here."

"He deserved it," I responded. "As you know well."

"Hmm." She conjured up a flame in each hand. "Looks fine to me."

I looked around the arena again. At least half the participants were on the defensive, hardly able to conjure a spark. Bria herself wore a casual expression which almost masked her tired eyes and tense air. *Hiding something. Definitely hiding something.* "Where'd you learn to fight?"

"I had a good teacher."

Better than good, if the way she'd fought earlier was any indication. I'd never seen her overtly breaking the rules, and yet there was something different about the way she fought that set her apart from the others.

And then there was her inexplicable visit to the Citadel, which was supposed to be out of bounds.

"Are you *sure* you don't know any spirit mages?" The question escaped before I could quite think it through.

Her jaw tensed. "I know *you*. If that counts. Why, did you think you had to become buddies with the Death King to learn spirit magic?"

My mouth parted. She had some cheek, that was for sure. She couldn't possibly know about our lessons, but I needed to shut her down before she got any dangerous ideas.

"I'm in the Death King's employment," I told her. "That doesn't make us friends."

"No, because he isn't around," she said. "He's skiving off, isn't he? Not even watching his own trials."

"Are you sure you *want* this job?" I said, exasperated. "Because you're doing a great job of convincing me to kick you out."

"Thought it was up to the King of the Dead," she said.

"The final decision is." Hell if I knew if it was true, though. After all, he *wasn't* in the castle, though it was beyond me to figure out how she'd worked it out. "Have you been snooping around the castle when the Elemental Soldiers told you to stay put?"

"I saw most of it during the flood," she said. "I met your fire sprite, too. He's cool. Why did he get put in charge of guarding the hall of souls, anyway?"

"You met Dex." Okay, this girl was ringing way too many warning bells. "He got the job because he's the one person I trust to keep any potential saboteurs out of the castle. And if you're getting any ideas, then I'll gladly escort you to the jail myself."

Her mouth pressed together. "No need for that. I thought you wanted me to give you information about potential saboteurs, not accuse me of doing the same."

"If you know someone in here who plans to disrupt the contest—"

"I don't," she said, a little too quickly. "But I don't think Sledge was working alone. He has friends."

I glanced around, followed her gaze, and spotted another larger contender with a mullet haircut who could have been Sledge's younger brother, shooting fireballs at his cowering opponent. A questioning look earned a nod from her. *So it's him, huh.*

Before I went to confront him, I asked, "Do you know the location of the House of Fire?"

Bria frowned. "Why? If you want to ask them if one of their members is trying to wreck the contest, they'll throw you out on your arse."

"For one thing, a former friend of mine might be hiding with them." I was starting to regret bringing up the subject. "For another, I'm about fifty percent sure someone connected to the House sent assassins after me. Do you know them personally?"

And what about her side trip into the Citadel of the Elements?

Before she could answer, Ryan strode up to me. "We're resuming the matches. No magic. Bria, you're fighting Clancy over there."

"Put her against that dude instead." I pointed at the big guy, who was called Bark or something equally weird. Bria shot me an unreadable look before walking over to the other fire mage to start her match with him.

Did she know about the assassins who'd perished in the jail? Or was she entirely innocent? She definitely knew the House of Fire's location, but it sounded like there were more members of said House than I'd thought. If the House of Fire held as many people as the Death King's Court did, then I'd be hard-pressed to take them on alone. Besides, if Brant wasn't at their hideout and they weren't responsible for sending the assassins, I'd be putting my life at risk for no reason. Better to find the traitor among the contenders first. Then I'd find out who'd sent them.

The challengers' magic continued to malfunction, even with the regular combat rules in progress. It was like someone had flooded the arena again, except there wasn't so much as a droplet of water in sight. No matter how hard I searched the grounds, I found no signs of Harper's brother, either. I even ducked into the jail, finding someone had removed the assassins' bodies. No doubt the Death King had someone turning their bones into ornaments. Though it struck me that the creepy décor might be nothing more than a façade, to convince everyone that he was a terrifying monster.

How was I to know truth from lie anymore?

I returned to the arena to find Bria had knocked out her opponent, who lay sprawled on his back, his clothes smoking at the edges.

"He cheated using a cantrip," said Bria. "Gave himself a boost."

"Can anyone back you up on that?" I looked behind the arena to the gates, and a beam of light snagged my gaze on the other side of the fence.

The node. Someone's coming into the swampland.

I turned my back on the arena, leaving a bewildered Bria behind, and ran past the cloaked liches at the gate in pursuit of the shimmering node. As I veered in that direction, a dark shape appeared within.

I stepped right up to the node, reached inside it, and grabbed a solid arm, yanking the intruder on top of me. The two of us crashed to the swampy ground. Sledge snarled and grabbed at me, only for me to ram an elbow into his ribs.

"Back *again?*" I snarled. "Are you the one who's switching off everyone's magic?"

Fire spluttered from his fingertips. His mouth twisted, his eyes quite deranged, and he aimed a wild punch at my nose. I blocked with my forearm and drew the node's power into me, but he leapt out of the way of my attack with surprising speed. *How is he moving so damn fast?*

As he surged forwards, I kicked his legs out from underneath him. Energy poured from my hands and slammed his head into the ground. "Stay put, dickhead."

Sparks flew overhead, and Dex zoomed over. "You need to stop getting into fights when I'm not around."

"Thought you were guarding the you-know-what."

"Aria is there instead," said the fire sprite. "I wondered why you ran outside the gates. What's with him?"

Sledge let out a bellow of rage, but I grabbed a handful of his life force and tugged. His thrashing grew weaker, and when I drew another surge of life force from him, he flopped onto his back.

"Nice one," Dex said. "What're you doing?"

"Draining his life force." My grip faltered as he fell unconscious. "Crap. I should probably have kept him awake so he could tell us where he's been hiding out."

"Throw him through the node into no-man's land," said Dex. "Or drag him up to the Withered Oak. Maybe that'll get them talking."

"What did Bria say to you?" I asked. "She said you two spoke."

"Who?" he said. "Oh, her. She wanted to know why I was living in the castle. Frankly, it's rare that I find any human who bothers to notice the likes of me."

"You do realise she's a suspect, don't you?" I said. "She's

a rogue, with no background on record, and she's been snooping around the castle when she thinks nobody is looking. Right now, she's in my top three suspects for whoever's plotting against the Death King."

"Don't sound so accusing," he said. "It's not like I told her your address."

"You'd better not have." I looked down at Sledge, then opened my pouch, revealing my new cantrips. "Care for a little espionage once this guy wakes up? Someone sent him here to cause trouble, and I'm willing to bet it was either the House of Fire or someone else who wants to ruin the contest."

"Not fire-boy?"

"No, he ran away, probably for good." A bitter taste filled my mouth. "After everything I did for him. Dickhead."

"Told you not to bother saving his life," Dex said.

"Save the *I told you so's* for later," I said. "If I hadn't tried to campaign on his behalf, the Order would have found another way to make me into a target."

"They would," he acknowledged, "but that doesn't change the fact that fire-boy is a massive, pus-infected—"

"I'm *what?*" Brant himself stepped out from behind a bush, his arms folded.

In a flash, I drew on the node's power and caught him by the throat. "What the hell are you doing here?"

"I—" He choked out. "Dammit, I'm here to help you."

"Yeah, right." The glowing current of energy connecting us deepened, and while power flooded my veins, there was something that felt different about him.

I let go of the current, and Dex tutted. "You should have finished him off."

"Liv…" Brant broke away from me, gasping for air. "You're stronger than before."

"I'd take that as a compliment if you hadn't landed me in deep shit yesterday when you took off and left me next to the bodies of two dead vampires."

Dex whooped and cheered. "Don't you give ground, Liv. Not an inch."

"If I'd stayed at the scene, we'd both have been blamed," he said. "And I'd be dead."

"I know you're out for yourself alone, but it would be nice not to feel like you're kicking me when I'm already down," I said. "So the mages were lying about you not hiding at their base?"

"Who?" he said. "I'm not with any other mages. I'm staying at Trix's house."

"What?" I stared at him. "Trix would never let you stay with him after what you did. I'd appreciate it if you didn't lie to me, either."

"I'm not." He shifted uncomfortably. "Trix is still unhappy with me, yes, but when I mentioned you were in trouble, too, he let me lie low in his house so you wouldn't take the blame for my mistake."

The elf was way too forgiving, that was his problem. "Look, Brant, I'm not working with you again. You used me, you lied to me, and I swear if you don't tell me what the hell you're doing here, I'll fuck you up. Are you with him?"

He followed my gaze to the unconscious mage. "Who's he?"

"I'm taking a wild guess that he's with the House of Fire," I said. "I also know you were a member. Care to deny it?"

He flinched. "I haven't been back there in forever. Not since they let me out."

"Let you out?" I arched a brow. "What do they want with the Death King?"

He took in a breath. "Like the other Houses, the House of Fire is a prison for mages who step over the lines. I was incarcerated in there before I broke out and struck out alone, and so was Davies. That's how we knew one another. I wouldn't say either of us was a member of the House by choice."

A prison? The House was a prison? "I thought you and Davies met afterwards. When you started scheming against the Death King."

He shook his head. "No, we were both in the facility together. He won his way out by taking on the position of the Death King's Fire Element. I escaped by pure luck."

"Hold up," said Dex. "If the prison is for mages, who runs the place?"

"The mages who run the House don't give two shits about the rest of us," he said. "It's complicated, but the Houses were set up as an attempt to control the mages after the war, and to prevent any one House from rising to power. If the person infiltrating the trials is a member of the House, they're probably acting alone."

Damn. It seemed the House of Spirit hadn't been the only one to suffer punishment after the war. "So how did you meet Vaughn, then?"

"We were both runaways," he said. "He was from the House of Earth, and he and I fell in with the same crowd when we were on the run. I'm not saying he was a good person, but he and I faced the same choices. I just made a different one."

"Different choices?" I said. "You both chose to betray me, just at different times. He did it first, that's all. If anything, I'd have preferred it if you'd got it out the way without leading me along any further."

"I'll always regret what I did to you." His voice was soft, and I hated that it still tugged at the part of me which wanted to forgive him. "The Crow told us he planned to revamp the Houses and return them to what they used to be. They all suffered the consequences for what happened in the war. Four of them became prisons, and the fifth—"

"You knew the House of Spirit became the Court of the Dead." Disbelief struck me in the chest. "You *knew.*"

"He *told* you?" he said. "Why would he?"

"I asked," I said. "Maybe I was a little concerned that every spirit mage in the Parallel seemed to have met the same fate. It isn't like *you* told me why I was an exception."

That was why Brant had been so certain I'd be spared from turning into a lich myself. Unlike the Death King and his fellow liches, I'd been a normal human before Dirk Alban had found me.

Pain flashed in his eyes. "I planned to, but the Death King... he's killed people for less. It's not surprising that his liches are abandoning him."

"I suppose you know that they fell in with the Crow when he promised to use illegal magic to undo the curse?" I folded my arms. "Look me in the eyes and tell me the Crow is less twisted than the Death King is."

"He told you that, too?" His mouth pinched. "I know you don't trust me, Liv, but there's no way he would have given you that information for free. He wants to own you, too."

"Like you wouldn't do the same," Dex interjected. "I've

been living in the castle for weeks and His Deathly Highness hasn't laid a claim on me. If you ask me, you're just jealous because you've always wanted an army of liches."

"Forget the Death King," I interrupted, as Brant began to protest. "Tell me who ordered your release from the Order. That's who wanted to frame me, isn't it?"

He squeezed his eyes shut. "Holland is the one who fetched me, but I thought… I never knew there were spirit mages within the Order."

"Aside from me." I tilted my head. "Ever heard of the Spirit Agents?"

Puzzlement flashed across his face. "No. Why?"

"They were mentioned in connection with the Houses of the Elements," I said. "By one of the contenders."

"I don't know who they are." He shook his head. "Believe me, the House of Fire didn't tell me a thing. It wasn't until recently that I even began to consider that spirit mages might be a legitimate threat again, much less to the Order. I *think* Alban and Cobb and whoever else was involved in their sect were trying to organise some kind of coup to take over the Order from the inside, but they failed."

"They have contacts in the House of Fire." Another piece slid into place. "Of course they do. If the Order helped to arrange the punishment…"

"What is *he* doing out here?" Ryan marched over, and air blasted from their hands, straight at Brant.

With a yelp, Brant flipped head over heels and landed on his back in the dirt. "Okay. I deserved that, but—"

Ryan kicked him in the ribs. "You're going back to the jail where you belong, fire mage."

"Don't!" He cringed away. "I swear—I'm not here to

threaten your king. I never wanted to hurt anyone to begin with, not like Davies did. I wanted to save my own soul."

"That's a good argument for having it ripped out of you, if you ask me," said Ryan. "This time, permanently."

"Wait," I said. "Normally, I'd be all for it, but we need him."

Ryan shot me an incredulous look. "Since when?"

"Since the Order wanted me to take the fall for his escape," I said. "He knows about the House of Fire. Who better to help us find the traitors who are conspiring against the Death King?"

"I'd be more content to lock up *this* traitor, to be honest," Ryan said, hands raised.

Air magic sliced the air, and Brant leapt sideways into a bush. Leaves scattered everywhere, and I frowned at him. Brant didn't hide. Not when he could fight. The guy defined 'hot-tempered'. I remembered when I'd drained him earlier... he'd felt different than he had before, as though the Order had done more than kicked the fight out of him.

"Have you lost your powers, too?" I said.

"I—what?" He stuck his head out of the bush, hands held up to shield himself from Ryan's magic. "What do you mean?"

"Half our contenders are having trouble using their magic." I nodded to Ryan. "It's been happening all day. You too?"

"No." He shrank into the bushes. "Not like that. The... the Order did it."

Shock hit me like a lead weight. The Order had taken

his magic away. No wonder they'd assumed he wouldn't fight back.

"I can do worse," said Ryan.

"Wait." I stood between Ryan and him. "This isn't—look, the Order took his magic away. He's no threat."

Brant rose to his feet. "They did. Now I'm essentially powerless. If you want to lock me up, you can, but it won't solve anything. Believe me when I say you're in more danger than you can possibly know. The Order only spared my life because they didn't think I was enough of a threat, but you—"

Ryan raised their hands and levitated Brant into the air. "You tried to kill my master. You conspired with Davies to kill me, too. What do you have to say to that?"

A blast of fire shot over my shoulder. I cursed and spun around. "What the hell?"

"He's lying," said Ryan. "He's pretending he lost his power."

"I'm not," Brant said, eyes wide. "There's someone—"

Sledge leapt into sight with a bellow of rage, hands flaring with heat. I ducked a punch, fire singeing my sleeves, and found myself glad of my armoured clothing.

Ryan blasted him onto his back, and the swamp ignited at his feet. I backed out of range of the flames, calling on the node's strength, and power poured from my own hands. Sledge slammed into the mud once again, his eyes closing.

Then he got up, his movements jerky, flames igniting all over his body and burning holes in his sleeves.

"Is he losing control of his own magic?" I reached out and grabbed a cord of energy from within him, yanking on it like a piece of elastic. A trickle of life force reached me, but Sledge's eyes remained closed, as though something compelled him to fight even when he was barely on his feet.

Brant trod over to Sledge, ignoring the flames. His hand reached out and yanked a cantrip from around his neck. He winced, holding it up so I could see. "Don't touch this. It's hot."

"What is it?" I peered at the carved disc, but I didn't recognise the symbols on it.

"Trouble."

Sledge slumped back onto the ground, the fire going out in an instant. This time, he didn't rise.

Ryan levitated him into the air once again, then jabbed a finger at Brant. "You're both going to jail."

Brant didn't move. "I can't. Believe me, I know I deserve it, but that cantrip isn't the worst I've seen. I can help you."

"A likely story," said Ryan.

"Get him out of here first." I indicated Sledge's fallen body. "And—look, I need to get this cantrip to Devon. I bet she can figure out what it is. Brant…"

I shouldn't even be considering letting him walk away free, but as soon as he went behind bars, the Death King would step in and I could say goodbye to ever learning what he knew.

"He's not leaving," said Ryan flatly. "No way in hell."

"Then I'll take him back to Devon." And he'd better hope she didn't use a cantrip to blast his balls off for breaking my heart.

15

"I'm not working with him," Devon said. "And you shouldn't either."

The two of them had been arguing non-stop ever since I'd landed inside the house with Brant in tow, his hands tied up with one of Trix's all-purpose ropes. The elf himself had joined us a moment later, which made for a very crowded living room.

"Look, he was with the Order, *and* he used to be part of the House of Fire," I told her. "He knows—"

"He knows too much to be allowed to walk around free," said Ryan, appearing through the node to an exasperated look from Devon.

"Does it look like I'm free?" Brant looked up from the sofa, wiggling his bound ankles. "I can't even walk like this."

"Should I gag him?" said Trix.

"I'll light him on fire." Dex appeared behind Ryan. "Now he doesn't have any flames of his own, he's toast."

"Would all of you please stop jumping through the

node in the middle of my house?" said Devon, a muscle twitching in her jaw. "Isn't Brant a fugitive from the law? From the Order?"

"He's the vampires' problem now," I said, "and I can't say I know how vigilant they've been at searching for him."

"They're looking in the wrong place," said Brant. "They think I'm with my mage contacts."

"But instead you were hiding with Trix." I gave the elf an accusing look. "Why not tell me?"

Trix fidgeted. "I didn't think you wanted him to die."

My chest tightened. "I didn't, but the Order wanted me to take the fall for his escape so the vampires would lock me up. Anyway, Devon… there's a reason I brought him here."

She held out a hand and took the cantrip I offered her, which was still singed at the edges. "What is this?"

"That was on Sledge when he attacked us," I said. "It was like he was possessed or something. He kept fighting even though he was unconscious, and his magic was stronger than before. Brant claims to know what it is."

"I've seen them before," said Brant. "They're one of the spells the Crow was working on."

"And you decided to wait until now to tell us?" said Devon.

"I thought all his cantrips were destroyed along with the house," he said. "Maybe he had backups."

A chill raced through my blood. *The lich traitor claimed to be able to save the House of Spirit from eternal death. Might there be some truth to his claim after all?*

Devon turned the cantrip over in her hand, and then

she flicked a button on the side. Fire leapt from its surface, and the rest of us jumped back out of range.

"Whoa." I caught my balance. "Did those flames come from the device itself?"

"Must have," she said. "If it brought out Sledge's powers when he was unconscious, then it must be a dual-use cantrip. Reusable, too. Is someone still smuggling out cantrips on the side from the COS?"

I shot Brant an accusing look. "Well?"

"Of course you know about it." Devon turned on him. "What else have you been hiding?"

"I haven't," he said. "I never knew who the Crow had smuggling out cantrips for him, but it could have easily come from one of his secret storehouses. Don't ask me where they are, though. I really don't know."

"We'll ask Sledge," I said to Ryan. "When he wakes up."

"I'll see if my master can get answers out of him," said Ryan. "Wherever he is."

"I have an inkling I know where he is." Namely, the Order. The Order, who held even the formidable King of the Dead by a rope.

"Where?" said Devon. "I'm serious. If the Order shows up and finds him here—"

"They won't," I said. "He's here to help me with one specific task, and then..."

What happened after depended whether we were lucky enough not to be caught. But if he was telling the truth and he'd die if he went back to the Parallel alone, then the only option was for me to hand him over to the Death King again.

"What task?" asked Dex. "Grovelling to you?"

"Cleaning our house?" asked Devon.

"Whatever it is," Brant said, "I'll try my best."

I met his eyes. "You're going to help me find out who in the Order is responsible for sending those assassins after me."

Easier said than done. I'd got Cobb jailed, but he'd made a public incident which was all but impossible to cover up. The assassins had died before even admitting who they worked for, and the mages' hideout held no links to the Order. On the surface, the organisation seemed utterly free from corruption... and harder to breach than the House of Fire.

But there was someone at the Order who might be able to tell us who was pulling the strings. Cobb was the only person I knew who'd survived from among Dirk Alban's followers, who'd schemed to bring the spirit mages back into a position of supremacy.

"You can't be serious," said Devon. "The Order already took away Brant's magic, and your—"

"I know what they took." My trembling hands clenched. "But think about it. Who has all the answers, including my missing memories? Who has *Cobb?*"

Brant's face went chalk white. "You can't—"

"It's this or give yourself up to the vampires," I said. "I'll hand you over myself—or you can help me break into the Order's jail and find Cobb."

Cobb would know who in the Order was involved in the conspiracy... and he'd know where whatever remained of the Crow's allies would be hiding. Unlike Sledge, he hadn't been a thick-headed foot-soldier. He'd been deeply involved with Dirk Alban's schemes against the Order from the start.

The irony of the Death King and I working to save the

very people who'd ruined both our lives was not lost on me. But Dirk Alban's actions had left a trail of death behind them, and however cruel the Order's punishment had been, I had to believe that those of us who'd stood up to him had been preventing something much worse.

Now all I had to do was lie through my teeth to get answers from someone who'd lost it all at the Order's hands, and who would stop at nothing to take out the Death King.

I looked into Brant's eyes. "You got out of the jail once, right? You know the way around, don't you?"

"I guess," he mumbled. "But how are you going to get into the jail without getting caught?"

I reached for my cantrip pouch. "With these."

———

It took a solid twenty minutes of arguing to get Ryan to agree to my plan, and even now, Devon had her most judgemental face on. Brant, meanwhile, sat on the sofa wearing an expression which suggested he'd sell his soul for the Death King's ability to teleport away from us.

Ryan and Dex had gone through the node to set up their diversion, which left it up to me to wait for the signal. On cue, my phone pinged with a message from Ryan telling me they'd travelled directly from the Death King's realm to the node near the Order's base, and Dex was preparing to unleash his diversion.

I, meanwhile, would be going into the Order alone, with Devon and Brant waiting on the other side of the node. I turned on the invisibility cantrip and my body vanished from sight. My senses heightened as I turned on my second cantrip, and all sounds were amplified, along with my vision.

Brant tried to pull me into an embrace, but I stepped aside the instant his fingers brushed my arm. "I'll see you later."

Then I stepped through the node, drawing in as much of its power as possible as I did so. Trix stood on the other side, ready to go through and take Brant with him to the Death King's territory.

I headed towards the Order's HQ, waiting for Dex's signal. After a few seconds, a series of sparks flew from the lobby. Then Ryan's magic blasted the doors open, giving me a free shot to run in, still invisible, between the security guards and into the building.

Pandemonium filled the lobby as a series of loud caws broke out from the back yard. I spotted Dex soaring gleefully overhead, having freed every one of the confiscated vampire chickens the Order had on their property.

I walked through the chaos, my sense-enhancing cantrips warning me of anyone in my path, then slipped into the elevator and pressed the button for the basement.

A hand rested on my shoulder. I spun around, glimpsing the outline of Brant's shape with my enhanced eyesight.

"What are you doing?" I hissed. "If we get caught together—"

"We won't, because we can't be seen," he insisted. "I know the lower levels of the Order inside out, Liv. I'll make sure we get through without running into anyone."

"Where'd you get that cantrip?" He must have an invisibility spell of his own if he'd given Trix the slip. The sneaky bastard.

"The market," he said. "It won't last long, but it should be enough. If I get caught alone, I'll let them take me in so you can escape."

"That's a bloody terrible idea." I couldn't say I trusted him either, but he was here, and so was I. We had no choice but to go on.

The elevator ground to a halt and I stepped out into a bleak corridor with solid concrete floors and walls of metallic grey-silver. While I didn't like to admit it, it was nice having someone at my back who actually knew their way around this part of the Order. Last time I'd been here, I'd been caught in a fog of missing memories and couldn't recall anything substantial about the layout.

Pressure built at the back of my head the further I walked, as though a tight helmet slowly compressed my head around the sides.

"Can you feel that?" I whispered.

"What?" Brant murmured back. "Are you okay?"

A stabbing pain hit me behind the eyes. Images flickered to life in my mind as we entered yet another corridor, lined with heavy doors. Some doors were open, revealing blank-walled rooms. Interrogation chambers.

I've been here before.

The image of myself being steered down the corridor by Order guards flitted through my mind's eye, and cold sweat trickled down my spine. They must have brought me here after finding me at the scene of the crime. Beside Dirk Alban's dead body. In the next corridor, bars covered one wall, cutting off a row of holding cells.

Nausea swept over me, and for an instant, the lights dazzled my eyes and gave the impression of bloodstains on the walls.

The light flickered again, and Brant swore in a low voice. "Are you doing that?"

"Me? No." I could hardly see straight. My vision doubled, while the world swayed to the side. I leaned on the wall for balance, and a fresh wave of images flitted through my mind.

Walking through the corridor flanked by guards.

Standing inside a cell looking at the wall, blood still on my hands.

Dark shapes moving around me. Cobb walking across my path, his gaze fixed somewhere on his feet. When he heard me pass, he looked at me with his eyes simmering with fury.

I flinched away. At the time, he'd been a stranger to me, and yet now my thoughts from the present mingled with the memory, a chill raced down my spine. He blamed me for his fate... blamed me for getting him caught.

He blamed me for Dirk Alban.

"This is all your fault!" he screamed at me, and his voice merged with Dirk Alban's...

A sharp pain in my cheek brought me back to reality. I'd fallen against the wall, and Brant caught my arm.

"Liv? What's wrong?"

"Something about this place is hurting me," I whispered back.

Was it just the sense-enhancing cantrip I'd used, or was it the fact that this area was designed to contain spirit mages?

"Then we'll go back," he insisted. "It's not worth hurting yourself over."

"No—we must be close." I trod further down the corridor, each step bringing a spike of pain as Brant's fingers dug into my arm. "We're here…"

We came to the end of the holding cells and to another corridor containing a row of heavy doors, each inset with a small barred window.

The one on the right lay open, revealing an empty cell with metallic-coloured walls. I peered inside, bewilderment filtering through the fog in my mind.

Then Brant appeared out of thin air beside me, cursing under his breath. His invisibility cantrip had burned out— but what was with the empty cell?

Cobb. Had the Order traded him to the vampires, too?

"Looking for me?" said a soft voice.

Mr Cobb stepped out into the corridor. He wore a plain grey uniform that matched the colour of the cell, but he was smiling. His gaze flickered over Brant with obvious satisfaction.

Brant stiffened. "What the hell are you doing out of your cage?"

"I should be asking you the same question," he said. "I thought you were taken to the vampires to await trial, along with your beloved Olivia. Are you alone?"

"Yes," he growled. "Yes, I'm alone. Who let you out?"

He smiled, his eyes cold. "Didn't you hear? The Order judged that I was not in my right mind during the events of two months ago. They pardoned me."

No way. I looked from his cold stare to the box he carried, which contained a number of disc-like shapes gleaming with runes.

Brant backed up a step. "You can't be serious. You *murdered* Order personnel. You nearly started a war. Who the hell set you free? What did you bribe them with?"

I'd never admit it, but I found myself fervently glad Brant was here, if just because he was proof that I wasn't hallucinating Cobb's presence entirely. *They can't have pardoned him. No damn way.*

"The Order makes the laws, and they can be changed like… that." He snapped his fingers. "Isn't that why you were fighting for change? You wanted this. Unless you betrayed Olivia for nothing."

Brant let out a hoarse scream and threw himself at Cobb. The box of cantrips fell to the ground, and it took every ounce of willpower I possessed not to join in the fray myself. Neither of them had any magic, so they could only fight with their fists. *There must be something I can do.*

Cobb was already free, which meant his allies in the Order must be acting openly. We'd got here too late to stop Dirk Alban's allies, and revealing my presence would only hurt both of us.

I spotted a gleaming cantrip on the floor, which Cobb had dropped. While his attention was elsewhere, I picked it up, freezing mid-step when Cobb forced Brant backwards into the vacant holding cell. His mouth was bleeding, but his eyes glittered with triumph as he slammed the barred door on Brant.

"If you see Olivia before you die," he said, "tell her she would be wise to consider her options. If she gives herself up, we can guarantee the safety of her loved ones—all of them. If not…"

A chill raced down my back. Did he know I was hidden nearby? Perhaps he did. After all, Brant would have no real reason to risk his safety by coming down here alone.

"Fuck that," Brant spat. "It was your people who sent

assassins to kill the vampires' ambassadors, wasn't it? You wanted to free me so Liv would take the blame."

Footsteps pounded behind me. Cobb smiled, then he vanished. *Dammit, he used a cantrip.*

Two guards ran into view, and they zeroed in on Brant the instant he pushed his way out of the cell.

"Well, well," said the guard. "Look who's back. Guilty conscience?"

"I see you've put yourself back where you belong," said the other guard. "I wonder if any other fugitives have turned themselves in?"

That was my cue to leave. I backed through the corridor until I came to a fire alarm, then broke the glass. I ran as soon as the alarm blared out, my footsteps buried in the howling sound. I skidded around a corner, hardly noting the pain as my enhanced senses protested at the noise coupled with the sensation of having my magic suppressed.

Brant had bought me time, and if I showed my face anywhere in the Order, they'd connect my appearance with Brant's escape and lock both of us up. Cobb had vanished from sight—along with the cantrips he'd pillaged—and the best I could do was get everyone out of this building before he used them to mount an attack.

I set off two more alarms before reaching the elevator, slipping inside along with a guard patrol and trusting the blaring alarm to hide my heavy breathing. The two guards argued all the way up to the lobby, at which point I darted out and towards freedom. All I could do was hope that Cobb would get flushed out during the evacuation, but the fact remained that someone in this building had let him out of his cell.

Admittedly, Cobb was less dangerous on his own, invisible or not. He'd only managed to start a war because he'd had the Death King's soul and an army of liches on his side. Speaking of whom, I didn't see any sign of His Deathly Highness among the staff evacuating the Order's headquarters. Either he'd used his lich trick to vanish into the Parallel again, or he'd been elsewhere.

He couldn't possibly have known Cobb walked free... right?

I left the Order's headquarters and hurried back towards the node, my mind whirling. *Was Cobb seriously threatening my family back then?* Had he known I was there, and was he trying to imply that if I died, my family would live? It sounded like an empty threat, but who knew?

Nobody waited at the node, so I travelled through into the living room and found myself levitated into the air.

"Shit!" Ryan let go of me, and I landed in a heap on the sofa. "Don't scare me like that. I thought the Order took you."

"So did I." Devon backed up next to Trix, her eyes wide. "When Brant didn't come back..."

"They took him." I crawled off the sofa and straightened upright. "The Order took him. He gave himself up, but Cobb—he's free, and he's roaming around the Order at will."

"Whoa," said Devon. "They freed *Cobb?* What are they on?"

"Someone did, but I don't think it was a unanimous decision." I removed the cantrip from my pocket with shaking hands. "This is what Cobb was stealing from the Order."

"Huh." Devon flicked the switch, and my skin tingled, but nothing happened. "Weird."

"You just… hit the button?" Ryan said. "What if it had decapitated you?"

"It wouldn't have."

"Thanks a bunch!" Dex appeared in a flash of sparks. "You ditched me."

"I thought you'd already left after you released the vampire chickens," I said. "Nice job, by the way."

"You can't distract me with compliments," he said. "Where's fire-boy?"

"Gone." A hollow feeling filled my chest. "The Order took him. Cobb had an invisibility cantrip. He vanished the instant the guards showed up. But he was roaming around the cells for a reason."

"And risking recapture by stealing this crap?" Devon tossed the cantrip into the air and caught it again. "Must be valuable. I'll take it apart and see."

"Go ahead." Guilt swirled inside me. The Death King would be pissed at me for ridding him of the chance to lock up Brant himself, but I couldn't help wondering if *he'd* known about Cobb's escape. What were his meetings with the Order really about?

Was he involved after all? Surely not, given that they held links with the same people who had condemned the House of Spirit to a fate worse than death.

The Order had done that. The *legal* side of the Order. I understood why Cobb wanted to burn them all down, I'd say that much. But that didn't mean I'd let him get away with threatening my friends and family.

"I don't understand." Trix eyed the cantrip anxiously. "I thought the Order found him guilty."

"Someone in there overruled the decision." Which suggested he had friends in high places. "Not like we can give them a warning without ending up condemned ourselves."

He could do a lot of damage as a free man, but he still had no magic of his own—and it had been the Death King who'd been his original target. He'd needed his soul amulet and the magic which came along with it. Which meant there was a strong chance that at least one of the remaining fire mages in the castle had been sent by Cobb to finish the job his former allies had failed to complete, and to claim the soul of the King of the Dead.

Tomorrow was the last chance the enemy had to target the Death King's contest and bring their forces directly into his castle. Whether the Death King himself knew or not, we had to be ready for them.

16

I was too shaken by the day's events to sleep properly, let alone astral project. Going near the Order seemed like tempting fate, even though I wanted to know who among them had given Cobb the freedom he desired. Questions circled my mind like vultures, and I rose feeling less rested than I had before I'd lain down.

Downstairs, I found Devon sitting in the living room surrounded by bits of broken metal.

"Got the cantrip to work, then?" I asked.

"No, and now my other ones are playing up, too." She grunted. "Have fun with His Deathly Highness."

I groaned. "I still haven't told him why Sledge is in his jail, let alone this new crap."

Devon waved me off. "Good luck."

I stepped through the node—or I would have, if I'd been able to sense the current of energy. Instead, I remained standing in the same place. "Huh?"

"What?" asked Devon.

"The node." I reached for the energy again, only to find nothing waiting for me on the other side. "Did the node switch off?"

Devon frowned. Then she picked up the cantrip I'd taken from Cobb. "My other cantrips have been acting up all night. I wonder…"

"Wait, you turned off the node?" I said. "When you hit the button?"

"Must have," she said. "Why would the Order have something like that in their headquarters?"

"I don't know, but Cobb was carrying a whole box of cantrips." I couldn't think why he'd want to turn off nodes, but the guy didn't do anything without reason.

"Shit," she said. "How are you going to get to the Death King's castle, then?"

"I can use another node," I said. "I just hope the effect isn't permanent."

She frowned at the cantrip. "It might wear off by itself. Most cantrips do."

"Can I take that with me?" I reached out a hand. "I think the others should know what Cobb was stealing."

"Go ahead." She pressed the cantrip into my palm.

In truth, I didn't completely trust Devon not to run around shutting down the other local nodes out of curiosity, but the Death King needed to know about the most recent development. If nothing else, if someone tried to escape through a node again, it'd be a good way to bring them to a halt.

The nearest node to my house was a few streets away, which wasn't too much of a walk, but I half expected to find the Order waiting on the doorstep when I went outside. Even if they hadn't suspected me of breaking into their headquarters, I was on thin ice after Brant's escape already.

"Liv?"

I stopped walking. Oh, crap. "Hey, Mum."

"Are you okay, sweetheart?" she asked.

"Yeah, I'm just on my way to work." Wearing armour. Maybe I should have told her I'd got a new job at a Renaissance Faire. It had always been easier to pretend, ever since the Order had shoved its way into my life, leaving her daughter on one side and a stranger in her place. She knew I'd changed, but not how I'd got there.

"Is it busy?" she asked.

"Yeah," I said. "I've taken on an extra job this week. It's pretty much all-go, twelve-hour shifts until Friday."

"Was that the job you were asking me about?" She tilted her head. "It's with that young man who came to my house, isn't it? He mentioned wanting to hire you then."

"He did *what?*" The Death King and I had still been enemies at the time. Or so I'd thought. Had he seriously informed my *mother* that he'd wanted to hire me? "Wait, what else did he say to you?"

"Nothing," she said. "Why, what's wrong? You took the job, right?"

"Yes." How could I even begin to explain my weird relationship with the King of the Dead? "I mean, I'm surprised because I wasn't thinking of him as a potential employer at the time."

"Well, things can change quickly." She took a step closer to me. "Sweetheart, you might have gathered when we spoke on the phone that we're going through some big decisions lately. Elise and I."

"Oh?" I did my best to drag my thoughts away from

the Death King's absurd fixation on employing me, which had apparently begun five seconds after he'd realised I hadn't stolen his soul on purpose. "Like what?"

"Children," she said. "I know we have you, and you're wonderful, sweetheart, but Elise always wanted to be a mother, and we've been looking into our options. When I was married to your father, I wasn't exactly at a happy place in my life. If I had been, I might have considered having another child after you, but you know, life doesn't always go the way you plan."

"That's—great." I tried to inject some enthusiasm into my voice. "I know I wasn't around a lot when I was a kid. After I went away to the academy, I mean. And you and Dad had split up, and…"

"And dating wasn't going well," she added. "Until I met Elise. I admit we put the decision off, considering… everything."

Meaning: my dodgy memory and my fractious history with the Order. "Don't worry about me, Mum. Do it for you. If it makes you happy."

Elements knew one of us deserved some happiness in their life.

As for me, I had yet another reason to have stern words with the Death King. He'd better stay out of my life after Mum and Elise had their baby, or else he'd be down one spirit mage.

Mum and I parted ways, and I headed to the node, trying to get my thoughts back to the contest. Then I stepped through the node and landed outside the castle.

"What's going on?" asked Dex. "I tried to get into your house and hit a dead end."

"Devon and I accidentally turned off the node with a

new mystery cantrip I got my hands on," I said. "Turns out that's what Cobb was stealing from the Order."

He snorted. "What did the nodes ever do to offend him?"

"I don't know, but if he broke into the Order to steal them after tricking them into setting him free, he did it for a reason."

I walked to the castle with the strong feeling that I should have just waited for Sledge to wake up rather than trespassing in the Order's prison while Cobb was on the loose. But if I hadn't been there, I'd never have known Cobb walked free at all.

I entered the break room to find it empty aside from Ryan, who sat on the sofa, polishing their sword.

"Has my master visited you?" they asked.

"No, why?" I said. "Did you tell him about yesterday?"

"He's furious about Cobb's escape," they said. "I told him that Cobb claimed the Order pardoned him. I think he's going to see what they have to say to that."

"Is he at the Order's place?" I said. "I thought the contest was still on."

"There's only one round left, and then he can kick all the interlopers out of his castle," Ryan said.

"Except the person who wins," I added. "I need to talk to him, too. You know that cantrip I found Cobb stealing from the Order?"

"The one Devon turned on without knowing what it did?"

"That's the one," I said. "It turned a node off, Ryan."

Their eyes widened. "Why would Cobb want to do that?"

"I have no idea."

"Ryan," said Felicity. "Liv. We're needed outside."

Okay. Contest first. Deal with the rest later.

I walked alongside Ryan. "Have you spoken to Sledge?"

"He's completely insensible," said Ryan. "Barely awake, and too addled for an interrogation. I think that cantrip of his messed him up."

"Damn." Reading between the lines, His Deathly Highness hadn't been around for long enough to conduct an interrogation of his own. Not that Sledge was the highest priority, considering.

We went to join the other Elemental Soldiers in front of the arena, where the remaining contenders assembled.

"Today is all about teamwork," Ryan told me. "It's also the last round, so be prepared for the losers to kick up a fuss."

"Believe me, that's the least of what I expect to go wrong," I said. "So—teamwork. They have to work together to solve problems."

"Pretty much," said Ryan. "Glad Sledge is already out, or else he'd have caused no end of trouble."

"Don't speak too soon." He might be in jail, but he'd already tried to give us the slip more than once.

I moved closer to the arena, seeing the ground was covered with stone pieces of various colours and sizes. The goal, according to Cal, was for each group to assemble the stones into the right order like a jigsaw puzzle by using their magic to illuminate the patterns on the stones. Seemed straightforward enough, but I didn't put it past them to make trouble anyway.

I positioned myself next to the node to watch the contenders. As it became apparent, half of them still didn't have functioning magic. Lights flared up and went out, and dying flames flickered across the arena.

"Don't worry about your magic," Felicity called to them. "You have to solve the puzzles as a team."

As long as one person's magic was functioning enough for them to light up the puzzle, they would win. But why would someone still be intentionally sabotaging their rivals' magic at this stage?

Whatever the reason, the number of contestants had been cut down enough that I figured I'd try the process of elimination and see who among the remaining contenders *wasn't* losing their magic.

Pacing around the arena's edge, I zeroed in on Harper's group. *Is her brother hiding in here somewhere?* I'd failed to find him yesterday, but she barely seemed to be focusing on the puzzle. She kept fiddling with her hair and touching the scars on her face.

A bellow came from the jail. *Ah. It sounds like our prisoner is awake.*

I headed that way and halted in front of the liches guarding the entrance. Or I would have done, if the liches hadn't been nothing more than piles of smoky shadows.

Someone had turned the guards to ashes. Someone… like a deranged fire mage hell-bent on escape.

A glow snagged my gaze, and I halted in front of the node. Within its streaming current, another light shone from a human-shaped figure. A sprite. Dex?

No, not Dex. It was a water sprite, judging by the bluish-white colour, with long curly hair and wide blue eyes.

I reached into the node and grabbed the sprite by the scruff of its neck. "Who are you?"

"Help!" the sprite said, in a high feminine voice. "Help me!"

"You're coming with me."

I dragged the sprite along with me to the arena. Several contenders jumped to their feet, including Harper, who flinched at the sight of me with the sprite caught in my hand. "Mav! Don't hurt her."

"Come with me and I won't," I said.

She trailed after me, her head hanging low, while the others watched. Bria's eyes narrowed, and that gesture alone told me she was in on this, too… whatever it was.

I led the way into the main hall of the castle and through into the side room where I'd conducted the last questioning. The sprite didn't fight my grip, and she sank limply to the floor when I released her. "Care to explain?"

"I just wanted to win," Harper whispered. "We need the money."

"By suppressing your opponents' magic?" I said. "Did you flood the castle, too? Because you nearly got people killed."

"It was an accident," she said. "The water levels weren't supposed to get that high. I didn't know…"

"Didn't know what?"

Her eyes squeezed shut. "My brother gave me a cantrip to make my own magic stronger. I didn't know it'd affect her, too."

Before I could conjure up another question, the Death King himself strode through the closed door, his cloak swirling behind him. *At least he's actually here this time.* Harper's mouth fell open, her gaze darting from him to the door as though puzzling out how he'd walked through a solid surface.

"Come with me," he said. "Both of you."

The urge to tell him about Cobb hit me, but that would have to wait. Harper got to her feet, her entire body trembling.

"Please don't let him lock me up!" she whispered to me.

"Pretty sure I have no control over that," I muttered back. "You'd better hope this was your only crime, for your own sake."

I kept one eye on Harper to make sure she didn't run off, as we followed the King of the Dead into the empty hall.

With no apparent care for his effect on her, he turned to me. "Care to tell me what's going on here?"

"Harper is the one who caused the flood," I said. "She also had her sprite companion dampen the magic of the other contenders in order to win."

"I see," he said. "Did she give her reasons?"

"Except for her desire to win the contest? No." I turned to her. "Well?"

"I—" she broke off. "I needed the job for security. My brother and I are being hunted by a group of mages who used to belong to the House of Fire. If they catch us, we're dead. You don't know—"

"Olivia, escort her to the exit," he said, still without meeting my eyes. "I can trust you to expel the other traitors, can I not?"

"Yes, but—"

He turned and walked away, while Harper let out a soft gasp, swaying on the spot. Her sprite settled on her shoulder, making soothing noises.

"Come on." I beckoned to her. "The sprite, too. Be thankful he didn't order me to lock you up."

Sure would help if he'd stuck around long enough for me to warn him that Harper wasn't the only traitor. Someone had turned the liches to ashes, Sledge was throwing a tantrum in jail, and I doubted she was the only person in here with links to these mages connected to the House of Fire.

We walked out of the castle and descended the stone staircase into the grounds. Behind the arena walls, the other candidates cowered behind one another or stared in awe at the castle, no doubt because of their brief glimpse of the Death King. Most of them wouldn't have laid eyes on him before, considering he'd been absent for most of the trials. Hell of a way to meet the new boss. I wouldn't blame some of them for having second thoughts about this whole venture.

I snagged Ryan's arm on the way past the arena. "Take those two outside. There's still a traitor among the contenders."

Then I made for the node, treading carefully, one hand on my cantrip pouch. The light brightened... and I spotted someone lurking nearby. Bria.

I threw the cantrip at the node, flicking the switch as I did so. The current of energy vanished from sight. Bria spun around with a curse, a cantrip in her hand. Spirit magic blasted from my palms, causing her to drop her weapon, but she kept her balance with startling grace. I grabbed the cantrip where she'd dropped it. A paralysis cantrip, or something similar.

"Where'd you get that?"

She lifted her chin in defiance. "The Death King's storeroom."

Well, hell. "You and Harper were in on the same plan. Care to tell me who else was involved?"

Around us, countless liches filled the grounds, dark shadows cloaking them, surrounding the castle to protect their master. Bria's gaze flicked to the spot where the node's light had gone out. "What did you do? How'd you turn it off?"

"You aren't getting away that easily," I told her.

Light flared outside the gate, and Bria bounded to her feet. "Sorry, Liv, but I have backup."

She hurled a cantrip at my feet, then ran. I shook off the paralysis with a curse and ran behind her towards the gates, where the node outside had ignited. Figures filled the swamp outside—*human* figures, outlined in light. I skidded to a halt at the foot of the steps leading to the castle.

"Death King!" I shouted. "Greyson!"

He appeared, gliding down the steps, as one individual pushed through the crowd at the gate.

"Lord Blackbourne," said the Death King. "To what do I owe the pleasure?"

My heart gave a jolt. *Vampire.* I'd expected Bria's allies, whoever they were, but not them. They weren't working with the rogues from the House of Fire, were they?

"I wish to speak with you," the vampire lord said. "If you deny me, my associates will deny you the new Fire Element you desperately crave."

"Fine," the Death King said, a touch of impatience in his voice. "If you insist."

What the hell? Lord Blackbourne couldn't have betrayed us, too, could he? It made no sense.

"We have come here for justice," said Lord Blackbourne. "Hand over Olivia Cartwright and Brant Edwards, and we will gladly leave you to your games."

17

Nobody moved. The contestants remained in the arena, and I knew there was no point in hiding. The vampires had already seen me.

Of all the rotten timing. I should have guessed they wouldn't let the deaths of their emissaries go unpunished, but they must know I'd have nothing to gain from getting on Lord Blackbourne's bad side. Brant, though? He wasn't even here.

The Death King strode forward to position himself between the liches and the new arrivals. "Call off your cavalry, Lord Blackbourne. This posturing isn't necessary."

"Posturing?" he said. "Two of my ambassadors were killed while *she* was with them. And her fire mage boyfriend."

"He's not—" I cut off the automatic response. "He's with the Order. They recaptured him. Which you'd know if you'd asked *them* about why they let Brant out of their sight. They were trying to set me up."

"That's not what I heard," said Lord Blackbourne. "I was told you were looking to plead on the fire mage's behalf. Yet when I offered you the opportunity to bring him here, you killed two of my people and let him walk free."

"I didn't kill them," I said. "Assassins did. If they hadn't, I'd have come to talk to you right away."

"She speaks the truth," said the Death King. "As I told you, I arrived myself shortly after the fire mage fled and saw the assassins leaving the scene."

"The last I heard, they perished in *your* jail, which you neglected to mention to me."

Oh, *hell.* "They committed suicide rather than admit who sent them." Dammit, I did not have time for this crap. "Might have escaped your attention, but we're in the middle of kicking out interlopers who've decided to use the Death King's trials for their own ends. If you wanted to see me, you could have just sent an invitation."

The vampire bristled, but the Death King spoke up before he could eviscerate me for my rudeness. "She speaks the truth. I decided our safety was pertinent when I took the two assassins to my own jail. And if you don't mind, I have some traitors to expel."

I managed to refrain from gaping at him for his outright lie. Why was he covering for Ryan and me? He must really be confident in his ability to fend off half a vampire army. That, or he didn't think the vampires would turn on him.

"So I see," said Lord Blackbourne. "Is that more important than the well-being of your Court?"

The liches moved forward, as did their master. "I wouldn't threaten me, Lord Blackbourne."

Crap. They weren't seriously going to break out into a fight, were they? Did that mean the vamps had been against the Death King from the start? It made no sense for them to be, given that we'd helped them against the Crow, but it couldn't be more obvious most people were out for themselves alone. And they thought Brant and I had betrayed them.

Admittedly, I'd let the guy walk away free to save my own skin, only for him to sacrifice himself on my behalf again, but in the end, it had all been for nothing.

The vampires closed in, but the liches met them more or less equally. There were as many of us as there were of them, which left us at a stalemate. The liches couldn't die. The vamps were technically more vulnerable… but the calculating expression on Lord Blackbourne's face was not a pleasant one.

"Not a threat, Death King," Lord Blackbourne went on. "A reassurance. It seems many think you have lost your touch, so I wanted to let everyone know that I maintain control over the city of Arcadia. You, however, seem to be having trouble clinging onto this stretch of wasteland."

"You are misinformed." The two now stood almost face to face. "As you can plainly see, I control a substantial army, and I have no intention of letting your people overrun my castle. If need be, I will take you down by any means necessary."

I glanced behind me and to see most of the contenders were fleeing the arena through the back exit. I didn't blame them in the slightest. Except Bria had disappeared, too. Dammit.

Another light ignited outside the gates, and the vampires and liches alike turned in that direction.

"We're under attack!" someone cried out, and all hell broke loose.

The light brightened as energy surged from the node, raising the hairs on my arms. Ignoring the vampires, I ran out into the swampland, skidding to a halt near the node. Bria stood beside it, and a number of shadowy figures appeared within. Not liches, but humans. Humans, whose palms glowed with vibrant energy.

Spirit mages. Bria stood beside them, a knowing look on her face. The vampires, meanwhile, made no move to confront the new arrivals.

"Enough," said Lord Blackbourne. "Olivia Cartwright, come with me, and tell me where to find Brant Edwards so he can face justice."

I indicated the node. "I'm not sure I like the idea of your justice. You're working with a group of murderers and traitors."

"Murderers?" said one of the newcomers, stepping into view. "I wouldn't say that."

"Quiet, Miles," snapped the mage next to him.

Lord Blackbourne shot him a disgruntled look. "I would prefer it if you were to stay out of this."

He *knew* the spirit mages? Was I the only person who hadn't the faintest clue what was going on?

Lord Blackbourne gestured. "Get her."

Two vampires moved behind me, but the Death King glided into their path. The vampires skirted the Death King with blinding speed, but I dodged their grasping hands, energy shooting from my palms. The vampires toppled into the mud like falling trees.

The first spirit mage who'd spoken laughed. "Damn, she *is* good."

I sidestepped, blasted energy at him, and he deflected my attack. These were trained spirit mages, while I'd barely had one or two lessons. "Whoever you are, I'm not coming with you."

"You don't have a choice," he said. "Besides, I'm told we're not all bad."

Three of the mages approached me—not walking, but hovering above the swampland. Astral projecting. *Oh, bugger.*

I tapped into the node, drawing in its energy, but I'd never faced more than one spirit mage at once before. Never faced one head-on at all, in fact. The node's energy crackled in my hands, my hair standing on end and static creeping through my whole body.

"She's powerful—I told you!" One of them threw a handful of spirit energy at me. I ducked and returned fire, and the spirit mage deflected my attack with a wave of his hand.

Then a flickering movement in the corner of my eye resolved into a pillar of flames. Bria grinned at me from within. "Hey, there."

"You." I took a step towards her, but she moved dizzyingly fast, and then vanished.

That was an invisibility cantrip... but that didn't explain how damn fast she'd moved. Was she even human?

Energy slammed into me, knocking the breath from my lungs. I stifled a gasp as a familiar draining sensation grabbed me. The glowing ball of energy in the spirit mage's hands turned to a stream of light connecting us. I trembled, struggling to break the connection, and it took everything I had to hold myself together. He was ripping out my life force.

"Get her!" someone shouted.

A dozen threads of spirit energy slammed into me at once. Images burst behind my eyes, and the world faded out.

———

I stood, my back against the wall, as Dirk Alban shouted at me. "You ruined everything, Olivia…"

Then I came to alertness to find myself nose to nose with Miles, the spirit mage who'd hit me. His ashy blond hair was streaked with grime from the swamp, as was his face. His brown eyes glittered with amusement. "She wakes."

I pushed myself upright and bumped my head on the low ceiling. "Who the hell are you?"

"I thought you knew who we were," said Miles. "They call us the Spirit Agents."

What the hell is this? The room was bare of furniture, mostly because it was the size of a cupboard and contained nothing but a few dusty coats hanging from hooks. It seemed the Spirit Agents were short on cells to keep their prisoners in, because they'd shoved me into a cloakroom instead.

"What gives you the right to kidnap me?" I rose to my feet, but he raised a hand and sent a jolt of spirit energy into me. My back hit the row of cloaks, and a hook jabbed me in the spine. Ow.

This guy had real power. They all did. They'd learnt spirit magic somehow, away from the Order. It had never died out, not as long as these people kept it alive.

Too bad they weren't on my side.

"The vampires want you dead," he said. "This is the safest place for you to stay until they calm down."

Safest? He claimed to want to keep me safe? A likely story.

"They won't calm down," I said. "Not until the real killers are brought in front of them, but that's you, isn't it?"

"Me?" he said. "What makes you think that?"

"You kidnapped me and locked me in a cloakroom," I said. "And one of you tried to kill the Death King, too."

"That was a mistake," he said. "The two of us go way back."

"You do realise the vamps want me dead because someone stabbed their messengers and set me up to take the fall?" I said. "Besides, I was told you're a group of dangerous vigilantes."

He laughed. "Yeah, right. I'm glad our fearsome reputation is spreading, but we don't need knives to fight, and nor should you. Whoever those killers are, we're not associated with them."

"I was told you were," I said. "I was also told you were working with the House of Fire. So if you aren't with them, then who are you with?"

"The House of Fire?" He frowned. "Who told you that?"

Well... someone who just turned against us. For all I knew, Bria had been feeding me false information on purpose, yet the House of Fire *had* come up in connection with the criminals infiltrating the trials.

"Never mind that," I said. "How the hell are there so many spirit mages here? You're supposed to have died out. I thought the Order put everyone in the House of Spirit under a curse."

His mouth thinned, and a hint of emotion flashed in his eyes. "They tried to. They cursed everyone who survived the war in the hopes of wiping us out, but we're free spirit mages, born into families of other mages. It's more common than you'd think… as you probably know yourself."

"My family aren't mages," I said. "They aren't even practitioners."

"That would explain why you were so hard to track down," he said. "Self-trained mages are my favourites. You have balls, Liv. I can call you Liv, right?"

"This isn't *funny.*"

"No, it's tragic." A touch of pity appeared in his expression. "The Order genuinely thought that confining mages to the Houses and strangling all opposition would wipe us out. But we can't be beaten that easily."

An unexpected tide of emotion washed over me, momentarily dispelling my rage and confusion. These mages weren't from my past, and he didn't talk like a fanatic or a cultist. If I wasn't more concerned with getting back to my friends, I might have stuck around to find out how many more free spirit mages existed here and how they'd escaped retribution from the Order.

I swallowed hard. "Look, *if* you're telling the truth, then what do you want with me?"

"We offer a hand to all rogue spirit mages," he said. "It's only fair. You were hard to track down, which is why we didn't approach you earlier. Then we heard you were in Grey's employment."

"That ended with the contest," I said. "You and the

vampires decided to crash the party before I could finish my job."

"The vampires won't stop until you and the fire mage are behind bars," he said.

"They won't calm down until they see proof that Brant is *already* behind bars," I corrected. "The Order has him locked up in their cells. Lord Blackbourne and I have met before, and he has no reason to believe I'd lie."

"Except for the two dead ambassadors," he added. "I don't know why Grey's trying so hard to prove your innocence, but—"

"I didn't kill them," I snapped. "I thought *you* did. There's definitely a rogue spirit mage involved in this."

"I told you," he said, "it's not one of ours."

The door opened behind him.

"Ooh, she's awake," said another spirit mage, a dark-skinned woman with a streak of pink in her curly hair. "Excellent."

"Do I know you?" I said.

"You knocked me out cold earlier," she said. "Nice aim."

"Thanks," I said, totally bemused. "Look, I'm finding it hard to believe there are any mages who *aren't* double-crossing dickheads at the moment. What's your relation-ship to the House of Fire? Do you want to boot the Death King off his throne?"

"No!" Miles sounded genuinely insulted. "As for the House of Fire, I'm no fan of the shitheads who run that place. They get paid for incarcerating their fellow mages. Shockingly, it means most troublesome rogues are runaways from the Houses, but if any of them are after

Grey's position, I assume they got booted out of the contest by now."

"Why do you call him that?" I said. "Grey? Did you know him?"

"Sure," he said. "Before he became all…" He waved his hands in what I assumed was supposed to be an imitation of a lich. "We weren't close, but everyone knows the Death King."

I stifled an inexplicable laugh. "Yes, and he'll be pissed at you for taking me away at a time like this. I'm not kidding."

"I guess I don't blame you for mistrusting us," said the woman. "Spirit mages who don't find us tend to have short lives."

I looked between them, my heart racing. I shouldn't believe a word they said, yet something about them struck me as sincere. Maybe it was because I'd always had to keep my guard up around people who didn't know about my magic. These people, though… they were just like me. Yet they'd somehow escaped punishment at the Order's hands. Jealousy slid through me like a knife. They'd had one another while I'd had nobody at all.

Yet this situation struck me as far too good to be true. There'd be a catch. There always was.

"Look, as nice as it is that you haven't tried to kill me yet, I have to get back to my friends," I said. "I think Lord Blackbourne ought to be taken to the Order so he can see I was telling the truth about Brant's imprisonment."

That wouldn't absolve me of being accused of murdering his fellow vampires, but he knew I was a spirit mage. Why would I fight with throwing-knives instead?

I took a step out of the cloakroom, but the two spirit mages blocked my path.

"No leaving the house," said Miles. "You're staying here until we say otherwise."

"I don't think so." I stepped up to him, feeling my cantrip belt around my waist. He hadn't removed my weapons. Guess he must have assumed I fought with spirit magic alone, like he and the others did. "Move, or I'll be a lot less likely to give you the benefit of the doubt for kidnapping me. Where even are we?"

"Our base, in Elysium," he said. "You're a long way from home, Olivia."

"Don't call me that," I snapped.

"Why?"

Because the Order did… and the Death King. "I'm sick of people trying to kill me, and frankly I'm concerned for my friends. If the vampires don't guess I'm here, they'll go after my allies instead."

"The vamps won't harm anyone innocent." He glanced over his shoulder, and I took the opportunity to snatch up a cantrip.

The paralysing spell caught both of them at once, and I darted out of the room and into a corridor. They really had shoved me into a cloakroom—under the stairs, no less—and the door leading outside stood at the end of the hallway. A promising humming sensation permeated the air, indicating there was a node close by. Finally, some luck.

I pushed open the door and used a cantrip to seal it. That ought to hold them for a minute. Then I walked down the grassy path to the gate, spotting a group of chickens wandering around. *Are they vampire chickens?*

Who brought them here? I dragged my gaze away and put those questions firmly in the 'later' pile.

The unkempt garden ended in a high fence overgrown with spiky plants, and I did my best not to touch any of them as I pushed open the gate from the inside. Thankfully, it opened without setting off any alarms.

Freedom beckoned. Once outside, I broke into a run, following the humming of the node. Left, right, into an alleyway… oh, shit. Someone else was ahead of me, standing still as though waiting for me to catch up. I skidded to a halt as the Death King turned around to face me, wearing his human face. "Good, you're safe."

My jaw hit the floor. "I was kidnapped and that's all you have to say? Aren't those people the same spirit mages who attacked us the other day?"

"They aren't, but I don't have time to explain," he said. "Come with me."

"Then explain on the way." I walked after him, unable to believe his nerve. "Why the *hell* didn't you tell me you knew a whole house full of spirit mages who weren't turned into liches?"

"Because you had no desire to abandon your previous life," he said. "Most of them were born here in the Parallel."

"So you decided not to mention it was even an option?" My rage cooled a little as the truth began to sink in. "Being a spirit mage without turning lich, I mean? You let me think I was alone. That's not cool, Grey."

His steps faltered a little at the use of his name and he didn't respond for a long moment. The buzz of the node grew more intense. I was too shaken to appreciate the fact that I was visiting another major Parallel city for the first time in my life.

Finally, he said, "Lord Blackbourne has given us an ultimatum. We need to convince the Order to hand Brant over to the vampires."

"Again?" I said. "I'd ask those spirit mages to help, but I doubt they're thrilled at me for giving them the slip. Besides, you know how it turned out last time. The vampire ambassadors ended up dead."

But that wasn't the important bit. If the vampires got hold of Brant again, they wouldn't spare him. I didn't doubt that for a second.

We have no choice. This is the only way.

We had to go back to the Order and hope that they were in a cooperative mood this time around. Which seemed a tall order, considering how many others we'd managed to piss off today. Not to mention Cobb... *oh, damn.*

"I know what Cobb stole from the Order," I told him. "Cantrips that switch off nodes. I may have used one on the node outside your castle to stop Bria from inviting her friends in. That's why the spirit mages came from outside the gate instead."

"I see," he said.

"Is that all you have to say?" Unbelievable. "Bria ran off, along with her allies. Why did you ditch your castle at a time like this?"

"Forget Bria," he said. "I've dealt with her for now."

"What the fuck does that mean?" I halted mid-step. "And the Order? How do you know Cobb's allies won't have a team of assassins lined up to take shots at us if we set foot inside their headquarters? Is pacifying the vampires more important than staying alive?"

"Not at all," he said. "As for the Order, I am confident we won't be attacked while we're inside their headquarters."

"Because of your so-called special arrangement with them." A furious dam burst inside me. "They let you live—relatively speaking—and you don't threaten their control over the magical world, no matter how many people they hurt. That's how it is, huh."

"It isn't," he said, "but now isn't the time to discuss the Order. We have to go."

The node's current surrounded us, carrying the Death King and I away into the swampland.

The instant my feet touched the ground, mages surrounded us on all sides, hands blazing. Fire mages. *The runaways from the House of Fire.*

As if we needed any more enemies. *Did the Spirit Agents betray us, too? Were they lying?*

Davies strode to the front of the group of mages. "Whoever my replacement is, they're not going to get the chance to take up their position before they die."

18

The Death King looked his former Fire Element up and down. Then his gaze went to his companions. "I have to admit I'm surprised you found any allies among the mages, considering the Houses' well-known views on those who turn their backs on their own people."

He knew where Davies was hiding? I didn't know why I was surprised at this point. But while the Death King's manner was calm, a hint of impatience underlaid his voice. He hadn't expected them to show up here and now, when we had far too many enemies circling the gates already.

I glanced over at the castle, which appeared still and quiet. The vampires had gone, as had the Spirit Agents—for now, anyway. This should be Ryan's fight, if anything, but the other Elemental Soldiers must have stayed behind to guard the castle and prevent the other contenders from taking advantage of the Death King's absence.

"They know I always intended to bring you down," Davies said. "And this time, I'm not going to lose."

Davies's fellow fire mages advanced, hands flaring with bright orange light. None of them had been stripped of their powers. They weren't contenders. But then, why had they chosen now to strike? Had one of the Spirit Agents given them directions?

I really hated when my *too good to be true* assumptions ended up being on the mark.

Luckily, they hadn't picked the best place for an ambush. I reached into my pocket and threw a cantrip into their midst, freezing several of them. Then I drew on the node's strength, and the Death King did likewise.

Power blasted from our hands in unison, knocking the mages backwards. Their flaming attacks spun off course, setting patches of swampland on fire. Davies ducked behind his fellow mages to avoid being hit.

"Cowardly little shit." I flung a cantrip at two other mages, freezing them to the spot. The mages might be strong, but there was no way they could handle both of us at once. We already had them on the run, backing up to the node.

The node... where a shadowy form flickered into view. Then another, multiplying until a row of shadows filled the swampland.

"Death King," I warned, pointing. "We have company."

More liches emerged from the node, joining the fire mages. Oh *damn.* Maybe ditching the Spirit Agents had been a mistake.

At a command from the Death King, his own liches flowed from the gates to join the battle on our side. Davies raised his hands and blasted flames over the mages' heads, right at me. I deflected and the attack hit a lich, turning it to dust. Heat singed my face as Davies sent another blast of fire my way, his mouth twisting with hate. The heat rose, and he didn't seem to care that his allies cringed away from his blazing hands.

"You're dead, Liv," said Davies. "Like Brant will be when I find him."

"You won't find him." So that would explain why Brant hadn't returned to join his allies from the House of Fire after his escape... it seemed Davies inexplicably blamed him for his predicament. "And you're way down on my list of concerns, mate. Who's calling the shots here? Have you really been hiding in the House of Fire all his time?"

Twin streams of fire burst from his hands, colliding in front of me as I conjured spirit magic to my hands and blocked his attack. The ongoing burst hit two liches, disintegrating them. Yet the forces emerging from the node didn't slow. If anything, the Death King had underplayed how many of his allies had defected.

Why? What do they have to gain from siding with the rogues?

More liches came from the gates to join the fight until I could no longer tell who was on which side. The mages fought with fist and flame, and while the Death King fended them off, a group of them had reached the castle gates—only to be met with an army of wights on horseback. The wights trampled through the fray, sowing even more confusion.

"What's in it for you?" I traded blows with another mage. "Why side against the Death King? It sounds like his House is the only one which is remotely fair to its members."

"He's a liar and a murderer."

Before I could ask what in hell he meant, a flash of blue light ignited, and a semi-transparent figure flitted into view.

Harper and the water sprite ran up to us, the sprite's magic crashing onto the nearest fire mage like a tidal wave. Behind her, Dex flew over to join them, waving at me.

"Where have you been?" I said.

"Around," he said. "You won't believe—"

"You." Davies advanced on Harper, flames flickering between his fingertips. "Thought you'd come back, did you? I could have given you a far better deal than the Death King, you know."

So he was the one who'd been threatening her? Couldn't say I was surprised.

Harper gave him a defiant stare. "I'm not your lapdog."

Davies indicated to his liches, who surrounded her on all sides. "You made your choice."

"Hey!" I ran behind him, but the liches already had their prey in their grip.

Harper's scream reverberated in my ears as I found myself nose to nose with Davies. He laughed coldly. "Don't look so hurt. She was dead the instant she turned on me."

I punched him hard in the face. Blood spurted from his nose and the pain in my wrist and hand were totally worth his stunned expression.

"I thought you were saving your revenge for Brant." A smirk appeared on his face. "It was worth taking my place at his side to see your reaction when you found out who he really was."

Another punch, this time to his mouth. "I always knew *you* were a bastard."

He laughed, spitting out blood. "He still hoped to save you. He should have guessed the Order would never let you walk free. Even the Death King knows they want you dead no matter who comes out on top."

What? "The hell are you talking about?"

"The Death King, of course." He choked on another laugh. "The only reason he even gives a shit about the Order being taken over is because he knows the instant the Order falls, you're dead."

He was lying. He must be. "You're full of shit, you know that? The Death King doesn't even like me. Besides, I'm pretty sure whoever's leading the coup in the Order wants everyone dead who isn't a traitorous scumbag."

"The Order could have used you," he said. "Even with your memories gone, you might have been given a second chance, if you hadn't taken his side. You should listen to the Death King more often, given all he does for you."

"Are you *jealous?*" I said. "He gave *you* the opportunity of a lifetime, and you threw it away."

He spat out blood. "I picked the winning team, Liv. The Order *and* the Houses are finished, including the House of Spirit. I got out while I could. If you weren't so ignorant, you would have done the same."

"Davies!" Ryan's furious cry rang across the swampland.

I let Davies go and he sprang to his feet, just as Ryan's attack slammed into him. He flew several feet into the air, yelling, blood streaming from his nose. Ryan screamed and released another attack, and Davies hurtled through the air—right into the Death King's waiting grip.

His fist entered Davies's chest and withdrew in another instant, glowing with light which dissipated on the wind. Davies's lifeless body fell to the ground, eyes half open, while I reeled at the suddenness of his demise.

Around us, the sounds of the battle were quietening, the arrival of the Elemental Soldiers and their leader spurring the fire mages to flee. Those who were still alive, anyway. The Death King's army had triumphed. And yet the victory felt hollow.

"Olivia," said the Death King. "You need to go home before the vampires come back."

I wheeled around to face him. "Did you know? Did you seriously know the Order has wanted me dead all along?"

"One side believes you are like Alban and too dangerous to survive," he said, without looking at me. "The other sees you as a threat to their own plans."

"Which you know about." I stepped towards him. "I could report you to them, you know. For not warning them."

"Why do you think I was there?" The unexpected despair in his voice stopped me in my tracks. "They refused to take my word for it. Cobb's allies hid too well, and they're in every level of the Order's ranks. They've been waiting for years for the chance to restore the Order of the Elements to what it used to be… with the spirit mages at the head."

Impossible. *Impossible.* "Are the Spirit Agents involved?"

"No," he said. "They're likely to be targeted, however, if the Order does indeed end up falling. I cannot say I didn't try to warn them."

"You might have warned *me*." The words snapped out, my voice brittle. "Half the upper room already wanted me jailed for life. Even Cobb and his allies only wanted to use me because he'd lost his own spirit magic. I guess this time they've decided they don't need me after all."

"Olivia." He took a step towards me. "I wouldn't do anything rash. The vampires—"

"Need to see the Order, who want me dead. Which, I assume, Lord Blackbourne already knows." I caught sight of the other Elemental soldiers removing the bodies of the fallen mages. "If you're going to use that as an excuse to reach out and offer me another position in your service as long as I don't ask the wrong questions, then you can get fucked."

I walked towards the node, remembering belatedly that it no longer led to my house now I'd accidentally turned off that node. Which, no doubt, the Death King had known, too.

"I'm sorry it turned out like this," I said, without turning around. "I almost understand why you did it. But I'm done apologising for shit other people did to me, and I'm done letting you manipulate me. I'm going to warn my friends."

I entered the node, my mind spinning like the current of energy, and landed on the street down the road from my house. Then I walked home, my rage simmering and then fading as the day's events hit me like an avalanche. One way or another, there was no turning back from this.

Maybe I'd been too harsh on the Death King. It wasn't like he'd known I might have wanted to join up with the Spirit Agents, given the chance, and besides, they hadn't exactly presented themselves as on the straight and narrow, either. There was still the question of which spirit mage had attacked us through the node on the first day of the trials. The fire mages had only fought alongside liches, not spirit mages.

The closer I got to home, the tighter the vice clamping around my chest grew. The Death King hadn't been blackmailing me at all when he'd hired me. He'd wanted me to take a job working for him because it was the only way I'd be out of the Order's reach. Even if I'd ended up losing my soul and turning into a lich. Which, ironically, would have been safer for me than the alternative.

But in the end, the enemy would always have tracked both of us down. There was no point in wondering how things might have gone if I'd made a different choice.

For now? I needed to be ready to fight.

I made my way to the shop and unlocked the door. Devon wasn't in, and the lights were off. The node was still dead, too. Unease skittered down my spine as I made my way through to the living room. Devon wasn't in there, either. She'd gone.

I checked my phone. No messages. That wasn't usual at all.

They took her. Someone took her.

19

Dammit. Who had taken Devon captive? The Order, the mage survivors from the battle, or the Spirit Agents? The Order was most likely, but if they hadn't openly turned against the Death King yet, they'd outright deny it if I strode in there and demanded they give her back.

I needed backup.

As though conjured by my thoughts, a knock came from the door. I tensed, then went to answer, reaching for a cantrip as I did so.

Ryan held up their hands in surrender. "Whoa. I'm not here to attack you. I didn't want to leave you alone with so many people out to get you."

"I figured." I drew in a breath. "Devon is missing. I'm almost certain the Order has her, but I don't know if their coup has gone public yet. Cobb, though… he might have figured out I'd used one of his cantrips on the node and realised I saw him at the Order yesterday."

"Shit," they said. "Some of the fire mages might have

survived the battle if they got through the node in time. Maybe they're the ones who took her."

"The fire mages don't know Devon," I said. "The Order does—and Cobb threatened my friends and family already. Have you seen Trix?"

"No," they said. "Not recently. Maybe he's home in the Parallel. Do you want me to fetch him?"

"I'd prefer not to risk *his* life, either, but I don't think even the Death King can get me out of this one," I said. "Unless Devon's at the school reunion, which is where half the Order's staff will be tonight at any rate."

"Tonight?" they said. "Wait, you mean the academy?"

"Yeah," I said. "You went there?"

"I did, but you probably don't remember," they said. "I can't say I particularly like the idea of going to a reunion."

So we'd all been there at the same time, and yet we'd never crossed paths. Not that my memory would cooperate anyway. I was still missing too much.

"I doubt Devon's really there," I added. "She hated school as much as I did."

Ryan pressed their lips together. "Okay. I'll go with you to the Order... but the vampires are still looking for you."

"I figured," I said. "I notice they didn't give us a hand during the battle."

"Vamps aren't fans of fire," they said. "Liv... I'm sorry. And I think my master is, too."

I didn't meet their eyes. I couldn't think about what Davies had told me, not with Devon missing and the growing suspicion that the enemy had taken her as bait. If I'd challenged the Order yesterday, I might have avoided this... but let's be real, they'd never have taken any accusation lying down. Walking in without the Death King as backup wasn't appealing, either, but the reality was that he had less influence over the Order than I'd ever believed. I was on my own in this one.

"The node is still blocked," I said. "We'll have to use a different one."

Ryan and I made our way to the node down the street. As we walked, Ryan said, "I'll go back and fetch the others, but we need a meeting spot."

"The node near the Order will do, as long as nobody is waiting outside, but I don't think they will be," I said. "They'll all be on their way to get drunk at the school reunion."

Ryan went through the node first. I counted down from thirty seconds, then I stepped through and approached the Order's base.

Two unfamiliar guards stood outside the door when I walked up to them. "Hey. Have you seen Devon?"

"No," said the man on the right, who looked like he was part shifter. "What are you doing here? Aren't you supposed to be in the Parallel?"

Did everyone hear about the vampires? Surely not.

"The Death King sent me home from the contest early," I said. "Devon is missing. I want to speak to someone who can tell me where she is."

"She isn't here." He loomed over me. "You should go."

"I don't think so." I peered past him into the lobby, but I didn't even see anyone on the reception desk. Were most of the staff at the reunion? "I need to speak to Mrs Carlisle, head of the Retrieval Unit."

"She's not in." He looked me up and down. "Aren't you the one whose mind was addled by a spell?"

At one time, his words would have made me leave, contrite, but not this time. I shoved past him into the lobby, ignoring his look of outrage… and found the place deserted.

Deserted, aside from the sound of footsteps on the stairs. I backed towards the door to shout a warning to Ryan, but it was too late. Mr Cobb walked into the lobby, his footsteps echoing on the polished floor.

"So it *was* you," he said. "I take it you finished off those rebel fire mages?"

"With the Death King's help." I turned to the guards, who hadn't budged an inch. His allies, then. "Who the hell in the Order agreed to work with you? You had their people killed."

"Some here remain loyal to the original Order, despite everything these pretenders did to us." He trod along the polished floor towards me. "Others were easy to persuade. There are always some who are open to bribery, and others who see the futility of allowing the new Order to remain intact when its very foundations were built upon our destruction."

"You're talking about the spirit mages." My throat closed up. "But they didn't all die. The survivors are in the Court of the Dead, and yet you tried to kill their leader when he's as much of a victim as you are."

"Do you truly believe that?" he said. "To think you've allied yourself with someone who turned on his own… but I suppose you still don't remember your own history."

A hollow feeling formed inside me. *What more didn't they tell me?*

"Enough taunts," I said. "Tell me where Devon is. I swear, if you've hurt her—"

"I have no reason to harm your friend," he said. "I simply wanted her out of the way, and she gladly saw my reasoning. A school reunion is hardly torture."

"That's where you sent her?" Disbelief laced my tone. "Then what the hell are you doing here, waiting for the Order staff to come back so you can gloat in their faces?"

"Liv." Ryan pushed past the guards, who blocked their way with snarls of warning. Yelps followed when Ryan's magic levitated them into the air, and Dex flew into the building, pursued by two sprites.

"You're outnumbered, dickhead," he told Cobb.

Aria flew in behind him, along with the water sprite, and the three sprites circled Cobb. *He must be here for a reason. He couldn't have known I'd show up, with half the Parallel hunting me down.*

His eyes narrowed at Dex. "I beg to differ."

The elevator doors slid open and a number of people ran out into the lobby. All of them wore the same faded grey uniform. *They're prisoners.* Cobb had set them free.

Cobb gestured with one hand. "Take her."

The former prisoners swept through the lobby like a tide. A fair few ran for the exit, but others circled me, their eyes pale and their faces lined. *The Order took their magic. Like Cobb.*

Hands grabbed for me, and I reached for my cantrips and set one of them off, paralysing the nearest mages. Then I called on the power of the nearby node, and magic filled my veins and spilled out, crackling like an electric charge.

"Stop her!" Cobb snarled. "Don't kill her. I won't have her power wasted. Turn her off."

A cantrip snapped, and the ceiling lights sputtered and

died. At the same time, my own power went out like a light switch. I went rigid with shock, numb, unable to feel the power of the node in my veins any longer.

He turned off my magic. Those cantrips he'd stolen didn't just work on nodes.

Hands seized my shoulders. I fought every step of the way, but strong arms lifted me off the floor and propelled me across the lobby.

The elevator doors closed, and then we were travelling down, and further down, as though into the very centre of the earth.

The doors opened, revealing a corridor lit with fluorescent lighting, panelled in metallic silver. Cold concrete touched my feet and a familiar pressure hit my skull as they dragged me along and pushed me through a glass door into a room as cold as a refrigerator, containing only a metal table and several chairs. Not a cell... but shivers ran down my arms and the pressure on my skull worsened. This wasn't the first time I'd seen this room.

I'd sat here during my interrogation after Dirk Alban's death.

"This is a holding cell for spirit mages," said Cobb. "I was stripped of my magic in a similar room. No doubt you were held here, too, if you remember."

Two mages pushed me into a seat, and cuffs snapped into place over my wrists and ankles. "You want to strip out my magic, then?"

"Why waste a good thing?" He gestured to someone out of my line of sight. "Bring in the other one."

I struggled and squirmed but the chair held me captive. "You're living on borrowed time, Cobb. Keep telling yourself you have the upper hand. It'll only last until the people upstairs realise what's going on down here."

"There is nobody upstairs," he said. "The council were called out on an urgent meeting, and they assume everything they left behind is in working order. We have already seen to it that the Order is ready for taking."

That can't be. It can't be that easy. Yet if there'd been spirit mages in their forces all along, waiting for their chance to take back the power they believed they'd been denied… maybe it was.

"They won't allow this," I said. "The other Order branches will find out."

"Not before it's too late for them to do anything about it." He halted in front of the table, studying me. "They don't believe we're a threat. They made the same mistake with the Houses, and even with the Death King, when they punished all of them for the events of the war. Some of us refused to capitulate. We could have been allies, Olivia, if only Alban had trusted me enough to tell me he was training you as his successor."

His successor? "That wouldn't have changed the outcome. He's dead. And you're nothing."

His jaw tensed. "Not for long."

The door opened, and a second man was dragged in and deposited in the chair opposite mine. Cuffs snapped into place on his ankles and wrists. The two men who'd brought him in retreated, and the glass door slid closed.

Three of us remained… Cobb, me, and the stranger in the chair opposite. A man with tan skin, greying hair, wide eyes brimming with fear and pain.

Cobb moved behind his chair and held up a round,

gleaming soul amulet. Then, with a cold chill of certainty, I knew what he was going to do.

"Remove her soul," said Cobb, "and I will take her powers for my own. You know what will happen if you say no."

The spirit mage's eyes were wide, his hands bloody where he'd tried to free himself, but he was obviously as trapped as I was. Had he been the Order's prisoner, before Cobb had freed him?

Cobb smiled. "I would have preferred for Greyson to be the one to do this. It would be much more fitting. But it seems he is less loyal to you than he is to his own subjects. He hasn't even come to your rescue."

A chill rose to my skin as he released the cuffs on the spirit mage's hands, lifted his arms onto the cold metal table, and pressed the round shape of a soul amulet into his palm.

"It shouldn't take long," he said. "You won't feel a thing, Olivia."

He took the spirit mage's free hand and pressed it to my shoulder. At once, coldness washed over me like an icy wave, and I found myself dragged out of my body as the soul amulet called me, drawing me into its embrace.

No.

I dug my heels in and resisted with all the strength I possessed. The spirit mage tugged harder, sweat standing out on his face, but I refused to give in.

"If you fail," Cobb said to him, "you die, and I'll find someone else to do it. It shouldn't be too hard."

Once my soul was in that amulet, it was game over, but the spirit mage would pay with his life if he failed. I needed to stall, but he'd switched off my spirit magic, and my allies were trapped upstairs, surrounded by an army.

The spirit mage's cold touch brushed against me, and a stream of energy appeared, connecting us. Chilled magic filled me, and my eyes widened. He wasn't draining me. He was throwing me a lifeline.

This time, when I floated free of my body, I let myself be tugged towards the amulet. Then I spun around, as I'd done when the Death King and I had fought the liches, and thrust my own palm into Cobb's chest.

Powerless I might be, but I had a damn sight more than Cobb did. Energy flowed from him to me, and his outraged exclamation was lost in the humming sound of the fluorescent lights dying.

Backup had arrived.

"Liv!" yelled a voice from outside the room.

Dex. I reached for his warmth and the sparks of his fire magic appeared in my own hands. The spirit mage let go of the amulet, and when Cobb whirled on him, I directed the fire at his own feet.

His yell of pain was music to my ears.

I floated back into my body, as the other spirit mage leapt from his seat. With his free hands, he reached for one of the unused chairs and hurled it across the room at two former prisoners, who backed out through the glass doors. The spirit mage hobbled across the room and grabbed a key the guard had dropped, using it to free my wrists.

"Thanks." I took the key from him and undid the cuffs on my ankles, handing him back the key so he could do the same. Outside the room, the sprites flew around the corridor, distracting the former prisoners.

Cobb flew at me with a roar of fury, but Dex's power was still in my hands, and a jolt of fire blasted from my palms. I shoved him into the chair, and the cuffs snapped into place once again.

"You won't survive this!" he bellowed, fighting against the restraints.

"You don't have the Death King's soul this time around," I told him. "Now, tell me. What did you do with Devon?"

"Her?" he said. "I told you the truth. She's at the reunion. Perhaps she'll still be alive when you get there."

Shit. He must have sent more of his allies to the reunion—where most of the Order's employees were, their guard down and their weapons left behind.

The spirit mage and I left the room and shut the door on Cobb, finding the corridor almost deserted. So much for loyalty. It seemed most of the prisoners had made a run for it while they had the chance. I reached the elevator first and caught my breath as we rose towards the lobby.

"How'd they get you?" I asked the other mage. "Were you in the jail?"

"Not for long," he said. "I was with the Spirit Agents, and the Order caught me when I was on a mission here on Earth. I'm Sean. You're Liv Cartwright, aren't you?"

"That's me," I said. "Word of warning: there might be more enemies upstairs. Cobb freed all the Order's prisoners."

"Fool," he said. "Some of them were locked up for good reason. I'll try to hold them off. You should warn the other Order members. I take it you know where they are?"

"Unfortunately." The elevator ground to a halt and the doors slid open. I walked out, to find Ryan standing over the bodies of several fallen prisoners. The sprites flew out behind me, and Dex soared across the lobby with a loud whooping noise.

Ryan looked up. "Where's Devon?"

"At the school reunion, apparently," I said. "Along with more of his allies."

Cobb's imprisonment downstairs wouldn't last forever, but that room was more secure than anywhere else right now. Enough to hold him until I got to Devon and the others.

I just hoped I wasn't too late.

The spirit mage and I parted ways outside the Order. I had a million questions I wanted to ask him, but finding Devon and warning everyone at the reunion had to come first.

"Thanks for saving my neck back there," he said.

"Likewise," I said. "Will you be okay? The Spirit Agents… you know how to get to them, right?"

"I know where they are," he said. 'Thank you."

He took off for the node, while I noted Ryan's raised eyebrows.

"He's one of the Order's spirit mage prisoners," I explained. "Cobb tried to force him to strip out my soul, but it backfired. The other prisoners, though—they ran off."

"They're the least of the Order's problems." Ryan looked up and down the street. "What did you do with Cobb?"

"Cuffed him to a chair in the Order's dungeon," I said. "I can't be in two places at once, and he saw to it that everyone who might be an ally isn't there at the Order's base. Something about an emergency council meeting. As for the reunion, I'm almost certain it's a trap, but I need to get Devon away from them."

"I'm more concerned the vampires will catch up to you," said Ryan. "Do you want to go ahead to the reunion alone? I can find Trix and the other Elemental Soldiers and be ready to fight, if Cobb's people make a move."

"And me?" Dex said. "I want to meet all your ex-classmates."

"Feel free to come, but don't even think about setting anything on fire," I said. "Unless I tell you to, that is."

In other words, if Cobb or his people made an appearance again. The odds of that happening were much higher than I'd like, given his comments about Devon.

Ryan glanced over their shoulder. "I can find my master, but the Order—"

"I know they have a hold over him," I said. "I should have guessed. And I know I shouldn't have yelled at him, but I'll apologise later, if I get out of there alive. I doubt the Order will believe me about Cobb unless I can get someone with authority to vouch for me. Someone who isn't locked in a cell after attempting to rip out my soul."

Dex snorted. "If you ask me, he was bluffing. The worst that can happen is that Big-Toothed Dave asks you out."

"His name is Gap-Toothed Dave, and I hope he doesn't, given that he's engaged." An entirely different kind of dread gripped me at the thought of walking into the school reunion dressed in the Death King's armour and covered in swamp water and mud, but what choice did I have?

Dex flew alongside me as I walked towards the hotel hosting the event. The thump of old-school nightclub music pounded in the air, while smokers in skimpy dresses and smart suits mingled outside the doors. Yes, I was definitely going to draw attention, but I had my Order ID on me even if I wasn't exactly dressed up for a special occasion.

The guards on the doors looked at the black mark, then at my face. "Olivia Cartwright."

"That's me." I put on a false smile, biting my tongue so as to avoid asking why there was more security here than at the Order's base.

The guard eyed my muddy boots and tutted. "Go in, then."

Dex perched on my shoulder as I walked through the doors. "What a bunch of snobs."

"Better not say that to their faces."

I scanned the crowd. Most were people I only vaguely recognised. Practitioners, for the most part, as mages rarely stuck around long enough to graduate. I side-stepped a group of ex-students, suppressing the urge to shout out that Cobb had tricked everyone into letting him escape and now he had the run of the Order's headquarters while they were drinking champagne. Not that it would do me any good if I did. Short of bringing the man himself with me, I had no proof to speak of.

Dex whispered in my ear, "There she is."

I spotted Devon talking to Judith French of all people, who wore a red dress which would have looked lovely if her expression didn't give the impression that a dog had crapped on her shoes. Gritting my teeth, I made my way over.

"Hey," I said to Devon.

"Oh, it's you," said Judith, in tones that suggested I was a slug someone had left on the dance floor. "What's that outfit supposed to be?"

"I'm surprised you're not taking advantage of everyone's absence to gain favour with Cobb." The words escaped before I could reel them in.

Shock blanked out her disdainful expression. "Cobb?"

Okay. She's not involved. But someone here must be, and there was no way to tell from outward appearances. "Cobb tried to take over the Order while everyone was here. I locked him up for you. You're welcome."

"You're lying," she said. "You have a really sick sense of humour, you know that?"

"Feel free to believe whatever you like." I inched closer to Devon, giving her a *what the hell?* look. I'd thought she'd rather deal with a marathon session of paperwork than show up here.

Judith turned away from me, muttering something uncomplimentary under her breath, and left.

Devon shook her head. "Please tell me that was just a joke so you could get rid of her."

"I wish I could say it was," I murmured. "But someone ensured only Cobb's allies remained at the Order. He let the prisoners out, too."

"Olivia Cartwright?" said Mrs Carlisle, halting behind Devon.

Hoping she hadn't heard me, I fixed on a smile. "That's me. I'm surprised so many people showed up."

"Yes, even Greyson is here."

My heart skipped a beat. "Who?"

"Greyson Beaumont," she said. "You know him by a different name."

The Death King stood by the doors, his human face on and his usual dark cloak and armoured clothing replaced by something that resembled a tuxedo. My mouth fell open. *What is he doing?*

Devon's nails dug into my arm. "The fuck?"

Mrs Carlisle stepped past me. "Try to behave, won't you, Olivia?"

I didn't answer. I could think of a dozen more important things the Death King might be doing rather than walking through a gawking crowd of our former classmates.

"I'll see what he's doing here," I murmured to Devon, then I wove through the crowd towards the Death King.

For a heartbeat I wondered if he'd pretend not to recognise me, but maybe he suspected I'd throw a glass of champagne in his face if he did.

"What are you doing?" I hissed. "Whatever happened to the Fire Element contest?"

"I sent the remaining contenders home," he said. "The contest is over, and the winner has been selected. I thought I might find you here."

"What about Lord Blackbourne and the vampires?" I spoke in a low voice, conscious of several nearby heads turning in our direction, and others leaning to whisper to one another. "Are they still looking for me?"

"This doesn't seem like their scene." His arm came around my shoulder and I startled, then several cameras flashed. Laughter sounded.

Heat swept up my neck. Someone had taken a photo of me with the King of the Dead when I looked like I'd come back from comic con via an outdoor mosh pit. And I'd thought nearly having my soul ripped out would be the worst part of my night. I wished I could pull off the Death King's trick and vanish on the spot.

"Do people not know you're dead?" I whispered. "What planet have they been on?"

"Earth."

"Hilarious." Under normal circumstances, I might have reacted differently to him making a joke, but I would have happily traded anything I owned to make the rest of the crowd disappear so I could get a straight answer from him. "I need to talk to you alone."

Whispers trailed us across the room, but I hardly noticed or cared. As we neared a corner with fewer people standing in it, I leaned closer to him.

"Cobb is locked in a spare room in the Order's dungeon," I whispered. "He freed every one of their prisoners, and half the Order answers to him."

"I'm aware of your dilemma," he said, his own voice equally quiet. "I'm also aware that there are several assassins concealed among the guests in this very room."

Shit.

I spun around to look for Devon. Then the ceiling lights went out, and the music ended with a sputter and crash. Exclamations rose from among the crowd, while Dex landed on my shoulder. "What's happening?"

"Assassins." Then I shouted, "Everyone out! Now!"

Screams broke out, and the guests surged towards the doors. I looked around for Devon, but the crowd was too thick.

"I warned them of a potential attack," the Death King said, "but they refused to listen."

My mouth parted. I didn't doubt he spoke the truth. His standing with the Order had unravelled, layer by layer, until nothing more remained but Greyson Beaumont, ex-academy student and ally of the dangerous spirit mage, Olivia Cartwright. The Order trusted him no more than they trusted me.

I spotted Devon making her way through the crowd and squeezed past a group of panicking graduates to her side.

"Are you okay?" she said.

"Yes—and no. We have to get out—"

Orange flames flashed in front of the doors, and a fresh wave of screaming swept the crowd. *Crap.* The survivors from the battle must have come straight here.

The crowd parted as Sledge walked through, surrounded by a rising inferno. *And he has his cantrip back. Just great.*

He pointed a hand, and the inferno swept towards us. Skin and clothes caught aflame, the stench of burning flesh made me gag—and the three of us vanished at the same instant.

I staggered, reeling, on the swampy floor outside the castle. Devon landed at a crouch, screaming in pain. Her hands were burned red-raw.

"Shit!" I grabbed for my cantrips, but I didn't know if a simple healing spell could undo that kind of damage.

"Bring her with you—quickly," ordered the Death King.

I helped Devon to her feet as the Elemental Soldiers moved towards us. With their help, Devon and I made our way through the castle's back door and into the break room. Devon collapsed onto the sofa with a whimper, and

I took a cantrip from my pouch and used it on her hands. The burn marks faded a little and she slumped against the cushions, tears streaming from her eyes.

"This should help with the pain." Ryan came over with another cantrip. "How did Sledge get out of the jail?"

"He sneaked out when we were fighting the fire mages," Felicity said from beside the door. "He must have had another cantrip."

"Or someone helped him," I muttered, thinking of the other fire mages who'd fled the castle to pick a fight with the Order. How many people had been killed in the attack? "The Order might blame us for this. They'll see the fire and assume the mages are to blame."

"There are already rumours about a gas explosion," said Ryan. "That's usually what they run with in the event of a fire mage's magic gone awry."

"Why'd they attack the Order?" Felicity looked between us. "What the hell is going on over there?"

"Cobb," I said. "He used the reunion to cover up an attempted coup and sent the fire mages to attack the guards while they were off-duty. I locked him in the Order's dungeon, but he already freed his friends. Maybe I should have brought him here instead.

"If you hadn't gone to the reunion, your friend would be dead," said the Death King. "I would go and fetch Cobb myself, but I would rather he wasn't imprisoned here in my castle."

At least I'd made one good call by leaving him behind, considering Cobb's first target would be the hall of souls.

Devon groaned, stirring. "Ow… my hands…"

Even after I'd used the cantrips, the burns were still red raw. Powerful fire mage magic like Sledge's might have permanent effects, and if she was unlucky, she might never be able to make cantrips again. And I'd already lost my job at the Order. Even if we survived this, how could we move on?

Cal ran into the room. "Someone is at the gates."

I turned away from the sofa. "Who?"

"I'm taking a wild guess that it isn't an ally," said Ryan grimly.

"I'll handle them," said the Death King. "You three—stay alert. There might be more fire mages hiding in the swamp."

Instinct told me to stay beside Devon, but a more pragmatic voice in my mind told me that the person at the gates was most likely one of the vampires, and that I'd be better off giving myself up to Lord Blackbourne than letting anyone else take the fall.

The Death King and I reached the gates, where the liches on guard duty parted to allow us to see the visitor.

"It's me," said Brant.

The Death King *moved*. In a heartbeat, he had Brant by the throat, a stream of energy connecting the two of them. Brant struggled and kicked out feebly.

"Wait!" I said. "Look, now is not the time to be strangling our allies."

"This man is no ally of yours." He flung Brant across the swampland, where he sprawled on his back in the mud. "He's here for a favour, or to beg for shelter again."

I looked at Brant. "Tell me you aren't here to steal anyone's soul."

"I'm not," he said. "There are some horrific reports coming in from the Order. Something about an explosion at the reunion?"

"Your fire mage friends," I said. "Working with Cobb. I locked him up again after he tried to rip out my soul. He set you free, too, didn't he? You might have warned me."

"I didn't know he'd stay at the Order," he insisted. "I thought he was coming here. Besides, Cobb isn't the one you should be worrying about."

He rose to his feet, and this time, I was the one who grabbed his life essence. "Tell me who it is, then."

"I don't—I can't." He leaned back, eyes bulging at the sight of the energy current connecting the pair of us.

"Then you're going to help us find them." I clenched my hand over his life force. "Davies is already dead, and if you don't help us find your allies, you'll be next."

Behind him, the node outside the gates lit up from within. The Death King glided in that direction, and I braced myself for a fight.

A vampire emerged from the current of energy, hardly a hair out of place.

"There you two are," said Lord Blackbourne. "I hear you're wanted by the Order, Olivia. And I see you have Mr Edwards with you, too."

I didn't move. "If you want someone to blame, then look for Cobb. His allies took over the Order. I locked him in the Order's dungeon, if you want to find him."

"I heard about the attack at the reunion," he said. "However, you cannot possibly expect me to believe the Order—which endured the spirit war and was instrumental in bringing down the perpetrators—would fall so easily."

"They've been taken over from the inside," I said. "And there have always been people wanting to reverse the decision made at the end of the war. Dirk Alban…"

"I seem to remember you were involved in his scheme yourself," said the vampire lord. "Is this a confession?"

The Death King stepped up to him. "I would prefer not to have to set my guards upon you, Lord Blackbourne. I have already told you my opinion on Olivia's innocence—"

"She's as innocent as you are," he said, "which is to say —not at all. This deception is frankly tiresome to watch, and does you no favours, Grey."

Anger flashed across the Death King's face. "Believe it or not, the Order stands poised to fall, and if anything, you should be seeking new allies, not alienating them."

"That is why I am asking you for these two individuals," he said. "Edwards and Cartwright are wanted for questioning for their involvement in the deaths of two of my allies. If they're innocent, they can tell me in person."

"Oh, for the Elements' sakes," I snapped. "A bunch of rogues from the House of Fire killed your allies. The same people which formed an alliance with Cobb."

Brant stepped forwards. "You can take me with you, but leave her out of this."

"Very well." Two vampires stepped in behind their leader, seized him, and vanished into the node.

"Hey!" I advanced on Lord Blackbourne. "Cut that shit out. Brant wasn't the one who killed your people. You must know that. He's—"

"A former inmate of the House of Fire," interjected Lord Blackbourne. "If you wish to speak for him, come with me."

The Death King spoke in a low, deadly voice. "I wouldn't."

A chill raced down my back. Devon lay injured in the

castle, but there was nothing more I could do for her. Brant, on the other hand, was on the cusp of being sentenced to death, and the vampires might be the only allies I had left outside of the Court of the Dead.

I needed them on my side.

I met his eyes. "I want to make a bargain of my own."

"A bargain?" The vampire's teeth flashed as he smiled. "Enlighten me."

"I'll go with you, if you promise not to declare war on the Court of the Dead," I said. "We have a common enemy, one who's bound to strike you next. If you want my help, don't attack my allies."

"In that case," said Lord Blackbourne, "I'd like to invite you to come with me."

He took my arm, and an instant later, we passed through the node and emerged in front of the vampires' council house. Brant was nowhere to be seen. Locked up, no doubt. I warily followed Lord Blackbourne into the red-carpeted hallway. As usual, old-fashioned lanterns lit the way into a wood-panelled room filled with plush red chairs and a long wooden table.

Lord Blackbourne walked into the room and indicated for me to follow. Not a cell. Good start, then.

"I'm glad you saw things my way, Olivia," he said. "Greyson can be stubborn, but he must understand that your life isn't worth the safety of his people."

"You're looking at the wrong enemy," I said evenly. "The Order has been attacked from within. I didn't believe it at first either, but Cobb freed every one of their prisoners and sent his allies to attack the school reunion. The Order's staff need to be warned, but they wouldn't take my word as proof."

"A dilemma we have faced ourselves, recently, with the Crow case," he said. "I have to confess that it was rather difficult to believe one of our own was once a spirit mage."

"Not to me," I said. 'It didn't take me that long to conclude it was a vampire pulling the strings."

"The Crow was never a mastermind," he said. "He was a follower, despite his ambitions, just like Cobb."

"Speaking of Cobb, he's only going to be in jail for as long as it takes his allies to realise that he's down there and send someone to set him free, which isn't long enough for my liking." I reached into my pocket and pulled out the empty soul amulet. "Cobb had a spirit mage he freed from jail and he was going to put my soul in this. He'd have succeeded if the spirit mage hadn't helped me instead and my sprite hadn't shown up."

"Your sprite?" he said. "I have to admit, I'm surprised that talent came back to you first, given everything you've forgotten."

"What's your point?" I said. "I'm getting a little tired of everyone dancing around the truth. Is it because spirit mages had some kind of affinity with sprites?"

"Yes," he said, "but you must know you have been connected to this scheme from its inception."

I narrowed my eyes at him. "And why is that?"

"Because you killed Dirk Alban," said Lord Blackbourne. "And Greyson Beaumont helped you do it."

21

I stared at the vampire lord. "You have got to be joking. I killed him? Wouldn't Cobb or one of the others have hunted me down for it if I had?"

But I had his blood on my hands. Or someone's blood.

"I doubt anyone told Cobb," he said. "I'm reasonably confident that he wasn't present at the time of Alban's death, though I don't doubt he blamed you for the loss of his own magic... hence his attempt to take it for his own."

I lowered the soul amulet, returning it to the pouch at my waist. "If you aren't sure, then how in hell do you know I tried to kill Dirk Alban? The Order wouldn't have spared my life if I had."

They would have arrested or killed my former mentor if he'd survived, but now I didn't know what to think. For all I knew, my dreams might have held a kernel of truth. Perhaps I truly had ripped out Dirk Alban's soul.

"I can't speak for the Order," he said. "You *were* young and easily led, and perhaps they thought you regretted allying with Alban, so they sought to right both wrongs at once and erase your memories."

My hands fisted. "How do you know? You weren't there."

"Would that I had been," he said. "The only surviving witness is yourself, and your memories alone conceal the truth of that fateful day."

"You can't bring back memories that the Order took away, so don't bother lying to me," I said in brittle tones. "Besides, what's the point in any of this? Why'd you bring me here, except to taunt me about my missing memories?"

"Because the truth of what we are up against lies in those memories," he said. "You're starting to remember, aren't you? Greyson said you often saw visions of your past during near-death moments."

"I thought you and the Death King were at cross-purposes at the moment," I said. "You mean to say you've been meeting up to gossip about me behind my back?"

"Our last meeting was before the regretful murder of our emissaries," he said. "After that, I realised we needed you in custody. You're too ignorant of what you can do."

"And whose fault is that?" I said. "The Order—who, I reiterate, are on the brink of being taken over by spirit mages hell-bent on domination. Won't that cause a major shakeup of your arrangement? They might even come for your territory, too. I wouldn't put it past them. Cobb already tried to take down the Death King."

"If you hadn't stopped him," he said "It is true that we owe you a debt... though it took me some time to work out how to repay it. I think your memories will be a good place to start."

"If you're saying you can bring them back—"

"There was a video recording of your trial which I think you'll find fairly enlightening," he said. "Greyson told me he thinks you might be in need of another reminder to trigger your buried memories."

"How did you get that?" Disbelief bled into my tone. "Electricity barely even works here. Besides, why would the Order record the trial?"

The vampires were loaded, though, and they had connections on the surface which would enable them to get anything they needed, if they wanted to.

Not only that, they'd been discussing my deepest secrets with the Death King without him breathing a word to me. Yet I didn't have the energy left to burn on hating a man who'd been faced with an impossible choice the same way I had.

And, if Lord Blackbourne was telling the truth, we'd been in this together from the start.

Lord Blackbourne reached under the desk and pulled a laptop from its case, which he deposited in front of me. As it loaded up, an image filled the screen, showing my own face. At seventeen, I'd had longer hair, and sat with my head bowed. I didn't look at the camera.

A chill wafted down my spine, and my whole body locked to the spot as a long-buried instinct urged me to flee.

"Do you deny using spirit magic?" said a low, masculine voice.

"No," said the teenage Olivia.

"You were found beside the body of a dead man," he said. "Did you kill him?"

"No," said the girl on the screen.

No. I denied it. But was I telling the truth? I didn't remember, even now.

"You will be spared death, on one condition," he said. "Your memories of learning spirit magic will be stripped from you and you will be placed under surveillance for the remainder of your time at the academy."

"Okay," whispered the girl.

Dread seeped through my bones. Then, darkness filtered in, and the world disappeared, to be replaced by a bloody wall made of cold metal. Unbearable brightness shone in front of me. A voice murmured in my ear: *"Let him go."*

Someone was talking to me, but I couldn't see the speaker. The brightness in front of me grew until I couldn't see anything at all, and I was aware that I was falling… falling…

"Liv. Liv, are you okay? Can you hear me?"

That voice again…

My eyes flew open to find myself leaning against the table in Lord Blackbourne's room. I jumped to my feet, shaking all over. "What the hell did you do to me?"

"Nothing," he said. "Whatever you saw was triggered by the video of your trial. It's not uncommon for that effect to come from reminders of the moment when your history was erased. After all, your memories of the trial weren't taken. I assume you blocked them out yourself. So… what did you remember?"

I shook my head. "Nothing that made sense. Voices… I recognised them, but not who they belonged to."

"You didn't see Alban before his death, then?" he asked.

"I didn't see anything except… blood. And—I was holding someone's soul, in my hands."

"Alban's soul?"

I don't know. Cold sweat coated my body. Once, I'd have said there was *no way* I'd ripped out someone's soul in cold blood, even someone like Dirk Alban. Even a murderer. But now?

"If I killed him, he deserved it." I raised my head. "Why does it matter so much to you? It was over a decade ago that he died."

"Because it is Dirk Alban whose ideas have inspired the current uprising within the Order," he said. "The cantrips the Crow was making were one of his ideas, too. If Cobb and the others lay their hands on the very instruments that started the spirit war, they could do a great deal of damage."

"Then you think Alban told me his plan," I said slowly. "Before he died."

Because he was training me to be his successor. Even the vampires had known.

"You, Olivia, might be the only person with insight into Alban's strategy," said Lord Blackbourne. "The Order likely knew it, too, and they assumed erasing your memories would also erase the risk. Unfortunately, it seems his ideas were spread through other means, and we have yet to capture a living victim to question."

"The two assassins committed suicide," I said. "The ambassadors... did you send them to spy on the Order?"

He inclined his head. "I hoped they might gain useful information from the fire mage, but I doubt he knows anything of import, either. The enemy would have disposed of him already if he did."

Unfortunately, I suspected he might be right. "He's a pawn. Like I was. Look, I believe you, but my friend is in serious danger, my family is under threat—and what did you do with Brant?"

"He's safer than he would be if the Order still had him," he said. "Without his magic, he's not much use to anyone."

My chest tightened. Remembering the Order's rooms brought me out in chills, especially given my more recent narrow escape. "You're right. He's not. I know he fought on the wrong side, but I don't think he deserves to die."

"You wish to make another bargain?" he said.

"Sure, why not." Recklessness seized me. "If you spare Brant, what would you want in return?"

"When you remember the information Alban told you before his death, you will tell us right away."

"You seem certain I'll remember." But he'd offered me a way out, and I trusted Lord Blackbourne to keep his word. Certainly more than the Order. "I'll do my best, but I can't make any promises."

Firstly, I needed to see to Devon's safety, and ensured Cobb returned to jail where he belonged. Which meant returning to the Order.

Lord Blackbourne glided across the room and opened the door. "Think very carefully, Olivia. There are more forces at play than you know."

"Or so people keep telling me." I stepped out into the hallway. "Thank you for sparing Brant. And I'm sorry about your ambassadors."

I walked through the corridor, feeling more alone than I ever had in my life. While part of me wanted to check up on Brant, a far more significant part wished I hadn't left Devon and the Death King alone when some of Cobb's allies were still at large and the Order was in disarray. The vampires might be our allies, but they'd leave the Death

King to fight his own battles alone unless something was in it for them. Besides, I'd wrangled enough favours from Lord Blackbourne already.

A knife soared towards me. I called on my spirit magic and deflected it, as the door to the council house burst open.

"You're under attack!" I shouted.

Two assassins circled me, faces masked, knives in their hands. I called on the node's power and blasted the weapons from their hands, as the vampire emerged from the council house with two allies in tow.

One of the attackers spat at Lord Blackbourne's feet. "This is for the Crow."

A vampire glided behind him and snapped his neck, but two more assassins ran in to take his place. I turned towards the node, alarm flaring inside me. If the enemy was here, they might well be attacking the Court of the Dead, too.

I wouldn't let Devon get hurt again. Lord Blackbourne might be pissed at me for abandoning him in a time of crisis, but what choice did I have? The vampires had numbers on their side, but if the enemy liches had come back—the Court of the Dead couldn't fall. I wouldn't let it.

I wouldn't let the Death King perish before I learned everything else he'd kept from me.

22

I ran out of the street and into the town square, past the Citadel of the Elements. Lord Blackbourne's words pounded in my skull. *You killed Dirk Alban, and Greyson Beaumont helped you do it.*

I skidded to a halt in the mouth of a side street, where two more assassins waited. Magic blasted from my hands, knocking them backwards, while bolts of fire shot over the rooftops. More fire mages?

Then Dex flew up to me, his hands sparking. "Can you go five minutes without someone trying to kill you?"

"Apparently not." Relief swept over me as Ryan and Trix walked towards me, accompanied by the other two sprites.

"The vamps let you go?" asked Ryan.

"Yeah, but the assassins came a moment later." I indicated the bodies on the ground and the flashes of fire spreading throughout the streets. "I bet they're on their way to the Court of the Dead next."

"They're coming from the citadel," said Trix.

"Um… what?" I turned that way, and to my utter astonishment, Bria emerged from the front door with a crowd of other mages behind her. "Oh, *shit.*"

"Liv?" Bria approached us, her hands blazing with fire.

"I guess you saved me the bother of coming to find you." I called the node's power to my hands and fired it at her, forcing her to dodge.

"Wait!" She ducked and rolled to her feet. "I'm on your side."

"A likely story." I used my spirit magic to knock the nearest attacker down, while Trix intercepted two assassins making their way from a side street.

Ryan's magic raised two more assassins into the air and flung them into Bria's path. Flames continued to spiral from the hands of the fire mages, but we must have taken a big chunk of their number out in the earlier battles.

I, meanwhile, made for the node, which glowed like a beacon against the darkening sky. The node brimmed with energy, and as I approached, several figures rose from within, their hands glowing. Spirit mages. *Are they with the Spirit Agents?*

The spirit mages circled the node, and one moved to stand in the centre of their group. A tall man with longish dark hair and deep-set eyes in a face lined with the merest trace of wrinkles.

"Causing trouble again, Olivia?" he said.

"Who are you?" I said. "Another dickhead from my past?"

"Not your distant past," he said. "You should know me, though, if you think about it."

His voice carried a resonance I found creepily familiar… the chill baritone of a lich.

No way.

Recognition hit me. The last time I'd seen this dude, he *was* a lich. Specifically, Hawker, the first lich who'd betrayed the Death King. Yet he looked human, even more so than the Death King did when he was masquerading as a living person. He wasn't wearing a mask or an illusion. He was alive and as solid as I was, judging by the knife he gripped in his free hand.

"I thought you were cursed." I stood my ground, my heart plummeting. "I thought the Crow's cantrips turned out to be fatal. They killed everyone who tried to use them. Besides, I destroyed his supplies when I blew up his house."

"You only destroyed some of them," he said. "It took many sacrifices, and much pain, but I am the first of my kind to walk in the light again."

No wonder I didn't recognise any of his allies. They were *liches*, or they had been. This time, they weren't decaying or falling to pieces. Or so it seemed.

"If you're using cantrips, don't they have a time limit?" I said. "Before bits start falling off you, I mean? The Crow had the best of them and even he fell apart in the end."

Though admittedly, he'd died because Brant had given him his own dud cantrip. Had one of his experiments really worked after all?

"The Crow was trying to do something extraordinary," said Hawker. "He was trying to reverse life and death… to make it possible for those of us from the House of Spirit to walk in the light again. And now we have succeeded in that goal."

I'd bet this was what the vampires had hoped I'd remember, or part of it, anyway. But it was too late now. Lord Blackbourne and his people would be lucky to survive, and in the end, the Crow's death hadn't stopped his goal's completion.

"Then what do you want with me?" I said. "Because I'm already alive. Unless you want to reverse that and stick my soul in an amulet like Cobb did, but that guy is a waste of space. He couldn't even manage to hang onto the soul he risked his life to steal."

"Cobb is irrelevant," said Hawker. "Those of us bound to the House of Spirit have suffered far more than he ever has, though we needed his help to take back the Order. I, meanwhile, intend to take back both realms for our own."

You're out of your mind. But he'd already lured away a fair few of the Death King's peers with the promise of returning them to the life they would have lived if not for the curse. Worse, it seemed at least some of the spirit mages were just as power hungry as the Order had always claimed as justification for their punishments after the war.

And that meant Dirk Alban had believed the same. *I guess I tried to kill him for a reason, huh.*

"You still haven't said whether you want me dead or alive," I said. "I have to admit I'm getting a bit pissed off at being left out. How do you know I won't make a willing ally?"

"You already chose Greyson's side over ours," he said. "Greyson, who trapped us, who punished his own kind, and bound us under his rule. Now his people will flock to my side when they see what I have accomplished."

"What, being a selfish bastard who's left a trail of dead

behind you?" I ignored the mutters from the other spirit mages, who'd spread out as though waiting for orders. "You don't have much of an army, either. Guess those cantrips need some fine-tuning."

He couldn't have an infinite number of cantrips at the ready, and they'd only work on one person at a time. Which made his army limited, at least in terms of living spirit mages. A dozen of them could give me one hell of a headache, but not if I brought backup. I couldn't think of anything better to do than to stall for time until the other liches showed up. Before they destroyed the Death King for good.

"You have no respect," he said. "You'd have been safer if you'd allowed Cobb to bind your soul to his. He has an incentive to keep you alive. I don't."

His hands glowed, as did his allies', and a torrent of energy surged towards me. I jumped backwards a heartbeat before it made contact, but the momentum nearly made me lose my balance. He might be alive again, but he was back in full possession of all his powers as a spirit mage. Like the others. No wonder they'd been able to amass a fighting force so quickly.

He advanced on me, away from the node, with several other mages forming a shield around him.

"Too cowardly to fight alone?" I said.

"Greyson uses this strategy himself," he responded. "He sees himself as the saviour of our House, as though he didn't condemn us to an eternity of suffering. As though he doesn't let his people lay down their lives for him. As though he didn't abandon you to the vampires."

"You're wrong." The Death King had annoyed the shit out of me for so long, but I didn't believe for a minute he'd let his people sacrifice their lives for him. "I chose to go to the vampires of my own free will. Just like you chose to abandon the man who stuck his neck out for you when half the Order would have seen you destroyed."

I reached for his life force, only to fetch up against a barrier. A shimmering current of light surrounded him like an invisible shield, fuelled by the energy flooding from the other mages. *So that's why he has them stand so close.*

He raised a palm, as did the other mages. Four currents of light collided with his own, and the combined attack sent me flying into the nearest wall. Hard brick cracked against my spine, and I bit back a scream.

He's strong. He's far too strong. The guy was just like the Death King himself—an enemy I shouldn't be engaging with without backup, let alone with four other fighters lending him their strength.

My back aching, I bolted into the street into the main square, which was still thick with fighting. Assassins fought mages—*spirit* mages. Hands aglow, they stepped out of the citadel and engaged the assassins in battle.

Wait a moment. They were the Spirit Agents. *Please say they're on my side.*

As Miles strode to the front of the group, Hawker and his allies turned on the new arrivals. "You again? I thought you were dead."

"Guess again," said Miles.

Bolts of energy flew left and right, and I got in a few hits of my own, knocking one of Hawker's allies off his feet. Yet I couldn't get near the man himself, not as long as he remained hidden behind a shield of other mages.

The bloody hypocrite. He has some nerve criticising the Death King's methods and then using his allies as pawns.

Bria ran among the Spirit Agents and fired off a blast of fire, knocking one of the assassins over.

"Hey!" I shouted at her. "Whose side are you even on?"

"Not theirs," she said.

"You tried to kill the Death King."

"We came to an understanding."

"You did *what?*" But it seemed she'd brought the Spirit Agents through the citadel of all places. Had they been hiding in there all along?

Before I could ask what she was playing at, twin bursts of energy collided overhead, forcing me to duck. Nearby, Sean was locked into a battle with one of the other spirit mages. He must have run straight to the Spirit Agents after his escape from the Order. He caught my eye and nodded, and the enemy thrust a palm into his chest, drawing out his life force.

I ran up to the attacker and shoved him off Sean, grabbing the current of energy in my hand. The enemy squirmed free an instant later, but breaking the connection gave the other spirit mage the chance to get back on his feet.

"Thanks," he gasped out. "Liv… you have to stop him."

Easier said than done. But I had to take down Hawker before he broke into the Death King's castle and destroyed him—or used one of those cantrips to bring *him* back to life only to give him a permanent death.

But what if that's what he wanted?

If the Death King got hold of Hawker's cantrips, he'd be able to break the curse and his people would be free. The curse would be over. Yet in the process, they'd lose the protection inherent in being liches. It wasn't up to me to make that choice for them, but it sure as hell wasn't up to Hawker. And if I let him and his allies continue, they would finish what Dirk Alban had started and bring about the deaths of everyone I cared about.

Hawker and his four spirit mages advanced through the crowd, blasting aside anyone who challenged him. Sean moved in behind me, beckoning to another spirit mage, and two others moved in front. Their hands glowed, forming a shield around me.

Surprise jolted to my core. They were imitating the positions of Hawker's followers and loaning their power to me. This must be a spirit mage fighting formation for a reason, and sure enough, I felt the bolstering strength of four separate currents of energy as I aimed an attack straight at Hawker.

He spun around, and our twin currents of light collided. Our shielding mages faltered one by one until just the two of us remained.

Hawker's eyes narrowed. "You can't beat me using spirit magic alone, Olivia."

No. I couldn't. I reached into my pouch, but instead of a cantrip, I found myself holding the soul amulet Cobb had tried to use on me. Inspiration struck.

Time to find out if I was spirit mage enough to pull this off. Hawker had no shield left. I wouldn't have a better chance.

I gripped the soul amulet in my palm as I advanced on him, calling magic into my hand. He did likewise, and we circled one another.

Then I reached up and grabbed for his soul. Energy

slid into my hand and I tugged, hard, but my grip slipped before I could grasp it.

Guess I'm not strong enough yet after all.

Then another hand joined mine, and a dark presence stepped to my side, cloaked in shadow.

The Death King had arrived.

23

The King of the Dead joined me against Hawker. My fingers grazed the spirit mage's soul, but alone, I couldn't even strip out his life energy. Two people were better than one, though—and the Death King hadn't come alone. Liches emerged from the node to battle those who'd turned on their master, and the air was soon thick with flying balls of energy.

"So you decided to stage a war in the city of Arcadia instead of coming directly to me?" the Death King said to Hawker. "I took you for a fool, I admit, but not a coward."

"Forgotten Olivia's betrayal already, Greyson?" he said. "Did you know she always planned to turn on you after she'd killed Alban? I suppose the missing memories are a convenience in this case."

"Stop talking," said the Death King in a low, deadly voice. "I should have killed you the instant I suspected you coveted my position."

"Oh, but you're too fond of giving people second chances," he said. "Aren't you? Even her—"

The Death King slammed into him, cutting off the rest of his sentence. My hair stood on end with static as the two spirit mages—one living, one dead—collided in a clash of bright energy that blurred my vision. Darkness and light fought for dominance, while my grip tightened on the amulet. If I bound Hawker's soul, I'd also turn him immortal again, which might end up being a downside. Instead, I shoved it back into the pouch and threw a paralysing cantrip at him from behind.

The cantrip fizzled out on contact, while Hawker held the Death King at bay. "You can't hurt me, Olivia. I'm far more than a simple human this time around."

Chills washed over me. Then my body froze, locking to the spot as two liches closed in. Hawker shot me a wicked smile of pure malice.

"Stop—that." I reached wildly for a source and drew on the nearest fire mage's magic. The heat unfroze my limbs and fire blasted from my hands, setting the liches aflame.

The Death King advanced again, shadows darkening around his edges in a manner that made him look more demonic than I'd ever seen him. Yet Hawker had him on the defensive. The two were master spirit mages, but Hawker had one advantage: he didn't care who he hurt. Streams of energy flowed from the nearest mages to him, friend and foe alike. He was draining them all to boost his own strength.

His attack smashed into the Death King like a freight train. I found myself flung backward, off my feet. I hit the ground hard, rolling upright to find the Death King next to me, feet braced on the ground.

"Are you okay?" I wheezed.

"He has too much resilience for a human." He

remained upright, but his voice sounded as breathless as mine. "He's feeding off the others. If he pushes too far, they'll die."

"More of a problem for us than for him," I gasped out. "But—I thought you'd want this. The curse broken. Your people freed."

"That's not what this is." He straightened upright and caught his balance. Hawker had drained his life force, too. "This is his attempt to re-establish the spirit mages as the dominant force and restart the war they failed to win the first time around. I cannot allow that, and I cannot allow him to take over the House of Spirit."

Hawker strode towards us, a wicked light in his eyes and the lives of a dozen or more spirit mages fuelling his strength. "I said they follow a false king, Grey... it should have been me, not you. And it will be. When you are dead."

The Death King stepped into the way, and the two collided in a rush that sent a wave of ice crashing over me. Streams of energy spiralled outwards from their hands. The Death King was trying to drain him, but he simply held too much power.

Then a spiralling thread of energy appeared, linking my own spirit to Hawker as he drew my life force out of me, inch by inch. *No.*

I caught the thread in my hand, tugged desperately, but Hawker held fast, his power spiralling around him in circles. Like a node, feeding on the strength of the few mages still on their feet. One fell. Then another. Disbelief filtered through, but as the Death King had told me, once we were linked, there wasn't any way for me to survive.

"Liv!"

I didn't see who shouted my name. The buzzing of the node drowned out all other sound. The energy slid from my bones, from my blood, removing all sensation. With my last reserves of strength, I staggered towards Hawker and dropped to my knees.

My hand closed on a knife discarded in the dirt.

Sean ran towards me, diverting Hawker's attention. His fist shot out, yanking the life force from within the other spirit mage. With shaking hands, I lifted the dagger and thrust upwards into Hawker's chest.

Hawker staggered, and the current of energy stopped flowing between us for an instant. I dropped to my knees, drained, my vision blurring. Sean lay nearby, his eyes sightless. He'd given his life for me, and yet…

And yet I was dying. I slid out of my body, floating upwards, propelled by some instinct I had no control over. Hawker, still bleeding freely, turned heel and vanished in a flash of light.

The Death King approached, and it was strange to look down on him as he bent his head, his hands turning my body over. "It wasn't supposed to end like this. You were supposed to live."

He rose to his feet, gripping the soul amulet in his hand. Then his gaze locked onto where I floated, detached from my body. A dreamlike sensation took hold as he reached out, his hand closing on me… on my soul. At once, I stopped drifting, held captive in his hands.

I didn't hear the question he asked, but I nodded. I didn't know what else to do. The world kept fading around the edges, while all sensation disappeared—except for one voice. Quiet. So quiet.

"Liv—Liv. Please, Liv."

I'd heard *his* voice, in my last memory before the Order had caught me.

"It was you," I tried to say, but I was no longer able to speak. Not even when he held up the amulet, not even when I felt myself fading away beneath its surface, and not even when I looked down and saw my dead body turn to ashes which blew away on the breeze.

Then the world faded to nothingness.

24

As though from a deep sleep, I came to alertness to find myself floating in the middle of the hall in the Death King's castle. My feet didn't touch the polished floor, and when I looked down, only darkness filled the space beneath me.

"I'm dead." The words should have felt heavy in my mouth, but I couldn't feel much of anything at all. I was dead. A lich. Immortal, eternal, and bound to stay here forever.

I might have cried, but I didn't have tear ducts. Didn't have eyes either. I was nothing more than a floating shadow. Even my emotions felt muted.

On the plus side, I was still here. I still existed. Which was more than others might say.

"Oh, good, you're awake." Dex hovered in front of me. "And you're like me. I guess we'll both have to play NPCs now."

"Did you have to remind me?" Like I didn't have enough reasons to lament my new bodiless existence.

How was I supposed to join in with D&D night in this state?

"Hey, you get to live forever, at least," he said. "I didn't know what I'd do without you."

"That would be really heart-warming if I wasn't *dead*."

Two more sprites approached us. At Aria's side floated a semi-transparent blue-white sprite with long hair and a mischievous expression.

"Did you take in that water sprite who rigged the trials?" I asked Dex.

"Her master was dead, so she didn't have anywhere else to go," he said. "She says her name is Mav."

"And Bria? What about her?" She'd fought on our side, but I'd lost sight of her in the battle. I might have more pressing concerns than what in hell *her* game was, but I had all the time in the world now.

"Funny thing, that," he said. "On second thoughts, I think I'll let his Deathly Highness explain."

"Explain what?" I swore as Dex flew away, leaving me hovering in mid-air. "Come on."

Then I saw who was standing in the doorway, staring up at me. Devon, back on her feet. I flew down to meet her. "Hey, Devon."

Devon jumped. "Liv? Is that really you? It's kinda hard to tell, what with the mask and all."

"Crap," I felt my face, but if it was as shadowy as my hands were, no wonder she'd freaked out. "Guess I need to practice putting my human face on."

"Can't you ask the Death King to teach you?" she said.

"I haven't seen him yet." Not that I knew what to say to him. He'd saved my life and condemned me to death in the same instant.

And as for everything else that had come up during my vision of my past? I didn't know how to deal with that on top of the knowledge that I was never going home again. The world on the other side of the nodes had no place for liches.

"He's the one who did that to you," she said. "Right?"

"To save my life," I said. "Not that it helps. Hawker got away. So did Cobb and his other allies, and they probably have the whole Order dancing to their tune now."

"I know." She blew out a breath. "I haven't been back home yet. To be honest, I don't dare. The Order knows I'm on your side. Unless I can convince them otherwise, but…"

"But they might try to jail you again," I finished. "I'd lie low here, but it's up to you. You can leave, after all. I can't, not without falling to pieces."

"Shit, Liv," she said. "You're really… I mean, don't get me wrong, there are upsides. Like our expenses are way lower now."

I didn't quite manage a smile. What was I supposed to tell my parents? I'd never see them again. I couldn't return to the Order even if I wanted to. If I went back to Earth, I wouldn't survive away from the nodes. I'd fade away for good.

My heart seized. I took back all I said about liches being emotionless, because it didn't seem to be true so far. Then again, I appeared as much of a faceless monster as any of the living dead.

"I'm lying low until the dust settles," she said. "Doesn't hurt that half our D&D group is here."

"Wait, they are?" I floated after her as she led the way through the corridor to the break room, where I found several familiar faces. Trix and Ryan, Felicity, Cal… and Bria, wearing the uniform of the Fire Element.

"What the *hell* is she—?"

A hand caught my wrist before I could advance on Bria and demand to know what she was doing here. I rotated and found myself face to face with the Death King, armour and all. *There you are.*

"I need to talk to you," he said.

I shot Bria a glare she couldn't see, since my face was masked, and turned to the Death King. "If you insist."

I shoved Bria to the back of my mind and followed him out of the room. Now both of us hovered off the ground, he didn't tower over me as much, and we both moved at the same speed. We entered the hall of souls, which appeared as vast as ever, amulets filling the countless shelves and silence cloaking our steps.

"You never said it was this… dull," I said. "Death, I mean."

"I did tell you it wasn't something I willingly walked into."

Guess I didn't, either, in the end.

His tone made it hard to tell his thoughts, but the panic in his voice when I'd been on the brink of death came to mind. I wondered how well we'd known one another before, back when I'd been Dirk Alban's apprentice. Well enough for me to entrust him with helping me turn the tables on my ex-mentor, at least.

"You did," I said, "but I thought… I figured Devon at least would recognise me, but she didn't."

"No," he said. "I can teach you to conjure up an illusion of your former self, if you wish. You'll also need to decide where you want me to keep your soul amulet."

Oh. Right. That's why he'd brought me here to the hall of souls. I couldn't carry my own soul with me, not if I wanted to keep it where it belonged, anyway. Here was probably the safest place, and yet…

Silence stretched between us, taut as a wire. I wanted to scream and sob, and yet I felt as though a foggy cloud masked the emotions I'd once been able to express. Maybe in time they'd fade away entirely, along with all memories of being human.

"Where… whereabouts is it?"

He approached a shelf and pointed out an amulet, which looked identical to all the others. "I think here is the safest place for now. Nobody came in here during the battle."

"I suppose they didn't need to, now they're luring people onto their side of their own free will rather than stealing their souls."

"That was always Hawker's aim, I think," he said. "Clever of him, to turn himself on purpose in order to escape notice. He's one of the oldest of my Court, and few would recognise him as the man he was before."

"He hid among the other liches after the war," I said. "Right?"

He inclined his head. "The Order is rebuilding following the attack. I have yet to hear an update on Cobb's status… or his allies."

"Yeah. I thought so." It had all been for nothing in the end. I'd failed to save them, and I'd even failed to save myself. "What about Bria? You picked *her* as your Fire Element? I thought she was working against us."

"I'm going to have to ask you to trust my decision," he said. "Bria's connections to the Houses of the Elements will be invaluable in reforming my own House in such a way that there will be no more people leaving to join Hawker."

"Death King, I appreciate that you want to do right by your people, but the fact is, they're defecting because Hawker is giving them a chance to come back to life again. Unless you can offer that, you can't compete."

"He's offering them a lie."

"That doesn't matter on the surface," I said. "A simple lie can outdo the truth just by seeming easier. Most people don't want reality or brutal honesty. They want to be told they're right. And now they believe Hawker is offering them a miracle."

A miracle, with a hell of a sting in the tail. There must be a downside somewhere, one that would backfire on him in the end.

But if there wasn't? If there was the faintest chance that I'd be able to return to the life I'd known before, I didn't know that I could refuse it.

As it was, I was stuck here for the time being, and my best bet for survival was to blend in among the others. The Order didn't know I was still alive. Since Cobb had them under his control, that would be a blessing for once. They wouldn't be out looking for me. Which gave me a unique opportunity.

I would go and find where Hawker and his allies were hiding. I'd find the spell they'd used to bring themselves back to life. Not just to save the Death King, but to save myself, too.

This wasn't over. I might have drawn my last breath, but I would live again.

And this time, I would live as a spirit mage.

ABOUT THE AUTHOR

Emma is the New York Times and USA Today Bestselling author of the Changeling Chronicles urban fantasy series.

Emma spent her childhood creating imaginary worlds to compensate for a disappointingly average reality, so it was probably inevitable that she ended up writing fantasy novels. When she's not immersed in her own fictional universes, Emma can be found with her head in a book or wandering around the world in search of adventure.

Find out more about Emma's books at www.emmaladams.com.

www.ingramcontent.com/pod-product-compliance
Lightning Source LLC
Chambersburg PA
CBHW050810190726
48285CB00005B/1867